By Angel McCoy, Matthew McFarland, Joshua Mosqueira-Asheim, Aaron Rosenberg and Lucien Soulban

Credits

Written by: Angel McCoy, Matthew McFarland, Joshua Mosqueira-Asheim, Aaron Rosenberg and Lucien Soulban
Additional Material: Alan I. Kravit
Developed by: Justin Achilli
Editor: Carl Bowen
Art Director: Richard Thomas
Layout & Typesetting: Becky Jollensten
Interior Art: Mike Danza, Troy Nixey, and Christopher Shy
Front Cover Art: Christopher Shy

735 Park North Blvd.
Suite 128
Clarkston, GA 30021
USA

Front & Back Cover Design: Becky Jollensten

© 2001 White Wolf Publishing, Inc. All rights reserved. Reproduction without the written permission of the publisher is expressly forbidden, except for the purposes of reviews, and for blank character sheets, which may be reproduced for personal use only. White Wolf, Vampire, Vampire the Masquerade, Vampire the Dark Ages, Mage the Ascension, Hunter the Reckoning, World of Darkness and Aberrant are registered trademarks of White Wolf Publishing, Inc. All rights reserved. Werewolf the Apocalypse, Wraith the Oblivion, Changeling the Dreaming, Werewolf the Wild West, Mage the Sorcerers Crusade, Wraith the Great War, Trinity and Sins of the Blood are trademarks of White Wolf Publishing, Inc. All rights reserved. All characters, names, places and text herein are copyrighted by White Wolf Publishing, Inc.

The mention of or reference to any company or product in these pages is not a challenge to the trademark or copyright concerned.

This book uses the supernatural for settings, characters and themes. All mystical and supernatural elements are fiction and intended for entertainment purposes only. This book contains mature content. Reader discretion is advised.

For a free White Wolf catalog call 1-800-454-WOLF.
Check out White Wolf online at
http://www.white-wolf.com; alt.games.whitewolf and rec.games.frp.storyteller
PRINTED IN USA.

Contents

Introduction: Something Wicked This Way Comes	6
Chapter One: Sins of Morality	10
Chapter Two: Sins of Society	38
Chapter Three: Sins of Discretion	62
Chapter Four: Sins of Power	84
Appendix: A Conspiracy of Sinners	104

BEHIND EVERY GREAT FORTUNE THERE IS A CRIME.

— HONORÉ DE BALZAC

Heresy abounds in the modern nights, whether arising from immorality or amorality. These heresies, these taboos, transcend matters of faith. They are crimes committed in the darkest of hours by vile, selfish Childer of Caine. To some, the taboo is merely a transgression against the social order, while, to others, even the slightest breach of the Kindred's millennia-long legacy is the gravest matter, deserving of the Final Death. The heresies contained within — the sins of the Blood itself — take many forms. Are they quick paths to power? Are they rebellions against the ancient custom of the Damned? Are they heresies against the wicked nature of the Kindred — sins committed in the name of redemption? Only one answer is universally true: These secrets are open renunciations of the culture that surrounds the undead. Welcome to the lonely path.

Introduction: Something Wicked This Way Comes

A heretic is a man who sees with his own eyes.
—Gotthold Ephraim Lessing

For some Kindred, "merely" being Damned isn't enough. Here in the Final Nights, with the world careening rapidly toward a seemingly inevitable Gehenna, desperate times call for desperate measures. The Kindred sponsor cults, truck with malevolent spiritual entities and adopt anathema as their codes of morality. But why?

It's easy to dismiss such things as the actions of "evil" Kindred. It's easy to accept that Kindred are the spawn of the Devil, given to atrocity and inherently flawed. In fact, to a degree, these things are true. A Kindred who does not resist her nature will inevitably find herself in the clutches of the Beast.

Obviously, as the presence of sects and societies evidences, not all Kindred end up driven mad by thirst and rising at night only to kill. These Kindred are the exemplary ones who have risen above being monsters — if only temporarily. These Children of Caine prove that Damnation can be resisted as long as one has the strength and will to keep it at bay. Hopefully, your characters are among these Kindred.

But such is not always the case. Fatalism takes its toll on all Kindred, and some bear its marks more gravely than others. If the world is doomed, these Kindred reason, why resist it? Why not indulge in what you want? Lacking the drive to steel themselves against the Beast, these Kindred find themselves consumed by it. Shiftless, indolent childer of the modern nights all too often resent the undeath into which they've been dragged, and elders finally succumb to the weight of untold years and snap.

What of the ones, though, who *truly* place themselves outside the world of the Kindred. It's one thing to terrify one's vessel before feeding; it's another altogether to actively pursue the thrilling taste of the Amaranth. When one rejects the mores of the Cainite world consciously and consistently, he has become something other than a venal Kindred. He has become a heretic.

Making It Count

That's what makes **Sins of the Blood** necessary. These are the heresies that those who are committed to rejecting Kindred society observe. Anyone can be an iconoclast; it takes a unique person to be devoutly different.

To that end, this book isn't a roster of baddies to whack. In the moral gray scale that **Vampire** observes, these Kindred might even be *right* in certain convictions, even if other parts of their creed are wholly aberrant to the rest of the world. The most complex **Vampire** games don't have clear-cut good guys or bad guys — each Kindred is weighed by the merits of her individual actions. The most ravenous Sabbat may still choose to rescue a child from a burning building. An ascetic Toreador starving herself to deny the Beast and curtail her predations on the mortal herd might lose the strength to fight the hunger one night and leave a newlywed couple drenched in their own blood.

Even after placing a Kindred in a position of responsibility for her own actions, **Vampire** also accounts for the motivations of those characters. That's the crux of degeneration, of Humanity and Paths of Enlightenment. A character who simply "does no evil" doesn't become more "good." A character has to genuinely feel remorse, to fight the animal inside her earnestly. That Sabbat who saved the child from the fire — did he do it to preserve her life, or did he do it because leaving her there would be a waste of vitae that he could have otherwise had for himself?

These are the sorts of situations that **Sins of the Blood** proposes. These enemies aren't cardstock mooks to beat into submission. They're thinking, vital characters who have undertaken some action or philosophy that the rest of undead society had spurned. Take these general ideas and apply them to specific characters. Let the results we discuss herein be the outcomes of motives that your specific characters harbor.

Think about that. The antagonists with which you populate your stories might be the compelling antiheroes of another chronicle. This book is for players and Storytellers alike. We don't mean to suggest that every character knows each of the secrets in this book — far from it. What we mean is that a player's character who adopts one of the philosophies can be every bit as rewarding to portray as a rival upholding that philosophy would be to overcome. Consider characters in the doomed tradition of Doctor Faustus or the noble sacrifice of Sidney Carton. Perhaps a member of the coterie wants to seek Golconda despite (or perhaps because of…) the wicked nature of his fellows. Maybe all of the characters are heretics themselves, comprising a coterie on the run for its own survival. Maybe they make up the righteous party, pursuing the pariah themselves. The story elements in this book work for all sides of the equation.

The Questions of Scale and Frequency

Note that even the motives that drive a heretic to commit his misdeeds do not comprise the sum of that character. If a Kindred's esteem is high enough, well, perhaps we can forgive him his unfortunate taste for undead vitae. If the prince maintains a domain that doesn't jeopardize the unlives of Kindred, does it really matter that he upholds the principles of the Path of the Scorched Heart?

Just as we mentioned before, that these heresies don't automatically relegate a Kindred to the position of "bad guy to be whacked," neither do they always need to be the central focus of the character who observes them. Storytellers and players (that is, those players who can be trusted to do so responsibly) should feel free to use these ideas to round out characters, or to use them as building points to distinguish characters from one another. A Kindred scholar trained in the Socratic Method is going to create a radically different experience than a Kindred scholar who has gone autarkis in an effort to isolate himself in the Gnostic tradition.

Nonetheless, all of these practices are considered heresies for a reason. If every Kindred in a city had one or more of these characteristics, the characteristics would be part of the status quo and not really sins at all. Storytellers, employ the contents of this book. Players, don't assume that you need one of these aspects to make unique characters.

This book is about sublime concepts. These rarities and weirdnesses surface infrequently (at best) in a Kindred's unlife. Their status is tied to this rarity. Use them only where they contribute to a character or a story. Occam's Razor applies here. If you can achieve the effect of something in this book without actually using the mechanics of it (as with our aforementioned scholars), then, by all means, do it. Storytellers, you can also use this sort of thing to defuse the know-it-alls in your troupe, should you have them. Let them assume that the cold scholar is on the Path of the Scorched Heart, then reveal later that he simply had a very low Humanity and a very cagey Beast.

Evil! Evil!

Taking all that information into consideration, remember that these behaviors are proscribed. Sure, they work as flaws to empathetic protagonists, but they also work as good cornerstones for those fighting in the idiom of **Vampire**'s themes of morality.

Keep in mind, however, that it's entirely too easy to relegate heretics to the roles of stooges or mooks. Don't set up a blood cult only to have it populated by a score of generic, dull-eyed slaves. If you want a shooting gallery, send the characters to the state fair and let them practice with the air rifles.

All of the philosophies and practices in this book are intended for use with devout characters. In keeping with the morality theme, you'll have deeper, more believable and more valuable characters if you understand *why* they've chosen to do what they do. As a Storyteller, doing so allows you to blur the moral line for the players' characters, who are going to have to consider their actions rather than splatter the goons in knee-jerk "enemy" fashion.

In the end, though, you're free to make your own decision. You're not doing anything wrong as long as you and your troupe are having a good time. Sometimes, whacking baddies is good, old-fashioned, beer-and-pretzels fun. Do what thou wilt shall be the whole of this book.

How to Use This Book

This book tries not to lump its "sinners" into one anti-empathetic whole. We've broken the taboos into distinct chapters, making not only the sins different, but those who commit them as well.

Chapter One: Sins of Morality examines the complex code of Kindred ethics. It details a few new Paths of Enlightenment and what happens when one's morality erodes to the point of no return, and it takes a unique look — could there be any other? — at the exalted state of Golconda.

Chapter Two: Sins of Society considers the social taboos of the race of Caine. Considerations such as sect and those who refuse to associate with them, the autarkis, are discussed here. Also, the dreaded Amaranth receives a bit of attention, for those Kindred who don't mind slaking their thirst on their fellows in the urge to fulfill their own legacies.

Chapter Three: Sins of Discretion exposes us to those who break the Silence of the Blood for their own ends. Cults — from herds to religious heresies to a flock of adoring followers — are the topic here, for those Kindred who don't want to face the Final Nights by themselves.

Chapter Four: Sins of Power includes new Dark Thaumaturgy paths and rituals, as well as a few other secret rites that, while not infernal in nature, would certainly not endear their practitioners to her elders. A few new mechanical systems for players and Storytellers — new Abilities, Merits and Flaws — are also covered.

Finally, the **Appendix: A Conspiracy of Sinners** introduces us to a few Kindred who have taken this book's heresies to heart. From small organizations to loose global confederations, it seems that nowhere is safe from the blight of the Kindred or their sins.

A Brief Lexicon

When discussing those who would break the understood social contract of the Kindred, certain unique words arise. Whether objective or loaded, the diction of (and regarding) the Damned is just as evocative as their less verboten parlance. Kindred should be careful around whom they use these terms. In some fearful domains, just knowing about such unpleasant things is a sure way to earn the attention of a sheriff or Inquisitor.

Harmonist: A follower of the Path of Harmony.

Internalist: A follower of the Path of Self-Focus.

Suspire: The burst of insight or moment of clarity that allows a Kindred to attain Golconda. The Suspire is a final test that determines whether or not she attains this goal.

Tainted: Marked by the Devil; in obvious league with demonic powers.

Unforgiving: A follower of the Path of the Scorched Heart.

Wassail: The act that "snaps" a Kindred, reducing her morality to zero and placing her under control of the Beast; when a vampire "gives up" the last vestiges of the Man.

Wight: A Kindred whose Humanity (or Path) rating has dropped to zero. While most Kindred assume that such creatures are ravenous monsters in constant frenzy, such is not always the case. Each Cainite's Beast is different. While some are indeed raging fiends, others evince a low cunning or practiced survival urge.

Chapter One: Sins of Morality

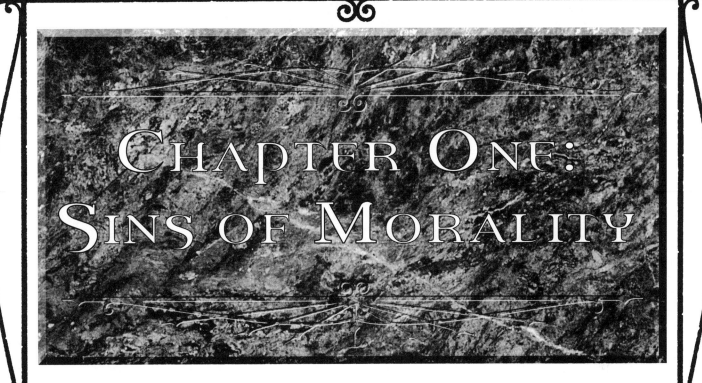

No man is a hero to himself.
—Ray Bradbury, *Something Wicked This Way Comes*

As I write this, I hear gunfire outside. I imagine it to be several blocks away, but I can never be sure. The sound echoes off the stinking buildings of this city, and the sounds I hear could just as easily be across the street. Wherever they originate, they mean the end of a life.

I remember a time when the death of a human being made a small sound, a death rattle. I have not heard such a sound issue from the throat of a dying mortal in many years. I can only imagine this to be because humans now die in such numbers that the individual's sound is lost amid the general din. I do not know. I am neither scholar nor philosopher.

In life, I was called Nehemiah. If I had a weakness, it was passion. I loved my wife and son so fiercely that it hurt sometimes. I cannot explain it. I could not explain even when I could remember the sensation, and it is long beyond my memory.

I am writing all this for a very specific reason, and the reader will bear with me, I trust. The reason for this treatise, essay, rambling — what you will — will become clear in the end. For now, only read and try to understand. It will, I assure you, not come easily.

By way of preamble, let me state that the Beast and how to protect oneself from its ravages is a concern for all Cainites. Even the most depraved among the kine is less a monster than the kindest — or, truthfully, most restrained — of us. In the pages that follow, I shall try to explain the mindset of a Cainite who forswears his humanity for other, more complex ethics. I shall also touch upon the fate of those who lose all control and become slaves to the Beast. The final and most important section of this work… will speak for itself, I think.

One anecdote before we begin, that of my Embrace. I was a fisherman by trade, as was my father before me. If I had a second love, it was the sea. One fine day, I sailed farther out than I ever had and, as sun set, found myself on a piece of land I had never before seen. I beached my small boat and lay down on the sand to sleep, not at all sure I could find my way home after dark.

I awoke to someone biting my throat. Ever a strong and alert man, I threw my assailant to the ground and stood. He regained his feet, and bared fangs. I sat down then. I knew that he was a monster and that I had no chance to fight him. He would take my blood if he so chose, and all I could do was resign my soul to G-d. I made one request of him, however. I asked him to take my boat back to my family so that my son could provide for my wife.

He sat down next to me, surprised at my courage and love. We spoke for hours, and he concluded, in brief, that my heart was too full of emotion and would eventually lead to my ultimate heartbreak and oblivion. Before I could protest (for that is all I would have been able to do), he was upon me.

I am sure, given my probable audience, I have no need to recount the sensation of the Embrace. I will, however, recount the last words I heard as a human being, before rising the next night as one of the Damned.

"Gone, gone the human soul," said my sire. And, oh G-d, how right he was.

When Humanity is Not Enough

For quite some time following my Embrace, I remained, for all moralistic purposes, human. It wasn't until much later that I came to follow one of the so-called Paths of Enlightenment. This is not uncommon, even though my sire had long forsaken any view that resembled human more. In those nights, the Paths of Enlightenment were rudimentary at best. The Camarilla and the Sabbat were not to be for many years, and a Cainite's method of chaining the Beast was often a chore undertaken alone. The key to keeping one's sanity was usually a key that a Cainite forged himself.

Now, however, a Cainite who wishes, or simply has no choice but to leave his humanity behind, usually receives instruction. So what then, the reader might well ask, is typical of a nascent Path-follower?

Normally, age is a factor. A Cainite normally retains a human viewpoint for some years after the Embrace, simply because the adaptation to nocturnal existence, coupled with the draconian horror of Cainite politics (the irony of the term "Kindred"— implying as it does camaraderie and fellowship — never fails to amuse me) is quite enough to contend with. But as the Cainite ages, he finds that everything he knows is dying. His mortal family, if his sire has instructed him well, knows nothing of his transformation and believes him dead. Any friends he had among the living have long ago forgotten him and gone on with their lives. As he goes along, night-to-night, he will eventually kill. And that is the turning point.

Consider, for a moment, the taboos that every culture the world over has regarding death. Whether the experience is meant to signify a terrifying judgment followed by eternal suffering or bliss, or a journey to another place without such qualifiers as pain or pleasure, death involves removing a being from human contact completely and forever. Every human being that I (for example) have killed has not simply vanished with no trace, but left behind others who mourn, weep and, in most cases, wonder where their loved one has gone. The first time a human dies under the fangs of a Cainite, that Cainite sleeps fitfully the following day. That human will never again enjoy a meal, a walk, a breath. He is gone forever. The immense responsibility of what he has done weighs heavily on a Cainite's shoulders.

Oddly enough, that burden does not compound with multiple victims, but becomes all too easy to bear. The more mortals who die to slake a Kindred's thirst, the easier it becomes. And as humanity changes, in the Cainite's sight, to a rabble of walking, chattering meals, the Beast rouses and thrashes against the Cainite's mind. As it takes time for a Cainite's moral rectitude to slip so low as to be a noticeable problem (particularly if the Kindred was, in life, a principled man) the young among the Damned are rarely recruited to follow Paths of Enlightenment.

Simple depravity is not enough, however. One thing that all Paths have in common (the ones that I have studied, at any rate) is that fools are not welcome to tread them. Any idiot can learn to enjoy slaughter, but the strength of intellect required to understand a Path, even one so deceptively direct as the Path of Honorable Accord, is beyond many Cainites. Likewise, a fool who believes, even as his undead flesh knits after a wound, that nothing beyond the physical world matters and that no G_d or gods exist does not have the spiritual capacity necessary to follow a Path. Those who are degenerate *and* stupid or shortsighted often end up as one of the ravenous fiends I shall soon discuss. Those who are nearing madness but still have the presence of mind to do something about it, however, may come to the attention of a teacher.

Paths in the Camarilla

Before entering into a discussion on the nature of this instruction, it behooves us to consider the difference between a Camarilla Kindred who chooses a Path over the more familiar precepts of human morality and a Sabbat Cainite who does so. Among the Sword of Caine, human morality is ridiculed outright. After all, reasons the Sabbat, mortals are indeed only cattle, and their lives are worth little. Why, then, should the mighty predators seek to emulate their prey, except as a means to lure them closer?

A good question, that. The answer is a matter of logic. Whether they choose to admit it or not, all Cainites were once mortal. In its dogmatic denial of humanity, the Sabbat hastens the path to the Beast considerably. Therefore, it becomes necessary for a Sabbat Cainite who does not wish to become a mindless, uncontrollable horror to follow a Path much sooner. (The Sabbat, after all, nominally espouses freedom of thought, and the Beast strips that freedom in short order.) In the Sabbat, a teacher might approach a promising candidate while that candidate is still a neonate. (Ancillae, I have found, are rare in the Sabbat.)

In the Camarilla, however, a neonate following a Path is unspeakably rare. In fact, I have heard of only one such Kindred in the history of the Camarilla, a gifted philosopher and alienist (what would now be called a "psychiatrist") Embraced into Clan Toreador in the late 19th century. As I understand it, the combination of the Rose Clan's heightened perceptions and rapture, plus his own rather obtuse thought patterns, made normal comprehension and morality impossible. Within five years of his Embrace, his sire made arrangements for him to receive tutelage in the Path of Death and the Soul. The fact that his sire was (and still is, to my knowledge) a member of a major city's primogen spared him some ridicule when word got around that he practiced "necromancy," but not much. As far as I know, he now exists as a recluse, watching humanity die around him, taking notes and startling other Kindred with a fatalism that impresses even the undead.

Following a Path in the Camarilla, therefore, definitely marks the practitioner as a kind of outsider and raises questions about Sabbat influence. That makes a certain amount of sense, of course, given that the first Tradition of the Camarilla (and the only one that speaks at all of the Kindred's relationship to mortals) states that Cainites, the undead predators of the night, must blend in with those mortals. Naturally, doing so necessitates an ability to relate to mortals, so many Kindred who, in pre-Camarilla nights, might have eventually been instructed in a road of morality suited to their ideals or found their own such road, now strive to remain humane, when they are, in fact, far from human.

So, to sum up a Camarilla Kindred's position, should he decide to follow a Path: He is a member of a sect that espouses human morality *as a way to remain hidden among mortals* (rather than for actual ethical concerns). That sect is composed of, pardon my language, vampires. Vampires are not human. Yet, our hypothetical Path-follower is ridiculed, suspected and quite probably interrogated at length for attempting to comprehend and exist within the boundaries of his undead existence æ in effect, for refusing to pretend to be something he is not. It would be safe, then, to assert that most Camarilla Kindred delude themselves beautifully, although I'm quite sure that such an assertion brands me a heretic.

What can such a Kindred do to avoid persecution? Join the Sabbat, naturally! However, I don't recommend this method (for reasons I will discuss momentarily). What I do recommend is that a Kindred who wishes to disguise the fact that he no longer follows the same moral track as the kine simply not make a show of it. Spiritual and moral discussions aren't entirely uncommon among Kindred (our condition begs some speculation, at least), and indeed, many Paths of Enlightenment hold knowledge and its pursuit as sacred. However, many of them also teach that keeping one's secrets is a wise idea. While such is the case for any number of reasons, ongoing survival is the best of them.

Does this mean that a Path-follower in the Camarilla should become a recluse? Not at all. A secretive Kindred is assumed to have something worth hiding. Unless one's Path specifically precludes or inhibits contact with others, it is wise to play the nightly social games that the Camarilla so loves. Appear at Elysium, become part of a coterie, should you feel so inclined. Appear honest before your prince. If the city in which you dwell hosts any elders who predate the Camarilla (and who still show their faces at Elysium), an insight into the vampiric condition might actually impress them.

If the secret is revealed, as it were, the exposed Path-follower is in a distinctly delicate position. He can expect visits from the Camarilla in the form of archons, asking ever-so-politely where the Kindred learned his ethical precepts and if, indeed, he or his mentor is a member of the Sabbat. On that topic, members of the Sabbat will certainly want to know why a Kindred is practicing "their" moral codes (yes, the Sword of Caine really is that arrogant, I've found), and they may send their own investigators. The Camarilla is nothing if not paranoid, and suffers no hypocritical delusions about behaving with tolerance toward such "alternative faiths." Elders, of course, will probably seek blackmail before persecution, if possible, but such is the nature of the Jyhad. Elders usually seek blackmail before *anything* that would benefit them less.

If an inhuman (if not necessarily inhumane) Kindred can fool his fellows by simply behaving "normally" around them, what about fooling the mortals themselves? How does a Kindred avoid detection (for the Masquerade is practiced by Cainites the world over, regardless of their politics) if he is dedicated to a higher purpose than subtle predation? Sometimes, the same principle applies: Avoid the mortals, but when one must interact with them, one does one's best to blend in. Of course, followers of some Paths are better able to adhere to this principle than followers of other Paths. The Path of the Feral Heart, for example, encourages its followers not to kill unless absolutely necessary (although a Beast's reason for exercising such restraint is quite different that a Man's). The Path of Death and the Soul, however, prompts its followers to kill at any time, as long as ample opportunity for study follows. Some Paths encourage contact with mortals; some hold it as a sin. The wise Kindred is wary. The kine can "feel" the malignant presence of the Beast in those who follow Paths. Although they may not know exactly what it is they face, mortals have an uncanny knack for knowing that it is some sort of predator.

When the act of keeping one's nature secret from the throngs of humanity clashes with the reverence one must show to one's Path, it is unfortunately the Path that usually gives. At heart, Cainites are selfish creatures. The ultimate act of selflessness, it can be argued, is to suffer or die for one's beliefs. Very, very few Cainites are willing to do so. (In fact, the only Path that I know that espouses honorable sacrifice is the Path of Honorable Accord — most others hold it a sin not to protect one's unlife in any way possible.) Even if co-existing alongside mortals is distasteful to a Noddist, the sheer number of mortals makes doing so inevitable at times. Although constant contact with mortals may push the Noddist further from his goal to be more like Caine, practicality and morality do not often mesh well. While difficult to avoid committing around mortals, the odd "sins" of many of the Paths of Enlightenment do indeed push the Cainite closer to the Beast. Therefore, in an attempt to avoid having to make a choice between sin and survival, many Camarilla Kindred use ghouls and other lackeys to carry out any business that requires mortal contact.

Paths in the Sabbat

On the other hand, Cainites of the Sabbat leave *humanitas* behind much more readily. This becomes problematic, since very few mentors are available for a young Sabbat on the verge of losing his mind. As I've stated, most Sabbat Cainites are neonates and elders, and, as always, elders have little time to instruct neonates. I suspect that if the overall survival rates of the Sabbat were higher, many more of them would follow Paths of Enlightenment, and far fewer would fall to the Beast.

I mentioned earlier that even if following a Path of Enlightenment is the only recourse one has against the Beast, avoid going to the Sabbat to learn. One reason I caution against the Sabbat is that although Paths are more common there than in the Camarilla, a would-be supplicant must still search for a patron. Trying to find help in the Camarilla means incurring a prestation debt, which, while inconvenient, is far preferable to the debt one incurs finding help in the Sabbat. Before a Sabbat Cainite will accept a student, that student must almost always be a member of the sect. Therefore, in exchange for aid in staving off the Beast, one agrees to give up one's freedom and join a fanatical army (which, ironically enough, claims to fight for freedom).

That said, the Sabbat certainly has the largest concentration of Path-followers, so what of them? Few elders of the sect remain true to human precepts, I'm sure. One

What Paths Work?

Certain Paths, as Nehemiah mentions, are easier for Camarilla vampires to follow than others.

- **Path of Caine:** As it directs its followers to avoid mortals and diablerize Kindred who cultivate their Humanity, this Path is probably not a wise choice for a Camarilla character.
- **Path of Cathari:** A Camarilla vampire who treads carefully could conceivably follow this Path, though she might appear to be sorely lacking in morality, especially at more enlightened levels of this Path.
- **Path of Death and the Soul:** The compassionless, lethal Necronomists rarely bother with the Camarilla. Their need to study death, often by causing it, draws too much attention. It's not out of the question, however, and of all the Paths, this one is probably the one most likely to be adopted by an elder who needs a moral compass.
- **Path of Evil Revelations:** Welcome neither in the Sabbat nor the Camarilla, the Corrupters fester in both sects. (That doesn't make them any more viable as characters for players except in certain chronicles, however.)
- **Path of the Feral Heart:** Arguably the oldest Path in existence (with the exception of Humanity), this Path is still practiced by some nominally Camarilla elders, and it could conceivably be passed on to younger Kindred. However, since the Path disdains politics, a Beast character would need a good reason (such as survival or protection in numbers) to join a coterie.
- **Path of Honorable Accord:** Although this Path is considered a Sabbat staple, its roots predate the sect. Therefore, an occasional Camarilla Kindred can be found among the Knights.
- **Path of Lilith:** This heretical Path isn't really endorsed by the Sabbat, and its practitioners are more concerned with enlightenment than sect politics. Likewise, the Path's precept against killing actually makes the Camarilla a more palatable choice for the Bahari than the Sword of Caine. (After all, the Lilin in the Camarilla can claim that regard for life prevents her from killing and not be laughed at too openly.) As the Camarilla holds Caine and Lilith to be mythological beings rather than actual historical figures (for the most part), even an open Bahari would probably be regarded as a deluded scholar rather than a dangerous heretic. Even so, the fact that this Path is so rare means that few Camarilla Kindred ever hear of, much less practice, the Path of Lilith.
- **Path of Power and the Inner Voice:** While Kindred do practice this Path (if rarely), it is commonly held only by elders who can appreciate its nuances and truths fully.
- **Other Paths:** The Paths of Night, Paradox and the others listed in **Vampire: The Masquerade** are practiced chiefly by members of the clan that espouses them. However, occasional members of other clans (and therefore other sects) find their way down these roads as well.

of the sect's guiding principles is to abandon all pretense of humanity. Elders have had centuries in which to realize this, but even after the bloody rituals and the mystic truths that Curse of Caine bestows, the neonates still find becoming something other than human a rather tall order. Oh, they do make a great fuss about "juicebags," of course. However, I see a strong similarity between them and teenaged mortals who bluster about not being afraid to die as they engage in demonstrations of "chicken" and other amusing pastimes. The young Sabbat talk, as they say, a great game, but for the most part, they must swallow their horror when they see vessels hung from rafters. Whether the horror stems from a lingering regard for life, or from a feeling of, "There, but for the grace of God, go I," it must be averted if the Sabbat is going to survive his first decade and not lose his mind.

No Sabbat clan is really more or less likely to follow a Path. The Lasombra and the Tzimisce, the founders and leaders of the sect, each have their own "pet" Paths, and I will soon discuss these further. In general, the question of whether or not a Sabbat Cainite can follow a Path is largely up to the individual in question. As long as the Cainite is competent and in good standing with the sect, he can probably find someone to teach him.

Once a Cainite begins to follow a Path, he may learn to disdain other Cainites who still cling to their humanity. After all, while they only talk of truly becoming inhuman, the Path-follower has taken action toward this goal. Meanwhile, his still-humane (so to speak) packmates may begin to see him as haughty and inscrutable. Sabbat packs have splintered simply because one member becomes so committed to his Path that the pack's purpose is disrupted.

The Others

Several clans follow Paths created for and by their members. While I am not a member of such a clan, I have had opportunities to study and converse with several such practitioners, and I feel it is in my best interest to relate what I have learned regarding these Paths.

The Path of Blood

The Assamites have undergone serious changes in recent nights. First, their curse fell, and I was disappointed to see that many of them reverted to their bloody predations of nights past. However, as the din from that occurrence begins to fade, I see that a significant number of Assamites have joined with the Camarilla. I do not predict, however, that this will mean a significant rise in the number of Dervishes that the Camarilla boasts.

To my knowledge, the Path of Blood is commonly taught only to those Assamites who achieve greatness within the clan by converting or taking the blood of "infidels." Therefore, those Saracens who have immigrated, as it were, to the Camarilla are unlikely to bring the Path's tenets with them. This Path is rarely proselytized outside the Assamite fold with any piety. Its followers do not often seek non-Assamite converts (even though the Path's code of ethics makes provisions for such), but I suspect that this reluctance is more because the Assamites are selfish than because they actively want to exclude others. It resembles a religion more than a simple ethical Path, as those who have crossed ways with a "devout" Dervish can well attest.

The Path of the Bones

In the nights before the Camarilla and the Sabbat, as I recall, another clan held the mantle of the "Clan of Death" and practiced a Path similar to the one that some Giovanni now espouse. Since I did not join Kindred (or Cainite) politics with any real interest until after the Giovanni rose to their current position, I have no idea how closely their Path of the Bones resembles its predecessor. I do know, however, that this Path is rare, even in the clan of its inception. Cainites with interests in death that are so deep-seated as to require morality based around it usually follow the Path of Death and the Soul, although the two Paths are superficially similar.

The Path of Night

Although rumors exist that this Path is truly ancient, descended from teaching of Caine (or Lilith, depending on the whims of the speaker), it is muddled and difficult to follow. I suspect that it was pioneered by young Lasombra around the time of the Anarch Revolt. Like the Path of the Bones, it is rare, and it is more common among a specific, rather pedestrian mindset (that the Kindred are horrific, indomitable monsters who fulfill their purpose by feeding on mortals) than within any specific clan. I imagine that the only reason that young, dispossessed Caitiff of the Camarilla haven't begun following this Path is its lack of accessibility to them.

The Path of Metamorphosis

I find this Path fascinating. The basic precept of the Path, as I understand it, is that the undead condition is not an end at all, but a step along the way to a final change. It's an interesting thought, but if one considers the source (Cainites who are capable of changing their forms at will) one can certainly see its ideological roots. Wishful thinking? Perhaps.

But then, the Tzimisce are the *only* vampires commonly capable of such changes, so a nagging feeling arises that perhaps they know something that the rest of us don't. (The Beast Clan is capable of change, up to a point, but the change is the same each time. The Tzimisce, however, are capable of changes limited only by their skill or imagination.) The Tzimisce's special Cainite gifts, perhaps the impetus for the Path of Metamorphosis, seem to spread easily from contact with their blood; I have seen entire Sabbat packs demonstrate its knowledge. So why, then, do the Fiends keep their knowledge hidden so carefully, when the tool of enlightenment (as they see it), the ability to change, is so easily spread?

The Path of Paradox

I confess, I am somewhat contemptuous of followers of this Path. Several of them once attacked me in Ulm, apparently after tracking me for some time. They spoke of "correcting the *maya*" and that my "*swadharma*" was to die at their hands. I escaped with my unlife, but I managed later to isolate one of them and extract some knowledge from him. In the end, I let him go. By attempting to destroy me, he and his fellow Shilmulo were attempting to correct what they perceive as a great wrong to the karmic cycle. Since I had fought them off and escaped, they concluded that they must have been wrong about my purpose within it.

Be that as it may, this Path is not practiced solely by the Ravnos. This is probably good for the Path's survival, given the recent destruction of most of the clan. The Shilmulo with whom I spoke indicated that sometimes members of other clans would Embrace mortals who were capable of understanding the cycle, and who therefore made good candidates for the Path of Paradox. I pointed out to him that basing possible members of a decidedly inhuman Path on what those potential members did as humans was fallacious. He, like many devotees of a belief system, did not have an answer for me.

The Path of Typhon

Some Paths are philosophies, some are religions. Most of the Paths espoused by one particular clan are more like religions. The Path of Typhon is one such Path.

I have never heard of a non-Setite Kindred pursuing this Path, and, given that their chief goal seems to be paving the way for their "god's" return, I can't imagine that there are any who do. Chief among the Path's virtues are solidarity and obedience, which means that the followers have strength of purpose behind their reprehensible actions. A drug dealer who sells poison in order to gain comfort and status is understandable, if not commendable. A drug dealer who sells poison in an attempt to garner followers for an undead god, however, is to be feared (or, if possible, burned).

Walking a Path

Now that we have seen what following a Path requires, what it may do to the standing of a Camarilla Kindred, the necessity of Paths in the Sabbat and the nature of the more familial Paths, perhaps we should examine just what following a Path means to any given Cainite.

First of all, consider the notion of "sin." In my breathing days, the greatest sin was worshipping a false god. Indeed, the Torah is rife with gruesome depictions of what happens to those who insult the One Above. Some religions prohibit alcohol, some pre-marital intercourse and so on.

An atheist would doubtless be surprised and perhaps amused by the various activities precluded under the heading of "sin." Often, a reason exists for the activity in question being declared sinful that has no bearing whatsoever on the religion in question. For example, the custom of eating fish on Fridays stems back to the Church wishing to give the fishing industry (such as it was) a boost, yet asking any teacher of Catholicism the reason for the practice would yield a far different answer.

Many sins, however, stem from taboos that any mortal would find obvious. The acts of murder, rape, theft and so on would seem to be "naturally wrong," regardless of the religion in question. Consider, then, that a follower of (for example) the Path of Death and the Soul holds the taboo against murder to be as misplaced as a modern pagan might hold an unwed Catholic's abstinence from sex.

Likewise, an adherent of the Path of Caine considers befriending a mortal sinful. The reasoning for this is sound enough if you happen to be a Noddist, but for the rest of the world, such a taboo might seem doomed. Because Caine, the first murderer, was outcast, and you seek to emulate him, you shun the mortal population? The Noddist calmly answers, "Yes." A Path follower cannot expect the world to share the things that he finds holy or unholy. In fact, only a follower of the same Path will sympathize or advise him. Following a Path is a lonely road, especially after the initial tutelage is over.

Consider, too, the difficulties of following a Path versus remaining "humane," which are presented merely by the fact that the mortals still control the world. Mortals make the laws in accordance with their beliefs. When a Cainite forsakes his *humanitas*, he also often forsakes mortal law and custom. Having survived long enough to see law and custom change dramatically, I can say with some assurance that such things are typically transitory. That does not, however, stop the mortal authorities from investigating murders, especially murders with an "occult" twist to them. And, despite the United States' vow that they shall make no law stopping a citizen from practicing a religion of choice, I seriously doubt that such an argument would absolve a defendant of a murder charge.

My point here is that humanity's precepts are often observed, much like many human religions, more by inaction and denial than by action and acceptance. A Christian may feel that he is following his religion if he resists the temptation of the flesh, but a Beast that does not hunt when the pangs of hunger strike — even if circumstances indicate that abstinence may be safer — is not being true to its fundamental nature. As I stated, many Paths of Enlightenment hold study and knowledge as sacred. However, one cannot acquire knowledge simply by denying ignorance. The active, even aggressive pursuit of one's ethics is something that few mortals (especially Westerners) are prepared to undertake. Such is especially true if the Path is based on esoteric knowledge that requires travel, patience and bargaining to acquire. So much simpler to play at being mortal, to avoid doing the things that, while living, one would have avoided. Comforting, certainly, but ultimately futile, as humanity's precepts sour after one reaches what would have been the 200th anniversary of one's birth and realizes that mortals are going to die, each and every one, regardless of what or who kills them. That realization, in and of itself, marks a slide toward the Beast, and it is truly inevitable.

When the Beast Wins

The slide toward the Beast ends in only two ways. First, the Cainite may meet Final Death. This is, needless to say, not the first choice of most Cainites. The only other possibility, however, is even less palatable: The Beast wins and takes over permanently.

Most young Cainites have never seen one of the pitiful wretches whose sanity and self have been subsumed. They hear tales from their sires, stories of Kindred who stalk the night, feeding on whosoever crosses their paths, eventually brought down like mad dogs by their own kind or by hunters. These stories are essentially true but somewhat misleading.

Indeed, most Kindred who succumb to the Beast become nothing more than mindless brutes. In Greece, the peasants called them *vrykolakes*. Mortals saw them as hideous, bloated monsters, and they knew countless folk remedies for slaying or incapacitating them. Mustard seed scattered about the house would delay such a creature. Thorns would bar them entrance, as they were deathly afraid of them. Needles stuck through a corpse's hands (or eyes, or stomach; the legends vary, of course) immobilized the dreaded *vrykolakes*. Of course, a true Cainite ignored these petty defenses, fed upon whom he chose and left no one the wiser. However, these remedies actually seemed to turn the ravenous *vrykolakes*.

I have traveled the globe over the centuries, and I can say that one thing nearly every nation on Earth has in common is a legend about vampires. The actual forms, capabilities and desires of the undead vary in legendry from place to place: The Greek *vrykolakes* bears little resemblance to the Malaysian *langsuir*, aside from their common diet. As any relatively venerable Cainite can attest, mortals misinterpret the facts almost willfully, so it comes as no surprise that their legends are a far cry from the truth, as are most of their preventive amulets. However, in the case of the mindless Cainites (referred to as "wights" in some elder Cainite circles, and it is this appellation I use for them here) most of these folk charms prove quite useful. A mountain rose placed on the chest of a Swiss wight immobilizes the creature. A stake through the heart, debilitating to any Cainite, may well destroy a wight (as opposed to simply paralyzing it). Why exactly does this occur? I have heard several theories, some arcane, some scientific, but none seem to cover the fact that, regardless of the Cainite's age or the potency of his blood prior to losing his mind to the Beast, superstitious mortal precautions have full effect (or at least some effect) on a wight. I humbly submit my own personal hypothesis on the matter. Recall, dear reader, that I am neither scientist nor scholar. My data is drawn almost entirely from personal experience and trusted sources.

(The reader might be interested to know that the word *wight* is used to refer to either a supernatural horror [rarely specified any further] or simply a human being. It is not without a certain irony, therefore, that a term that encompasses both what a Cainite was and is should be attached to the filthy creatures that are so representative of the failure of the Kindred's quest to cope with his human mind.)

As a Cainite loses his sanity to the Beast, he also loses his will. I do not refer here to ego, but to the *anima*, the questing instinct that elevates thinking beings (living and undead) above the animals. Add to this the fact that Cainites are inherently mystical beings (or "supernatural" ones, if you prefer). We are capable of feats that are simply outside the realms of science (with all due respect to the eminent researcher, Dr. Douglas Netchurch). As sanity fades, will disappears, and all that is left is instinct — and,

for lack of a better term, the curse. Wights are creatures driven by primal urge and divine damnation, unable to ponder their curse or to truly suffer from it. Therefore, the One Above opens the way for mortal remedies to hold these creatures at bay or destroy them, thus sending them on to whatever punishment awaits.

As further evidence for this "divine intervention theory," as it were, I present the thin-blooded. Rumors now circulate that this "last generation" of Cainites are incapable of siring new childer, but such Cainites suffer from the curse less harshly than most. I have heard stories of Kindred surviving the sun's rays for long periods of time, of Kindred eating and drinking mortal food and even of Cainites siring mortal children. (A note, however: This idea is not new. The Serbs had legends of creatures called *dhampyr*, who could fight the undead when no one else could see them. A fairly convenient way to make money, as it turned out. The *dhampyr* fights the invisible vampire, then collects a fee from the relieved citizenry. But I digress.) In any event, one common (though by no means universal) thread between the thin-blooded whelps of tonight is that common superstition often affects them. I personally met a young Caitiff who felt himself barred from crossing a bridge — just like the legends of old, which state that the Damned cannot cross running water under their own power.

But, the reader no doubt notices that in the case of thin-blooded (but still sane) Cainites, superstition seems powerful, but the actual Curse levied by G-d (including the fear of sunlight and the ability to consume only blood) seem lightened. Why is this? It is my contention that these thin-blooded Kindred are not beyond redemption, that a way "back to life," so to speak, exists for these unfortunates. Exactly how this redemption might be achieved, I am not certain. In any case, redemption is beyond the comprehension of the wights, and it is to them that I now redirect my focus.

Unlife as a Wight

Of course, I can only guess. However, every Cainite has some indication of what it is to be one of these mindless horrors, for every Cainite knows what it is to fall to madness. The frenzy brought on by hunger or rage is almost certainly what a wight feels constantly.

This is not to say, however, that every wight spends its time lurching about for victims. Were that the case, the Masquerade would not have stood firm as long as it has. Wights are not intelligent by any means, but remember that they operate by the basest instinct of all: survival. In losing their human will and soul, they have become truer predators than any still-sentient Cainite. A predator, after all, never gambles with its life. It does not enter a fight it doesn't think it can win. It feeds on the weak and the sick, and — despite wives' tales about cats æ does not toy with its food. Cainites do all of these things, arguably to stave off the weight of eternity. Wights, having lost their sense of time (how can an animal recognize time's passing, after all?) do not succumb to ennui, and thereby avoid the political and social entanglements of Cainite existence.

This rather animalistic pattern of existence goes a long way toward explaining how wights continue to exist in the modern nights. They do not, as a rule, frequent the human herds, as they are clearly no longer human. Instead, they slink through the sewers, wander through the barrios and ghettoes, avoiding prey until it is time to feed. Then, they single out a victim, immobilize or kill him outright and feed at their leisure. They make no effort to clean up after themselves, of course, and this is often how they are discovered. A life expectancy (so to speak) of more than a year is optimistic for a wight.

But exceptions do exist, of course. A man (or woman, I suppose) who was strong-willed and rational in the first stages of unlife may become a very dangerous wight indeed. Such a wight might experience "moments of clarity" during which a semblance of sentience returns. Such sophisticated abilities as language, of course, are impossible to recover, but the wight may well remember how to fire a gun, lock a door, or even start (if not drive) a car. Like amnesiacs, who tend to remember physical skills rather than verbal labels (that is, forget the word "car" but still retain the ability to drive) wights sometimes surprise pursuers by taking action that would seem beyond their capability to understand. Indeed, it probably is. While pursuing a wight once in New York City, I was very surprised when my prey grabbed the pistol from the belt of the policeman it had recently fed upon and fired at me. I don't believe, however, that the wight had any real idea what it was trying to accomplish; it continued firing even after the pistol was empty, and when I got closer, it dropped the pistol and attacked with its bare hands, completely forgetting the gun.

I occasionally refer to wights as the "remains" of Cainites, but exactly what remains? As stated, memories and skills sometimes remain in rather spotty fragments. A wight may or may not hunt familiar grounds æ I have seen cases in which wights fled the city of their previous unlife, a well as cases where the wight haunted the Rack of her city like a hideous ghost. Personality remains to varying degrees. For example, if a Kindred is, in "normal" unlife, the sort who enjoys testing his limits by experiencing pain, the wight that he becomes may well derive an odd pleasure from wrestling with its prey, allowing it to fight him for a moment before biting. This sort of personality retention, however, is by no means something to bet on. Ordinarily, the person whom the wight once was is subsumed, with only habitual or vestigial behaviors arising occasionally.

The gifts of Caine, however, are another matter. Over time, I have had opportunities to study with members of various clans, and indeed, when boons are offered me, I almost always take payment in instruction. Therefore, I feel myself qualified to discuss the mechanics (metaphysically speaking) of various undead proclivities.

Take, for example, the Kindred's heightened aspect of charisma. This beguiling skill relies chiefly on force of personality and the ability to inflict it upon others. One of the early abilities it confers is the power to frighten off an assailant simply by snarling at him (a superb skill to have, I might note, when one is walking in unsavory neighborhoods and does not wish to sully one's hands). This would seem an ideal resource for a wight. Little true skill is required, after all, and the effect is not unlike a cat making her fur stand on end to appear larger and more dangerous. But what of the other skills under this supernatural umbrella? The power of seducers and leaders, in the hands (and more importantly, the mind) of a wight? As even the rankest fledgling knows, the basic principles of any given Kindred edge are the first because they are the simplest to master. But they are simpler only because of frame of reference: The fledgling is learning to flex new muscles, so to speak, and he is learning by a combination of blood-borne instinct and instruction. Conversely, supernatural "physical" acumen, while common only to some clans, is basic enough that any Cainite can learn it without instruction. A wight seems to transcend the traditional learning process with regard to such advantages and exercise only those abilities that aid its survival (hence, exhibiting Dread Gaze while never learning to produce Awe).

While a still-sane Cainite is bound by clan and teacher with regard to learning new powers, a wight is bound by clan (to a point) and necessity. Undead gifts that have no practical use to the wight fade from memory almost immediately, whereas those that aid nightly survival become honed to dangerous levels.

For example, many years ago, in what is now Slovenia, I became aware of a wight that had wandered out into the countryside and taken up residence in a small village. The townspeople (devout Christians for the most part) lived in fear of the predator that sometimes stole into their children's windows. Of course all manner of superstition sprung up around that practice. Some believed that a demon from Hell had come to snatch the next generation of true believers. Others supposed it was the malevolent spirit of a deceased miser, and so on. (This miser, of course, was a Jew. Having watched this stereotype of my former faith appear and fester over the years, I am sometimes glad that my passions are deadened, else my enemies could follow the corpses of bigots to my door....) At one point, an otherwise well-respected widower was accused of lycanthropy, of all things. What never occurred to the townsfolk was that this creature was a predator, simply seeking the easiest prey. Children were too weak to fight, and they rarely had enough strength of will to call upon faith to save them (which may well have worked, recalling the pronounced effect of superstition on wights). I removed the wight from the village and discovered his former identity: a Toreador lately fled from Zagreb. After making some inquiries and tracing his movements back to that city, I discovered that at the time of his degeneration, he had walked among the undead for just under two centuries. During that time, he had mastered the art of preternatural senses, to the point that he could read the thoughts of those around him. Likewise, he had learned the secret of summoning others from great distances, but had never cultivated the third skill common to the Rose Clan, nor had he attained any skill in those curious gifts outside of his own clan.

However, when I tracked him down, he nearly outran me, a feat that few can boast. Twice I lost him in the shadows and had to call upon my own skill at heightening my senses (but meager at that time) to find him. After the hunt, I wondered how it was that a mindless beast could have learned the art of invisibility, when it baffles many more intelligent Cainites (I admit that it took me nearly a year to learn the trick of fading into shadows). Then I discovered that the former Toreador had attacked and fed on a Malkavian neonate before leaving Zagreb, and the progression became clear.

The wight, upon losing the last vestiges of humanity, lost his skills in supernatural sight and charisma. He retained only what he needed to survive: the ability to sharpen the five "natural" senses. However, his clan's affinity for speed was finally realized. Since it was "in the blood," so to speak, and necessary for his continued survival, he developed the ability instinctively. Then, upon feeding on the Lunatic, he found himself manifesting the power of stealth and honed the skill to the point where he could slip into a mortal dwelling without notice or alarm. This was all the wight needed to continue his unlife, and he probably would have continued preying on the children of the village until either bad luck, hunters or some supernatural force intervened. As it happens, his predations did not leave the townsfolk unaffected. The village stands to this night (though it has grown considerably, of course), and buildings constructed in the decade during and after the beast walked among them are notable in that few bedrooms have windows large enough to admit anything bigger than a cat or close enough to the ground that a man could reach the sill by jumping.

Hunting Wights

A Cainite who would hunt wights (and reasons exist for doing so, as I will explain shortly) had best remember that these creatures exist in a state akin to constant frenzy. They do not feel pain, and a wound that does not incapacitate is usually ignored. A Cainite who had powerful blood during his "normal" unlife loses no potency upon becoming a wight. The shattered remnants of a Cainite only seven times removed from Caine is a wight seven times thus removed. Combine whatever strengths the wight had before its fall with its animal cunning and predator's instincts, and you have some inkling as to what cagey prey it can be.

For example, the fear of fire and sunlight æ quaintly called Rötschreck lately æ affects wights to a much higher degree. This is not to suggest that wights are cowards æ again, they are predators, and just as a wolf flees from the strange sounds and smells of man, a wight flees from fire with all its considerable strength. So, using fire to destroy a wight is possible, but understand that it will fly into a deadly frenzy, and it will literally tear itself apart trying to escape. Conversely, a small, hand-held blowtorch is superb as a routing device while stalking wights æ you can be sure that they will run *away* from the fire, no matter what. The only trick is keeping up.

Another caution in stalking these creatures should be obvious æ the Masquerade. Wights don't give a fig for it, of course, and they will invoke their undead gifts openly, feed on mortals, lift cars or whatever else they feel they must do to escape a hunter, no matter who is watching. Great care must thus be taken to drive wights away from populated areas, either toward water (again, most of them shy away from it) or into an enclosed area (any abandoned building, or even a closed business æ the idea is to restrict their freedom of movement). Most princes, if told of a wight within city limits, will "lend" a hunter the assistance of one or more neonates. Sometimes, the scourge of a city (if one exists) will draft fledglings into service. While this might seem a bit excessive æ an entire coterie for one animalistic madman? æ the reader should recall that the hunter or scourge has no way to gauge a wight's power simply by looking at it. The wight could be the remains of a neonate, certainly æ but as I mentioned, the wight could also be all that remains of a powerful elder.

This should make clear one possible benefit toward hunting wights. While diablerie is often regarded as demonic cannibalism in the Camarilla, Sabbat Cainites may well go hunting for wights with this end in mind. (Another possible goal is to capture the wight and release it into a shopping mall, I'm told.) Despite the propaganda, Camarilla Kindred do occasionally commit the sin of diablerie, and so hunting wights in groups is practiced not only to ensure success, but also to ensure that none of the hunters may claim the wight's soul as his trophy. Unless, of course, the wight is the subject of a full blood hunt.

I had the opportunity once to converse with a Cainite who committed diablerie upon a wight. Before succumbing to the Beast, the wight had been a devout Christian for many years, and indeed, that faith was the last bulwark against insanity. I asked the Cainite who consumed the wight if she had assimilated any of the wight's memories (I'm led to believe that this happens to diablerists fairly frequently). The following was her answer. The reader should recall that what she "remembers" is quite likely the last memories of the Cainite as he lost his mind and became a wight.

"I remember a pit. Underneath me, a pit. My feet each on one side of the pit. I remember the pit growing wider and something in the pit, below, screaming. More like wailing, really. As though in pain from hunger. No reason to think hunger, but I think that's why it howled. And then it changed, and I remember holding onto a ladder or a rope, and slipping. And I kept trying to remember the words to the Hail Mary but I kept getting stuck after 'fruit of thy womb, Jesus.' And then I fell and the wailing was louder. And then I realized it was me wailing."

I have no idea how much of this is exaggeration. I should relate, in all fairness, that the diablerist in question is a Malkavian, which certainly makes me take the story with a grain of salt.

The next common motive for hunting wights, and the one commonly cited as primary, is to protect the Masquerade. Humane Kindred sometimes speak of protecting the citizenry at large from these horrors, but that, of course, is bunk. A wight left to its own devices will, sooner or later, be discovered by the mortal world, and Cainites of a certain age know well what happens next.

Some Cainites hunt wights for sport. This isn't an attitude I can say I understand. A prepared hunter (or a group of them) is usually more than a match for a wight simply because the hunters can expect the wight to respond to stimuli in a certain way. The danger here is much the same as that of humans hunting a big cat. If the cat decides that you are a threat, it will go to ground. If you corner it, it fights to survive. However, strength of weaponry and strategy usually prevails, unless the hunters have seriously misjudged their quarry's capabilities. Also, thankfully, wights are quite rare. Most Kindred will never see one. Those who do might not be able to distinguish it from another Kindred unless they see telltale evidence of its wretched mental state.

The safety of a city's Cainites is also a concern. Destroying the "mad dogs" of Kindred society is just as necessary for us as putting down true mad dogs is for mortals. While most wights do not attempt to feed on Kindred, occasionally one realizes that the blood taken from its own species is more filling than that of easier prey. I have never heard of a Cainite actually being diablerized by a wight, but that certainly isn't to say that it couldn't happen. I have no idea what effect this might have on the wight (and it isn't an experiment I'm prepared to pursue), but I hypothesize that it might either grant a moment of lucidity to the wight or, conversely, push the creature deeper into the depths of madness.

The final and least common reason I know of for hunting and slaying these unfortunates is mercy. The loss of sentience, of the consciousness that makes us thinking beings, is one of the most frightening things I can think of. Therefore, some of us (yes, myself included) track down the unfortunate wights and end their existence in hopes that they will know some peace in the hereafter.

Wight Packs

Diablerie aside, wights will attack other Cainites with the intention of feeding if they feel that they can do so safely. A Cainite who lingers over a meal might suddenly find himself struck from behind with a club (as wights intelligent enough to surprise Cainites are certainly intelligent enough to employ weapons). Such "cannibal" wights are more rare than their fellows, since their predator's instincts ensure that they shy away from such able prey. However, if two or more wights manage to find each other, a curious thing may happen. Rather than fighting, the creatures might join together in social groups analogous to wolf packs.

This only makes sense, considering that wights are descended from social animals. I have observed this phenomenon firsthand only once, but I have it on excellent authority that the case I saw was not entirely atypical. My experience in observing a wight pack in Detroit was this.

I was in the city hunting down a wight, the remains of a Sabbat mass Embrace. It had fled a battle with Camarilla Kindred and escaped. This wight would not have lasted long in any case — it was far too blatant about its predations and stories of a "cannibal killer" had already begun to surface among the city's poor. I found the beast, and began routing it away from inhabited areas so that I could dispose of it.

I herded it toward the river. Upon reaching the banks, I was surprised to see a figure running at the wight. The newcomer ran with a loping gait that did not seem at all human to me. Such being the case, I decided to see what the newcomer was and how the wight would react to it (and vice versa). To my surprise, the two beings sized each other up, and the wight I had been chasing ducked its head, apparently acknowledging the other as its superior. They then both turned toward me. Not wishing to lose this unique opportunity for study, I fled the area and doubled back to observe.

The second wight was obviously older, as I could see from its tattered clothes, and stronger. The two of them protected each other and hunted in tandem. Whenever they fed, however, the dominant wight would feed first, much like the leader of a wolf pack does. I would have been interested to see how a third wight would have affected the pecking order, but I was forced to destroy them both before either attracted attention from the local Sabbat or any mortal authorities. I can say, however, that the younger wight fought me with all its (considerable) strength when it saw that I meant to injure his companion.

The pack phenomenon is not universal, however. When two wights meet, the result is at least as likely to be a pitched battle between competing predators as it is the formation of a social group. This, too, is something I witnessed.

While traveling between New Orleans and New Iberia, I became lost and was forced to sleep the day in a roadside motel. I awoke that evening to something scrabbling at my arm as I rested under the bed.

After extracting myself from my (admittedly rather foolish) sleeping arrangement, I took stock of the intruder. It was obviously a Cainite, and its disheveled appearance and dull, animal-like eyes marked it as a wight. The only weapon I had to hand was a small pistol, and I doubt it would have done any good. As I was preparing to slow the beast using my temporal gifts, another misshapen creature entered the room.

While I had no way to guess the lineage of the first wight, the second was obviously the remnants of a Gangrel. Its eyes gleamed red, it sported blood-encrusted talons, and it had odd, patchy fur across its torso. I thought for a moment that these creatures were part of a pack (and I was beginning to reconsider my options) when the first wight launched itself at the newcomer. As it did so, I was able to observe deep furrows in its back æ clearly these two unfortunates had clashed before. They were more interested in fighting each other than bothering me, so I wasn't concerned for my safety. However, I did want to make certain that none of the other guests of the motel saw them or fell victim to their rage.

Carefully and slowly, I herded them into the bayou. They ignored me except when I attacked directly, and when I did, the one I attacked tried to run (considering itself outmatched). Finally, when both combatants were exhausted and wounded, I managed to subdue them and study them at greater length. I discovered that both wights had been hunting in the area, and each had been expanding its own "territory" until the two creatures happened upon each other. They had been hunting each other ever since, clashing when they met, with neither gaining enough advantage to win.

Storytelling Wights

The following information is intended for Storytellers who wish to use wights in their chronicles.

- **Morality:** A wight is simply a Kindred whose Humanity (or other morality) score has dropped to zero. As a result, the Beast is in constant command of the body. As mentioned previously, this command need not be a constant, blood-soaked rampage. The Beast can certainly be cunning when it needs to, and it is just this low animal sense of self that keeps the wight from simply destroying itself sooner, as is the case with most Cainites who suffer the wassail.

- **No pain:** Wights do not acknowledge pain from bashing or lethal wounds, and they soak such wounds at -1 difficulty. They suffer wound penalties only if the wounds stem from fire or sunlight, and even then, they typically enter frenzy (or Rötschreck) so quickly that pain does not hinder them.

- **Disciplines:** Wights do not learn Disciplines in the same way as most Kindred. Instead, they grasp the least complicated and most useful (to them) concepts of the Discipline in question — rarely over level three. For example, a wight developing Obfuscate would probably learn only the first two levels, as the third is too involved for its mind to grasp. The physical Disciplines (Potence, Fortitude, and Celerity) have no upper limit except the maximum dictated by the wight's generation. Out-of-clan Disciplines can be learned only if the wight already had some skill in the Discipline prior to degeneration, or he consumes at least five blood points from a vampire whose clan commonly exhibits it.

- **Animalistic:** Wights are nearly impossible to influence mentally or emotionally. All uses of Dominate and Presence (except Dread Gaze) receive a +2 difficulty modifier.

- **Appearance:** A wight can have an Appearance score no higher than 1. Nosferatu wights are often indistinguishable from "normal" Sewer Rats, which makes them all the more dangerous.

- **Memories:** How much a wight recalls depends on its Willpower rating. A wight with a Willpower score of 3 or less becomes a bloodthirsty monster, incapable of any real strategy or reason, hunting chiefly by animal instinct. A wight with a higher Willpower rating, however, can actually retain Abilities. For every point of Willpower above 3, the wight retains one dot of a given Ability. For example, a vampire with a Melee rating of 3 and a Willpower rating of 5 retains two dots of Melee.

The Alertness, Athletics, Brawl, Dodge, Intimidation and Stealth Abilities are not affected by this restriction. As wights have no Humanity, they cannot possess the Empathy Talent.

Note that some Abilities are inappropriate for wights regardless of their Willpower score. No wight will retain much mastery of Academics or Computer. Likewise, retaining a Linguistics rating only means that the wight can understand the languages it once knew (as opposed to actually speaking them).

- **Nature:** A vampire's Nature can influence his behavior as a wight. In general, if the wight does not perceive its unlife to be in direct danger *and* the wight is not hungry (its blood pool is more than 3/4 full), it will pursue interests related to its former Nature. For example, a wight whose former Nature was Architect may observe the old "count scattered grains of rice" myth or push dirt into piles around its haven, whereas a Monster wight will kill and kill again, no matter how full its blood pool is.

- **Generation:** Age and potency of blood are unchanged by the loss of Humanity. A wight can be of any age or generation. Older wights don't differ in behavior much as compared to younger ones.

- **Frenzy/Rötschreck:** Wights check for frenzy and Rötschreck at +3 difficulty. Most will flee fire or sunlight without bothering to resist the red fear.

- **Diablerie:** Consuming the soul of a wight is risky. Besides the usual Humanity loss, the diablerist must immediately check for frenzy (difficulty 8). Nightmares often plague the diablerist for months afterward. In addition, although the attendant "rush" from diablerie still occurs, decreased generation comes at a price. If the wight was of lower generation than the diablerist, the diablerist's player must roll Willpower (difficulty 7). If she succeeds, her generation drops by one, but she immediately gains a derangement (which one depends on the Storyteller's taste æ bestial ones are most appropriate). Wights will only commit diablerie if the wight in question has already done so (before becoming a wight) and is alone and undisturbed.

- **Superstition:** While the narrator of the preceding text greatly exaggerates a wight's increased vulnerability to superstition, many wights are indeed turned by garlic, crosses or other such "folk remedies" if the user succeeds in a Willpower roll (difficulty 8). If the user's player happens to have True Faith, the wight recoils automatically and flees if possible. A stake through the heart will not destroy a wight, but it does paralyze it as usual.

- **Wight packs:** Groups of wights occasionally behave as stated elsewhere in the text. The strongest becomes a sort of default leader, and the pack affects crude attempts at strategy (harrying prey like wolves, attacking *en masse* and so forth). Weaker wights will fight to Final Death to protect the leader.

I never discovered the identity of the Gangrel wight, but the other turned out to be a Ventrue and the childe of a New Orleans harpy. Said harpy, as it happens, offered to pay handsomely to keep the news of his childe's fate from the ears of his fellows. I had no desire to become involved with the harpies of any city, however, and so declined any reward for silence.

Cainites of all stripes are rare, of course, and wights even more so, which means that the odds of encountering either a pack or a feud are extremely slim. However, if something happens only once a century and one has seen the passage of 15…well, let me close my discussion on wights by saying that, like all wild animals, they are unpredictable and dangerous, and (obviously) have no moral limitations at all when it comes to survival.

Other Paths to Golconda

It would seem that Golconda is the logical extrapolation of *humanitas* for a Cainite. But what of the Paths of Enlightenment? Are they exempt from any possibility of redemption, simply because they chose the road that best suited them?

The answer is no. However, the possibility lies, I believe, in giving up the Path and rediscovering one's human ethics and morality. This process takes years, possibly decades, and given the inhumane nature of many Paths, this goal may be impossible to achieve. However, one's human side can be reclaimed if the vampire is strong enough to try.

As for those Cainites who attempt to reach Golconda (or a similar state) by reaching the pinnacle of their particular Path, I have no true idea, only guesses. I should think that some Paths might allow for it with a bit of heretical change to the Path's ethics, while some others (notably the Path of Metamorphosis) seem to have this sort of transcendence in mind as a goal. However, true Golconda comes from conquering the Beast and redressing one's crimes, not from a study of what it is to be a monster. I must, therefore, conclude that, although some kind of reward might await the followers of the Paths of Enlightenment, the reward is not the road of Mercy promised by Gabriel.

To Introspection

Golconda is hinted at in the *Book of Nod*: "…for even now there is a path opened, a road of Mercy, and you shall call this road Golconda. And tell your children of it, for by that road they may come once again to dwell in the Light." In that context, it seems to stem from G-d directly. However, it is important to note that the "God" of the *Book of Nod* is the same entity that both Jews and Christians worship (even if they themselves won't concede that point) and that some Cainites (my

Redemption?

I stated before that the final section of my manuscript would speak for itself. I also stated that only two avenues exist for Cainites who wish to defeat the Beast. In this last statement, I misspoke. One other method exists: Golconda.

I cannot speak the word above a whisper. That I still hold such reverence for the word æ for the concept æ might seem laughable to some, in the face of my…

No, I am getting ahead of myself. I must separate my experiences from the truth, divorce myself of emotion, as befitting one of the Unforgiving. Very well, then. The reader might well ask, "What is Golconda?"

Myths surround the word. Most of them are completely false; some are merely misguided. What Golconda is not, however, is a state of tolerance or acceptance. A Kindred who has reached Golconda is not, by conventional human morality, "good," "caring" or "tolerant." Golconda is not for the softhearted, as the discipline and self-perception it requires is phenomenal.

Golconda is *not* a state reached by following any one particular religion or faith. In my travels, I once heard a Kindred preaching that the true path to forgiveness lies in devout attention to the Five Pillars of Islam, that Allah would forgive those Kindred who followed the Muslim faith and reward them with Golconda. I actually broke my usual practice of strict observance with other Cainites and argued with him. How, I asked, could the Muslim faith be the way to forgiveness when that faith (like most others) was a product of a need for social change within *mortal* society, and when many Cainites (myself included) predate the religion's inception by hundreds of years to boot? He didn't have an answer for me, beyond the usual "Allah wills it so." Although I am not prone to bouts of strong emotion of any kind, that night I was overcome by disgust.

Likewise, no one sect or clan has any more information on Golconda than any other. The mysterious Inconnu are rumored to pursue Golconda, but they are also rumored to be the last of the Antediluvians, a group of demon-worshipping infernalists, the gatekeepers to Gehenna and so on. In all my centuries of unlife, I have never seen or heard from a member of this strange group, and I am forced to assert that they may not exist at all.

grandsire among them, reportedly) predate even Judaism. So, where did Golconda originate?

I spoke once with a member of the enigmatic Salubri. I am aware of the rumors surrounding their clan; I am also aware that many of these rumors can be traced back to the Tremere, and I prefer to trust experience over Warlocks. The discussion was brief, but the Cainite expressed an opinion that the founder of her clan actually discovered Golconda after extensive travel in the Middle and Far East. Since I spent the first several centuries of unlife among the Cainites of Jerusalem and the surrounding countries and never heard of Saulot or his involvement with Golconda, I am forced to doubt the veracity of that statement. However, I am also forced to concede that the woman who made the statement displayed an inner serenity much beyond her years (she confessed that she was little more than a neonate). I feel that the answer lies not in spirituality, but in science. For every action, an equal and opposite reaction follows. The action of a Cainite's slide into degradation, eventually ending in his Final Death or a brief, violent period in wassail, has its reaction in the Kindred's departed but still-extant soul crying out. The soul is immortal and strong, even if the Beast makes the Kindred's mind weak. Just as the Beast has its own end in mind — complete surrender to base instincts — the soul, too, has an ultimate goal, "to dwell in the Light."

I must apologize to the reader. Much of the preceding is my own philosophy, and I do not mean to offend. But, in following Golconda, dogmatic human religion has no place. There are no holy texts to offer prepackaged codes of behavior, no Pillars, no Commandments and rarely any teachers. The hardest step on the way to Golconda (aside, perhaps, from seeing the way at all) is the first one, because the seeker walks a dangerous road, alone in the dark.

The choice to make that first step is often done without knowledge or even rumor of Golconda. After all, the Camarilla regards it as allegory at best and a fairy tale at worst. The Sabbat, needless to say, scorns the very idea of penitence and remorse in favor of leading an unlife without regret. But sometimes, a Cainite sees something that makes him remember what it was to be mortal. It needn't be significant, but somehow, it touches a dead heart. A wedding, a birth, a death, a funeral, a child at play — the possibilities are as endless as the ways that mortal express their emotions. The point is this: The Kindred *remembers* the emotions, even if actually experiencing them is beyond his capacity, and he feels the burden of death and time that I mentioned in the first part of this writing.

This burden crushes the weak. The last memories of a wight might well include such a moment, but those who are strong enough to bear the guilt, and honest enough to identify it, find themselves acting on it. And this action is where the road to redemption becomes rocky.

Self-denial is not an easy thing for mortals, and is widely regarded as somehow virtuous. Fasting, abstinence from sex and so forth are seen as tools to grow closer to the Almighty. I'm sure I need not remind the reader of the effects of fasting on us. The hunger becomes more than we can bear. And so feeding for the penitent Cainite is an ordeal; many such Cainites turn to seduction or taking vitae from sleeping vessels, or even feeding on animals. In any event, a Kindred who seeks salvation must avoid killing at all costs, even in self-defense. The taking of a life is a sure method of losing all progress toward Golconda — and this includes murder by inaction (which means that Cainites attempting to find Golconda had best mind their associates carefully).

Most Cainites never proceed far enough on the path to see what comes next. Not killing mortals seems strange and unnecessary to many of us, and change comes hard to the undead. But a Cainite who manages finds that more than simple denial is involved. A Kindred seeking Golconda must first seek atonement.

Atonement, absolution, redemption, salvation and so down to the most basic of such concepts: forgiveness. In life, I had no idea how to forgive. I remembered slights against me for years, and nursed grudges studiously. As such, I never expected forgiveness, and my wife often surprised me by granting it to me when I stayed out on the sea too long, when I gambled with my earnings and so on. I was not a strong enough man to forgive.

I'm sorry. Only a few hours remain until dawn. I will see this through.

The supplicant must atone for any and all crimes he has committed. This can, in the case of younger Cainites, extend to sins committed while he was still mortal. In any event, atonement takes many forms. Perhaps the Kindred seeks out those he has wronged and simply confesses and apologizes. Perhaps he seeks to correct the mistake surreptitiously. Or, if there is no possible way to atone directly for an error (the Cainite fed on and killed someone and left him, and he has no way to find out the victim's name), the supplicant may seek to prevent crimes of a similar nature.

Again, note that the Cainite does not seek to atone because of responsibility, either to himself or to a higher being. The desire to repent *must* stand on its own — the Kindred must feel and display true remorse, else no progress is made. A Cainite who displays such behaviors openly eventually comes to the attention of a tutor. Whether that tutor chooses to reveal himself is another matter; it depends largely on whether the tutor feels that the supplicant would benefit by instruction, and indeed if the supplicant has any hope at all of reaching Golconda.

To reach Golconda, after all, requires denying the urges of and thereby triumphing over the Beast. One does not allow the Beast "controlled freedom," one beats it into submission. This means that a Cainite who cannot control the throes of frenzy or Rötschreck is not a candidate for Golconda. Self-control is paramount to attaining the state, as is self-awareness — one must be able to examine oneself honestly and ask, "Can I control myself? Can I deny myself? Can I forgive myself?" Not questions with easy answers, those. The tutor may choose to ask those questions for the supplicant, to place the seeker in situations where he will be tested. On the whole, however, the best lesson a tutor can give is one of hope.

The road, after all, is often thankless, and since mentors are rare and the road so very personal, it is very hard to tell that any progress is being made at all. At least when one violates a rule, one becomes aware of it — degeneration is much easier to track that redemption. A tutor can provide the benefit of reassurance and give the seeker some suggestions on where to turn next.

A would-be seeker should beware, however. Golconda, as stated, is personal. What might make one Cainite weep with guilt might elicit no real reaction from another. For this reason, mentors watch their protégés very carefully for some time before unmasking, if indeed they ever bother. If a seeker announces that he intends to seek Golconda and is rewarded with a mentor almost immediately, it is more likely that an elder has found a willing pawn than an enlightened Kindred has found a disciple.

And this brings me to another caveat of seeking Golconda: Avoid the Jyhad. The Jyhad is merely a plaything for ancients, a distraction from eternity. A Cainite seeking Golconda cannot afford such dalliances. The struggle with the anarchs or the Sabbat? The takeover of New York by the Camarilla? The war between Kindred and the strange Cathayans on the West Coast? All of these are of no import compared to (for example) a man being beaten to death by a gang in your own city. Cainites are beyond the strictures on killing as far as Golconda is concerned (though certainly premeditated murder is still premeditated murder, and I hardly need mention that diablerie likely prohibits any chance of reaching Golconda). Does this mean that contact with other Cainites is prohibited? No, not in and of itself, but consider the factors. If you spend time around Cainites who are not attempting to find Golconda (and it's rare that two Kindred ever attempt the road together), you are likely to have to prevent them from killing. You are equally likely to become involved in the sort of pseudo-political nonsense so common to the nightly existence of our kind, and this serves only to distract you from the business at hand. Golconda is a path best walked alone.

But then again, isn't the way to become strong to test oneself? And, if in associating with other Cainites, one finds these tests, could that not be a road to redemption? Actually, I'm sure it could. A coterie of Kindred (for attempting to reach Golconda while maintaining an active membership in the Sabbat is probably too much of a test) would certainly provide myriad opportunities to prove one's spiritual fortitude. Such a seeker would likely need to be in a position to stop any real atrocity that the others might wish to perform, but this could perhaps be masked by an over-developed loyalty to the Masquerade. And, that very Masquerade provides one necessary component to the path to Golconda — contact with humanity — that becoming autarkis might inhibit.

Mortals, after all, have the freedom that the seeker longs for. They have their base urges, true, but their base urges don't force them to fly into homicidal rages and consume the blood of whatever stands too near. Mortals are capable of such defining acts of selflessness, sometimes in the same hour that they betray those they love. That dichotomy, so grossly exaggerated in our state, is quite worthy of study and perhaps emulation. So, the seeker watches mortals, trying to return to something approximating his own human state.

This focus on humanity is one of the main reasons that the Sabbat detests the notion of Golconda so. They see it as regression, like a grown man wearing swaddling and seeking to return to infancy. But this really isn't the case. A human being never contends with the temptations that we do. Mortals have their own reasons to be strong, but they are tempted by food, greed, sex and so forth. Many of their temptations, while reprehensible in some places, rarely violate any basic taboos. Our temptation, our necessity — consuming the blood of the living — does exactly that. It is next to impossible to maintain our humanity without violating a law of humanity so innate and so sacred that it figures into nearly every faith in the world. And there is the old riddle of our existence, *A beast I am lest a beast I become.*

The seeker of Golconda responds to this riddle with a resounding "No."

We must survive, yes. We must feed, granted. But we are not bound to become a beast to stave off the Beast. This is why seekers of Golconda do not kill, and indeed some even ask permission to feed on mortals before doing so. The key to Golconda lies in denying that the Beast has power over the higher self, and giving in to the riddle is a victory for the Beast. It is akin to saying, "The Devil made me do it," and while the Beast is more a factor in the unlife of a Cainite than some improbable malevolent demigod is in the life of a mortal, the fact is that the Cainite owes full responsibility for the Beast's actions. Therefore, the only way to truly atone is to own the Beast and never succumb to frenzy, from hunger, anger or fear. It is not impossible, but the next thing to it.

When the seeker reaches this level of mastery of the self, a change surrounds him. His will becomes nearly indomitable; the mind tricks of the Ventrue, as well as the emotional manipulations of the Toreador and even the Malkavian skill of inducing insanity affect the seeker only slightly. The seeker is by no means immune to these powers, but he is resistant to them, as his mind has been trained to examine and re-examine his actions constantly for any hint of control by the Beast. Likewise, the effects of any standing blood bond are lessened considerably. Rumor has it that a seeker at this point may actually be released from the bond if he asks his regnant for freedom, honestly and without threat.

When the Kindred has atoned for his crimes, controlled the Beast and learned to make a final understanding of himself, the easiest parts of Golconda are over. All that

Attachment

Enclosed among these papers, the reader will find a letter from a mentor to a supplicant. Please treat it with care.

> *Tonight, I witnessed a great triumph of spirit. I saw possibility in you. Despite the way the fight ended, you are on the right path.*
>
> *To be sure, you may expect the ignorant brutes of the Sabbat to react the way they did. The paths they follow are their own; we do not seek to convert others. You stopped them from slaughtering those mortals; you did not fail simply because they didn't understand your reasoning.*
>
> *Please understand: Feel no guilt or shame over ending their unlives. I won't play G-d and state that they deserved it, but you acted truly and honorably. You warned them that you would defend yourself and you warned them of your age. They should have run. Instead they attacked. Please, please ~~~~ do not suffer for them. You have much yet to do.*
>
> *Lux Veritas,*
> *—C.*

lies ahead is the Suspire. This ordeal determines what the rest of unlife holds for the seeker. And we have now reached a critical place in this writing.

All Suspires are intensely personal trials, tailored for the Kindred undergoing them. They are meant to test the areas in which the Cainite's soul is weakest. They nearly always touch on some aspect of the seeker's clan. A Lasombra seeking Golconda might, as part of his Suspire, be forced to stare at an empty mirror and struggle to come to terms with what he sees (or does not see) therein. But clan alone is only part of the journey. At times, the ordeal is physical. Most supplicants undergo great pain through fire or sunlight, to test their strength in holding the Beast at bay. But the most important part of the Suspire is the journey into one's own soul, the long-departed soul that accompanied each of us until our sire drove it out with his vitae.

I cannot tell you of any other common threads between Suspires. There are none. The experience is meant for one being alone. I refuse to speculate further on what sort of test any given Cainite might endure; I am neither philosopher nor scholar, and such guesswork is beyond me. I can only tell you, with any clarity, of one Suspire.

Mine.

I had no tutor, not directly, so my steps on the road to Golconda were clumsy. All Cainites must overcome an aversion to feeling guilt, selfish beings that we are. My sire's blood saw to it that I had to overcome a deadening of all emotion. I had to reach past years of training in thinking and observing instead of feeling before I could even begin to understand Golconda. I had to forget all of my "progress" in the Path of the Scorched Heart, regain my human ethics, before any progress was possible.

It took me nearly a century to do so. A century of unlearning, of abstaining from killing any living or unliving things (except wights; I expressed my reasons for hunting them earlier, and I did and do feel that the world is a better place for their absence). When I finally was able to feel something again, it was a horrible, crippling guilt, stronger than anything I remember feeling since my breathing days. For nearly a century more, I tracked down descendants of my victims, when I could. I could not explain to them exactly what had happened, but I gave directions to the bodies of those I remembered. I funded (and, where possible, attended) funerals. I did not feed on human vitae for several decades, and then only out of sheer necessity.

The Beast has a weaker grasp on those of my clan than most, because of our deadened hearts. However, morality comes dear to us as well. So, where the hardest part of attaining Golconda for most Cainites might be mastering the Beast, for me it was finding my humanity.

I did. How is another matter. It certainly wasn't one event that opened my eyes, but little by little, I found myself longing for sunrise, which I hadn't done since I was a neonate. My two most common pursuits, music and swordplay, both of which I took up for practical reasons (namely honing my dexterity and coordination, and self-defense, respectively) I took to again with enthusiasm. I was engaging in these activities for the accomplishment I felt in learning or mastering new skills (or merely sharpening old ones) rather than always considering the practicality of such abilities.

And finally, I took up sailing again. Oh, the welcome I felt the sea give me when, for the first time in nearly three centuries, I sailed out to her on a one-man craft!

While on that boat, I entered the Suspire. It was much like dreaming, but without any hope of waking and seeing that everything was as it had been. I knew that, when I woke, whatever happened in the dream would follow me.

The dream began in Jerusalem, near my home. I was pushing my boat out to sea, and my son came running toward me. He asked to come with me. I had seen this scene before, I realized; this was the day that I would beach my craft and lay down to sleep on the sands, only to be awakened by Ezra, my sire. If I took my son with me, who knows what Ezra might do? And yet, if I refused him, my last memories of him (for I did not return home after my Embrace) would be of him disappointed and hurt.

I thought about this, and then promised him I would be home soon, to wait for me. It was a lie, true, but a lie that left him happy and anticipating. I sailed out, ignoring the dark clouds on the horizon. That should have been a clue that I was wrong.

The water became choppy as it had that day. The sky clouded over as night approached, and I beached my craft on an unfamiliar shore. I lay down to sleep, and found I could not. When a being walked toward me, I stood, expecting to see Ezra. Instead, I saw myself, after a fashion.

I saw myself as I would become: dressed in an expensive suit, peppered hair cropped short, watching everything with calm observance. My future-self approached, and asked why I had chosen as I did. I responded, "So that I did not disappoint my son upon leaving him."

He calmly asked, "No. Why did you leave at all?" And at that, I knew I had failed.

The Suspire is the final chance, the very last opportunity for a Cainite to right the wrongs of his unlife. At least, it was to me. Nothing I have done, not the wights I have destroyed nor the music I have created, none of this would equal the happiness I could have given my son and wife

Sins of the Blood

Storytelling the Suspire

The Suspire is the final step on the road to salvation, and as such, it might require a story by itself. If only one character in a coterie is seeking Golconda, perhaps representations of her fellows appear in the Suspire to test or guide her. If this is the case, the Storyteller should work with the other players and make sure that they know any hints that they need to drop or actions that their characters must take. The players must also realize that the Suspire is a personal experience meant for the character seeking Golconda. That character must be the star of the show during the Suspire.

So, what happens during a Suspire? Does the Cainite confront her worst enemy and battle to the death? Does the character meet God and beg for mercy? Is there a Holy Grail-esque symbol that the Cainite must find? The answer to all of these questions is… yes, if that's what the story requires. However, bear a few story considerations in mind.

While some Suspires do involve a physical challenge, even this challenge is symbolic. A fight scene might represent a Cainite's triumph over the Beast, whereas a scene that forces the seeker to endure fire or sunlight might be constructed to test her resolve and fortitude (not Fortitude). The true power of the Suspire lies in the inner journey that the Cainite undergoes.

What exactly happens during this journey is entirely up to the needs of the story. The Cainite almost assuredly has crimes that need to be redressed or regrets she needs to release, so bring them to the fore. You might choose to give the player a chance to symbolically rectify mistakes that her character has no chance of fixing in the "real" world. You might choose, instead, to present her with an entirely new problem based on what she has learned over the course of seeking Golconda. The Cainite might find herself forced to persuade a group of mortals to help her without the aid of Disciplines, appealing to their humanity. She might find herself confronted with the worst horrors humanity has to offer.

In any event, allow the player to justify her actions before deciding that her character does or does not pass the test and reach Golconda. There should not be a "right" and "wrong" way to complete a Suspire. Certainly, the Storyteller should have an ultimate goal in mind, but if the player finds a way to succeed during the challenge that sounds reasonable for her character, don't insist that the way you devised is the only path to Golconda.

had I simply *not left them* that fateful morning. Since the decision to become a Cainite was not mine, the only way I could rectify that mistake was symbolically, in the Suspire. But I did not. I took my Embrace as an immutable fact, and therefore left my family and sailed off to my doom once again.

When I awoke, I was lying on the deck of the boat. The sun was creeping over the horizon, and I had an urge to greet it. I did not, obviously. I slept on the boat that day, sailed back to shore that night, and began to contemplate what to do with my unlife.

It would be at once true and a bitter falsity to claim that I was lucky. True, I survived the Suspire with my unlife and sanity intact. Many failures are not so fortunate. Those who fail either fall to ashes or become a sort of wight, but without the desire to hunt. They simply wander about, lost in agony, until the sun ends their pain.

But on the other hand, I did not succeed, and there is only one chance at Golconda. Going on, knowing what might have been — this is probably the worst torture of all, and I have felt it before. The nights following my Embrace saw me lurking out of sight as my family slept, and me wishing with what passion I could muster that I might see them in daylight again, hold them close, teach my son to sail. I saw them again in my Suspire, and like Orpheus, that one sweet glance was all I had before my own lack of foresight doomed me forever.

So, what of the Kindred who completes his Suspire successfully? I know only that the Beast loses its teeth. The Kindred's unlife is forever free of frenzy for any reason. I have also heard that the thirst takes him much less frequently, as little as once a month, and that he becomes capable of improving his command of the gifts of Caine well beyond the norm. The requirements of purity are still there, of course: The Kindred cannot slip from his spiritual standards, but without the Beast, these standards are much easier to maintain.

Some Cainites who have reached this state choose to meet the dawn with their souls cleansed, but most remain, teaching, traveling, righting whatever wrongs they feel need to be addressed. Some leave all society and lead their unlives in the wilderness, although how they contend with Lupines is anyone's guess. Sometimes, they gravitate toward a seeker, almost by instinct, and help him down his own road.

Dear G-d, I so looked forward to doing just that. To being a father again, even in a loose sense. I have never sired — I remember enough about passion that I would never wish the curse of emotionless eternity on anyone — but I do miss being a teacher of any sort. Well, perhaps this writing will educate the reader enough to start him (or her) down the path. I sincerely hope so.

I close this treatise now. One hour and fifty-two minutes remain before sunrise; enough time to get to the docks and sail east.

You see, although everything I have heard and studied indicates that no second chance for Golconda exits, my Suspire taught me the danger of taking anything for granted. So, I shall consider this my second Suspire, in a way. If I am strong enough to endure the sun's rays, to suffer that pain and fear, perhaps I will once again "dwell in the Light."

If not… perhaps I will see my family again.

Either eventuality fills me with joy. I do not wish to consider the probabilities, nor the implications. I am through with observation. Tonight — today — I act. G-d go with me.

To you, the reader, I can only apologize if this writing seems rambling or improbable. I am sure that a true scholar would know how to arrange such an essay, but I am not a scholar. I am sure that a philosopher would quote the great minds of the ages as support for his thoughts, but I am not a philosopher.

I remain, simply,
Nehemiah,
Childe of Ezra,
Childe of Joshua,
Childe of Brujah

Paths of Enlightenment

Below are three additional Paths of Enlightenment. None of these Paths boast very large followings among any sect. However, occasionally a neonate emerges with enough potential to attract a mentor from one of these Paths.

The Path of the Scorched Heart

I feel no anger against you, although you have wronged me. I bear no grudge. However, since I obviously cannot trust you, it makes no sense for me to allow the possibility of you wronging me again. You understand.

—Nostoket, Gangrel of the Black Hand

Nickname: Unforgiving

Basic Beliefs: One of the Paths of choice in the now-defunct "True" Black Hand, the Path of the Scorched Heart prizes observation and logical thought over all. Strong emotion, contend the Unforgiving, is for the flawed, and it ultimately clouds judgment. Only hard data can be trusted, and this means data that are observed firsthand. Earning the trust of an Unforgiving is next to

ADDENDUM

Your grace, I found these papers exactly where you suggested I look. The clerk at the hotel seemed to expect me. I can only assume that this "Nehemiah" wished for you and you alone to be in possession of his last words. Judging from a curious story I heard on the docks last night, I believe he did indeed sail out to his demise. Two sailors spoke of a rumor they heard that a rented sailboat drifted toward the docks containing no trace of the man who leased it. All it did contain was a fine dusting of what appeared to be ash, an Italian sword (estimated value nearly 200,000 American dollars) and a genuine Stradivarius violin. (I have data to guess its value, however, should you wish me to procure it for you, I will do my best.) Both items show signs of recent use.

Please write me care of the hotel in Mexico City (you have the address, I believe) and advise me as to what you wish done with these pages, my prince. I wish to leave this country as soon as possible.

Yours truly,
Adam

impossible, since they consider that information that they glean from others sullied by those others' perceptions and emotions. Even if a follower of the Scorched Heart trusts someone, he trusts only that the person would not lie deliberately, which in no way makes him a reliable source.

The Path of the Scorched Heart originated within the strange bloodline claiming to be the original descendants of Brujah. Struggling to come to terms with the Beast, Brujah (so the legends say) decided that all emotions, negative or not, were tainted by the Beast's touch and so, therefore, were the actions of any Cainite ruled by her emotions. In cutting off the mind and soul from emotion — "scorching the heart" — Brujah hoped to find respite from the Beast.

The Unforgiving are wary of imposing their morality on others. What appears right or wrong may only seem so because the observer does not know the full story. Therefore, if a follower of this Path sees that something she perceives as immoral or otherwise wrong, she will attempt to prevent it only if immediate action is called for. Otherwise, she investigates, learns and then acts, secure that she knows enough to do so. A threat against her personally, however veiled, is treated as real. The Unforgiving do not like loose ends or subtle hints, and they are persistent in tracking down foes not because they bear grudges, but because they do not wish to chance having the foe come back to harm them later.

Needless to say, the Unforgiving detest the Beast. Succumbing to frenzy is considered a failure on the Path, as is falling to Rötschreck. The very fact that the Beast can be resisted indicates to the Unforgiving that it must be resisted. Since few vampires remember what happens when the Beast holds sway, no knowledge can be gleaned from it that isn't secondhand (and therefore tainted).

The Unforgiving tend to have long and near-perfect memories. They pay close attention to their surroundings, and they are superb listeners. Of course, they employ these talents largely to gain information that might be used to their advantage later. The Path prizes secrecy — if an enemy knows nothing about you, he is more likely to make mistakes when acting against you. Some of the Unforgiving make a brisk trade in selling information. While other Cainites may not know of this Path's existence, they soon learn that its followers are meticulously thorough in gathering data.

The Ethics of the Path

- Do not feel emotion. All emotion is clouded by the Beast's rage and therefore taints your view. Avoid fear and anger especially, as these are the tools of the Beast, and love, as it can be easily used against you.

- Trust only what you perceive. If a house is painted white on one side, you cannot assume that it is white on the other, as you cannot perceive it. Remember that around Cainites, even your perceptions can be fooled, so double and triple check everything before drawing conclusions.

- Never pass up a chance to learn a secret about another Cainite. Even if you never have to use the secret, simply knowing it will help you predict the Cainite's reactions.

- Do not kill mortals unnecessarily. Their emotions are untainted by the Beast, and therefore, they have much to live for. If a mortal has degenerated to the point that he behaves as a Beast-ridden Cainite might (serial killers, rapists, gluttons, etc.) kill him without hesitation.

- Consider carefully before trusting another Cainite, even to a small degree. Even another of the Unforgiving has her own agenda, and it may conflict with yours. Always be careful to define the nature of a relationship and never presume honesty or loyalty if such was never specifically stated. Likewise, you have no reason to display these characteristics to others unless you state that you will.

- Before taking any violent action, ask yourself if it is truly necessary. How would you benefit from another's death? If the answer is simply that it would make you "feel better," you are succumbing to the Beast's urgings, and you must leave the situation immediately.

Virtues

The Path of the Scorched Heart uses the virtues of Conviction and Self-Control.

History

As mentioned, this Path was pioneered by the clan founder of the Brujah. However, it wasn't codified as a true Path until the 14th century, when a True Brujah called Rathmonicus collected the beliefs and practices of the bloodline into a codex called the *Book of the Empty Heart*. While he himself was destroyed during the Anarch Revolt, the book survived to be re-copied and passed among members of the True Brujah, the Lasombra, the Giovanni and the Toreador. Perhaps three copies of the *Book of the Empty Heart* survive — certainly no more — in the collections of elder Unforgiving. The Unforgiving do not seek converts actively, and they typically wait to approach a candidate until she is an ancilla.

Current Practices

Only a handful of Cainites follow the Path of the Scorched Heart in modern nights. The Unforgiving are nearly invisible, since their ethics require patient watchfulness rather than extravagant action, though, so their true number may be higher than believed. When two of the Unforgiving meet, it is usually to compare notes or to share (or sell) secrets, rather than to engage in philosophical discourse. There is no true organization among the followers, but since so few exist, most Unforgiving know the rest at least by reputation.

Description of Followers

Most Unforgiving are observant, almost passive. They stand quietly in the back of the room, watching all that transpires, occasionally taking notes or speaking into a tape recorder. Modern technology doesn't frighten most Unforgiving, even the older ones, as they take the time to study and comprehend new devices rather than shying away from them. They tend to dress stylishly but plainly, not wishing to draw attention. When they do speak, they ask clarifying questions or make simple, obvious statements.

The Path originated with the True Brujah, and many of its followers are members of this bloodline. The occasional Lasombra (sometimes *antitribu*) follows the Path, as do some Ventrue. The Path even has a modest following in the Giovanni, though less among the clan's Italian branch than its American and Scottish families.

Following the Path

The Unforgiving repress emotion utterly. They rarely smile or laugh, but they do understand humor. They will gently (or not so gently, depending on circumstances) correct a Cainite who has his facts wrong about a subject, but they never contradict opinions, and they rarely argue such abstracts as religion. Killing comes easily, as guilt is ignored or suppressed, but the Unforgiving dislike killing that does not involve self-defense or ridding the world of destructive influences. They consider vampires to be inherently destructive, and they typically have few compunctions about destroying them. However, they do realize that the repercussions of such acts usually outweigh the benefits, and besides, the Unforgiving have much to learn from other Cainites. Some Unforgiving hunt down certain types of Cainites (Sabbat, wights, infernalists, etc.) while some merely observe and strike when necessary.

Common Abilities: Almost all Unforgiving have high Alertness scores, for obvious reasons. Many are also skilled in Investigation and Linguistics. Those who deal with other Cainites typically have high Subterfuge ratings as well. However, it bears noting that if an Unforgiving has occasion to learn an Ability, she usually will. Therefore, it is not uncommon for a very scholarly and pacifistic Cainite on this Path to know how to handle a gun (or even a more anachronistic weapon) with a great deal of skill.

Preferred Disciplines: Auspex is almost universal among the Unforgiving, regardless of their clan. The more data perceived, the more knowledge gained. Many Unforgiving also cultivate Dominate (for coaxing the truth out of reluctant witnesses) and Animalism (beasts see things that humans — and vampires — cannot). Often the Cainite learns one of the physical Disciplines, most frequently Fortitude, to aid in combat, should it become necessary. However, as with Abilities, a follower of the Path of the Scorched Heart learns whatever she is able, so making assumptions about an Unforgiving's capabilities can be fatal.

The Path of Self-Focus

No one controls you. No Vaulderie or bond, no Cainite's will, except your own. When you learn to quiet your mind and silence the Beast, you will see this.
—Juleidah, autarkis

Nickname: Internalists

Basic Beliefs: The Path of Self-Focus draws heavily on the Eastern philosophy of *wu wei*, or conscious inaction. The Internalists believe that deliberate attempts to change the world around them result in misery and failure. In effect, one must master oneself before claiming any kind of mastery of the world.

Internalists are not selfish in the sense that they don't care for others. They simply believe that meddling in other beings' affairs is dishonorable and wrong. It is one thing, say the followers of the Path, to aid someone who calls for help, but it is another entirely to endure pain or danger for someone who does not wish for such a savior. Pain is a learning experience, and "saving" someone from it is akin to robbing that person of knowledge.

The followers of this Path also believe that the answers to all moral and spiritual questions can be found within oneself. No teacher can answer a question for you. The best she can do is direct your gaze inward, where the wisdom lies. As such, some followers of this Path might claim that it makes a good starting point for Golconda. Most acknowledge, however, that as Golconda requires interaction with the world around the seeker, the Path of Self-Focus would only begin the seeker's journey.

Internalists place a great deal of emphasis on existing in the moment rather than planning too much for the

Path of the Scorched Heart Hierarchy of Sins

Score	Moral Guideline	Rationale
10	Making assumptions of any kind	You can never know enough.
9	Relying on others	Your actions are the only ones you can predict with certainty.
8	Acting rashly	Observe, think, calculate, consider then act.
7	Passing up an opportunity to learn a new skill or Discipline	You can never be sure what skills will be needed, so learn as much as possible.
6	Failure to kill a destructive mortal	Mortals are blessed with untainted emotions. Those who squander this gift do not deserve it.
5	Failure to end an overt supernatural threat (if possible without undue risk)	Mortals deserve to live without supernatural interference. However, it isn't worth dying over.
4	Killing a non-destructive mortal	There are sources of vitae that are more deserving of your attention.
3	Falling to frenzy or Rötschreck	To learn, you must remain objective.
2	Emotional outburst	What you feel is a weapon that your foes can wield. Do not present them with that weapon
1	Feeling strong emotion	The Beast feels. You do not. Deny the Beast, and it will wither.

future. As a Zen master once said, "Wash the dishes to wash the dishes." That is, say the Internalists, when performing a task, know only that task, not how it will affect them later, not whether it is good or bad, but simply completing it and doing it well. Doing so involves knowing a task for what it is, and clearing the mind of distractions such as hunger or the Beast's urges.

The Internalists do not seek to expunge or deny the Beast entirely, however. "Things are as they are" is a common axiom among the followers of this Path, and they accept that the Beast must be allowed to roam sometimes. However, a time and place exists in which to do so, and succumbing to the Beast at inappropriate times is considered shameful to the Internalists, since it suggests that they do not truly know themselves as they claim.

The Ethics of the Path

- The past and future are illusions; in truth, there is only now. Exist only in the moment.
- Know yourself, and understand that the Beast is part of that self. Know when to release the Beast and when to hold it in check.
- Learn your strengths and your weaknesses. Do not be like the carpenter who, when faced with a tree too large and twisted to cut down, called it useless. Instead remember that the tree was good for giving shade and shelter. Turn your weaknesses into strengths whenever possible.
- Overconfidence is a weakness and a conceit. Those who take pride in themselves are deluded; there is always someone who can humble you. Learn to identify such people, and be willing to learn from them.
- Judge others by actions, not by words. Words can have many meanings, but action reveals truth.
- Enjoy and learn from others, but remember that you alone are responsible for yourself.

Virtues

The Path of Self-Focus draws on the virtues of Conviction and Instinct.

History

The Path of Self-Focus in its current form dates back to the sixth century AD, when Middle Eastern Cainites and Asian vampires met and shared ideas. These ideas gradually evolved into a methodology reminiscent of the both Taoism and Zen Buddhism, made accessible and useful for Cainites. The "True" Black Hand brought this Path back to Europe and later the Americas, but it finds adherents worldwide. Indeed, the basic precepts of the Path can be found in several of the Dharmas now practiced by the Cathayans.

While it is unpopular among European Cainites, the Path of Self-Focus has a tiny but growing following among American Kindred.

Current Practices

Internalists may teach any student who displays promise in Taoist philosophy and grasps the basic precepts of the Path. Age is not normally a factor, nor is clan or sect. The Path's ethics are close enough to Humanity for an Internalist to exist among the Camarilla with little problem, while in the Sabbat, the followers are prized for their intelligent introspection and balanced nature. Since the very nature of the Path is solitary, followers rarely have any contact with each other outside of mentor-student relationships.

Description of Followers

Internalists, like the Unforgiving, are patient and perceptive. However, unlike the Unforgiving, they judge situations completely subjectively: How a circumstance relates to them is more important than remembering all of the minute details.

The Path of Self-Focus, also like the Scorched Heart, encourages its followers to learn many different skills. The reasoning is very different, however. While the Unforgiving learn whatever they can in hopes that it might be useful, the Internalists learn skills that complement or contrast their natural strengths, in order to learn more about themselves. Therefore, Internalists study fencing and poetry, calligraphy and martial arts, marksmanship and etiquette. Internalists are always respectful of others, and they would never presume to insult or dismiss someone based on beliefs or words. If someone acts against them, they defend themselves with as much or as little action as necessary. A stream, they point out, does not have to destroy a rock to move around it.

Members of nearly any clan or sect can study the Path of Self-Focus, provided they can find a willing teacher.

Following the Path

An Internalist spends some time in meditation every night. Every new sensation — feeding in a new way, learning a new skill, even suffering a wound from a new source — is grounds for inner contemplation. While other Cainites may find Internalists slow and overly introspective, they must admit that an Internalist knows exactly what she is capable of doing and does not push her limits so as to place herself in danger.

Internalists believe in a higher purpose to the world, be it in the form of God, ultimate meaning, an Oversoul or whatever ideal one chooses to apply. They also believe that the key to understanding this meaning lies within them, and that belief gives them a sense of hope that few other Paths can provide. Followers of the Path are honor-

The Path of Self-Focus Hierarchy of Sins

Score	Moral Guideline	Rationale
10	Overconfidence	Know yourself without delusion or ego.
9	Laziness of mind or body	When you stop contemplating yourself, you cease to learn and develop.
8	Failure to treat others as you would be treated	Show the ways of respect by example.
7	Relying on others	Although they may be strong, they cannot know your true purpose any more than you can know theirs.
6	Manipulating or controlling others (through Disciplines or the blood bond)	Thinking beings are not for you to own.
5	Struggling to overcome a weakness rather than turning it into a strength	Struggle creates conflict and moves you out of line with yourself.
4	Restraining the Beast unnecessarily	The Beast is part of you, and it demands focus.
3	Failing to spend some time each night in meditation	Like a muscle, self-focus grows weak with disuse.
2	Allowing outside forces to goad you into frenzy	You alone control your actions.
1	Being a willful slave	You must act as your own master. Even a teacher's orders must be questioned.

able and respectful, but they are quite willing to allow the Beast to rage if that is what is called for.

Common Abilities: Etiquette, Brawl (or Martial Arts), Expression (poetry or painting) — Internalists study anything that aids in understanding oneself and honing strengths or lessening weaknesses. All Internalists eventually acquire some skill at Meditation, although an initiate on the Path might not have an actual rating in the Skill.

Preferred Disciplines: The ability to leave the body and drift on the ether is something to which all Internalists aspire, therefore most learn Auspex, hoping to reach that level. Other Disciplines that rely on changing or augmenting the self (such as Celerity, Fortitude, Protean and Potence) are also considered worthy pastimes. Internalists that learn manipulative Disciplines such as Presence or Dominate usually do so as an experiential exercise and don't employ them except in self-defense.

The Path of Harmony

I am not a monster, I am a predator. Anything monstrous in the nature of a Cainite was already present before the Embrace.
— Will Baker, Brujah reformer

Nicknames: Harmonists

Basic Beliefs: Harmonists do not believe that anything that exists is "unnatural." Simply "being" means that an individual or force has a place. This includes vampires. Yes, the vampire's role in the natural order is somewhat unpleasant, but then, the rabbit would likely feel the same way about the fox. Harmonists have great respect for the natural order and their place within it.

Of course "natural order" is somewhat subjective. If vampires are meant to be a predator to humans, are they meant to keep the mortal population in check? If so, they are not keeping up with the times. Older Harmonists realize that the natural order is in a constant state of flux, and so trying to "preserve" it is an artificial notion. It can't be preserved, it can only be observed and realized. The earliest precepts of the Path of Harmony teach the Cainite to protect the world from undue disruption, which some interpret as attention to ecological concerns. As the Harmonist progresses on the Path, however, he learns that obeying the natural order is really a matter of walking the fine line between knowing when to act and when to leave well enough alone.

Harmonists also realize that they are predators in the unique position of being able to identify and understand their prey. However, they also realize that this understanding, if taken too far, can push them toward the Beast — exactly what happens when vampires attempt to retain Humanity as their moral code. Therefore, the Harmonists hold mortals in fairly high regard — but not as high as themselves.

The Ethics of the Path

• "Evil" and "good" are mortal attempts to codify events. They have no practical meaning, and they do not apply to your unlife.

• Human beings may be fascinating to watch and even to play with — the need to stave off boredom is an important one. However, you are not mortal any longer, so do not be fooled into believing that you are.

- The world is constant in a state of change; we are not. Adapt to the world's changes. It is our only means of survival.
- Do not sully your haven. This means that the neighborhood in which you reside should be clean and, if necessary, defended against rival predators and decay.
- We are the highest form of predator, as we have both human instincts and superhuman hunting skills. Hone both, but let neither overdevelop.
- Harmony is achieved by each aspect of existence fulfilling its role. As a Cainite, your role is that of a hunter.

Virtues

The Path of Harmony relies on the virtues of Conscience and Instinct.

History

Originally developed in the early 18th century in the Americas, the Path of Harmony combined elements of Native American beliefs and ideals gleaned from simply observing the world and the progress of humanity. The Path enjoyed some favor in the Sabbat for a time, and then suffered a recent schism with the sect. The Harmonists felt that the Sabbat's methods and ultimate ends were too destructive, both to the world and to the individual members of the sect. The Path split. Some members embraced their bestial sides and rediscovered the far older Path of the Feral Heart. Most of the remaining "true" Harmonists perished, left the Sabbat or learned to reconcile their faith with their sect loyalty (typically as nomads).

Current Practices

Harmonists make their havens wherever they feel safe. Most avoid Sabbat-dominated cities unless they are still members of the sect. Some claim membership in the Camarilla, whether they actually support the sect or not. While the Path draws more derision than open hostility from the Camarilla, the Harmonists have learned that it is simply safer to remain quiet.

Harmonists in the same general area do meet occasionally, if they are aware of each other. Young Harmonists occasionally influence ecological activist groups. Most Cainites on the Path, however, soon learn that no matter how "natural" the rural areas are, the territory is often already claimed. A smart predator respects a stronger predator's territory, so the Harmonists, despite accusations of "tree-hugging" by their former Sabbat brethren, keep to the cities.

Description of Followers

It takes a certain kind of Cainite to follow this Path. After all, a truly bestial vampire likely follows the Feral Heart, a humane one retains her Humanity. The Path of Harmony exists for those few Cainites who can find a balance between the two sides and retain it, interacting with the world around them without feeling guilty. As Harmonists progress, they realize that vampires are less predators and more parasites, and this realization actually makes co-existence with humans easier.

Harmonists may come from nearly any clan, but they are most common among the Gangrel, Nosferatu, Brujah and Ravnos. Since their Path coexists well with Humanity (and since the Sabbat feels that they are liabilities) there are more Harmonists in the Camarilla than in other sects in the modern nights, but even a statement like that is a matter of scale.

Following the Path

Unlike the Beasts, who have no sense of mercy or compassion, the Harmonists do not disdain such feelings. Humans have them, after all, and harmony entails keeping both the human side and bestial side of one's nature in check. However, if a Harmonist does not feel merciful, or if the situation seems to demand viciousness, she will do what is necessary. This attitude makes Harmonists unpredictable; the vampire who drank gently from a vessel and left her sleeping last week may tear out another's throat tonight. On the whole, however, Harmonists are among the more temperate of Cainites, even if they are only moderate by dint of the balance of extremes.

Common Abilities: Since the "natural habitat" of the vampire is the city, Harmonists are likely to acquire Area Knowledge, City Secrets and Streetwise, the better to know their territory. Most also have ratings in Survival and Animal Ken. Since Harmonists are expected to retain some of their human mindsets, Empathy is also common.

Preferred Disciplines: Animalism is seen as a good way to commune with the natural world, but it isn't required. Many Harmonists learn Auspex and Obfuscate (both good hunter's tools) and/or Presence (good for both luring and relating to humans).

The Path of Harmony Hierarchy of Sins

Score	Moral Guideline	Rationale
10	Attempting to alter the natural world	The world does not need your improvement. Don't try to play God.
9	Indulging in the Jyhad or playing too effectively at being mortal	Both human and Cainite societies are unnecessary for us.
8	Failing to hunt when hungry	Hunger makes harmony impossible because it is a distraction.
7	Pointless cruelty or kindness	Both are in your nature, but do not help or harm others without reason.
6	Not respecting a stronger vampire's domain	Predators do not seek danger.
5	Allowing gross disruption of the world	All things disrupt the world, simply by interacting with it. However, doing so deliberately is an attack on all things within the world.
4	Acting too human or too bestial	Acting too human makes it harder to kill when necessary; acting too bestial makes it too easy.
3	Refusing to kill if necessary	Better a dead mortal tonight than a live witch-hunter tomorrow. However, remember that even one dead mortal does not go unnoticed; discretion is paramount.
2	Feeling guilty about killing when necessary	All lives end; better they end to feed you than in some random or pointless way.
1	Grossly upsetting the natural world (vandalism, arson, etc.)	You have to dwell here, too.

Chapter Two: Sins of Society

The virtues of society are the vices of the saints.
—Ralph Waldo Emerson, Circles

Trapped between the great camps of the Camarilla and Sabbat rests a no-man's land populated by disenfranchised and expatriated Cainites called anarchs and autarkis. These social outcasts may protest such descriptions, but the fact remains that they exist as long as either of the major sects ignores them in favor of destroying the other. Once the scions of the Sabbat or the Camarilla's pillars decide to end these pariahs' existences, few of them will be strong enough to resist becoming ash. Fortunately, the Camarilla and Sabbat are often too preoccupied with one another to deal with what they consider rebel elements, so the anarchs, autarkis and occasional defectors trapped between Kindred and Cainite society exist by merit of reprieve. They are nothing to either sect but a perpetual nuisance and the occasional danger.

Knowing this, what brings Cainites to espouse this so-called unlifestyle? Why risk limited independence by angering two equally potent adversaries? The answers depend on whom you ask. Some shrug and claim that they enjoy the thrill; others launch into philosophical and political tirades against the two main sects and maintain that their actions are issues of choice. A candid few, however, admit that they had no alternative. Fate unzipped its pants, and they could do nothing but bend over and take it like a vampire.

Observers of the Cainite condition cite a variety of reasons for why Cainites may flitter in this social no-man's land. The Camarilla or Sabbat forced many into the fringes because of ideological disagreements, simple mistakes or unacceptable practices (a penchant for diablerie, slaking one's thirst on infants, etc.). Some enter this gray zone of their own volition because they either recognize their actions as "peculiar" or disagree with their blood kin's philosophies. Others are just drifting through with no particular allegiance (Uncle Tom to all, master of none).

Autarkis

By definition, autarkic means independent or self-sufficient, but in the modern nights, it is too often just another way of saying victim. While mortals hold romanticized views of loners as noble, independent rebels striking out against society — stealing from the rich to help the poor as it were — the truth is that Robin Hood never bit into Friar Tuck's neck for a nip of vitae. Autarkis are Cainites, first and foremost, and regardless of their intentions, they are every bit the Beast as their Camarilla and Sabbat cousins. By virtue of their solitary nature, perhaps they are even more the monster than anyone cares to admit. Regardless of whatever action deposited them on the fringes of vampiric society, they are convenient scapegoats for the nearest sect, easy targets for some youngblood looking to sharpen her fangs, and comrade to few.

For many autarkis, the Beast is a constant companion, and its voice grows louder with the passing loneliness. A few succumb to its impulses, surrendering to a cabin-fever-like frenzy. Others preoccupy themselves with indulgences best left untapped, while a rare handful possess the spiritual or mental wherewithal to stave off night after night of a haunted existence. Going mad is hardly romantic, so what drives Cainites into this state-of-being, what keeps them here, and what does everyone think of them? The answers are many….

The Seven Deadly Sins

A new bit of slang among some young vampires is "seven-D," short for the seven deadly sins. The practice began in the Sodom of cities, New York, among Sabbat packs, and it somehow fell into neonate usage with the city's fall. The namesake seven-D are often causes for young Kindred becoming autarkis, and the conceit ascribes the ways in which these Cainites managed to extract themselves from sect allegiance through choice or folly to one of the seven deadly sins.

• **Pride** — Few Cainites emerge from the Embrace proclaiming "I want to become autarkis." Well, perhaps not intentionally. The folly of the Embrace is that it instills a rush of power unequalled in experience. Many neonates and fledglings emerge from the change stronger, sleeker and deadlier than ever. Suddenly they are the lions of the savanna, seconds away from that burst of vigor that fells their antelope prey. Most young vampires are smart enough to keep their mouths shut and recognize the value of experience, age or their sire's claws. Others are not so well disciplined, and they overestimate their ability. They mouth off to the pack priest, insult a well-respected harpy or turn a fateful glare toward the sheriff. If they are lucky, someone slaps them on the wrist and they learn their lesson. Other times, response is quick and brutal, and the fledgling, neonate or even respected Cainite finds himself ostracized from sect society in a mortal heartbeat. Many autarkis who owe their banishment to pride have no one to blame but themselves. Their egos are their greatest adversaries, and someone decided to make an example of them.

Akin to this fate are those stubborn Cainites whose pride drives them into voluntary exile. Perhaps their sires or masters abused them once too often, or perhaps the vampire simply tired of serving as a pawn in the Jyhad or a foot soldier to the cause. Proud Cainites often chafe easily while in service to others, and they develop a "never-again" attitude before venturing off on their own. They rarely remain autarkis, however. Part of pride involves a dose of egotism, and vainglory cannot survive in a void. Cainites who suffered under the yoke of their sires often join the Anarch Movement, while those who believe that the sect never really appreciated their contributions usually become nuclei for cults of personality. Few return to the security of their sect unless absolutely necessary.

• **Avarice** — An iconoclastic elder of Clan Brujah once stated that avarice was a remnant of mortal folly. Avarice implies wanton, uncontrolled greed, which in turn implies impatience. To creatures who are virtually eternal, patience is often paramount to survival. Yet, some vampires still possess a mortal's scale of time, and they want everything now. Avarice is that clumsy sin. Autarkis burdened with impatience often earn adversaries through their heavy-handed attempts to accrue wealth, power or influence. They lie without discretion, steal without skill and play the Jyhad with the finesse of a drunkard. Along the way, they step on too many toes and reap an empty crop. Whether the sect casts the autarkis out because he did not warrant Final Death, or the outcast escaped before a lynch mob reached his doorstep matters little. His greed proved overwhelming and probably still remains a hindrance in his existence. These autarkis can never stay outside sect unlife, and they try continually to exert their influence where it remains unwanted. They often meet a quick end at the hands of sect vampires or by other autarkis who do not want them drawing the unwelcome attention of the Camarilla or Sabbat hierarchy.

• **Lust** — Lust is dangerous, for it implies that the Cainite cannot control his desires to possess someone else. Perhaps the autarkis craves the prince's harem of beautiful ghouls, or he cannot stop thinking about torturing and feeding from the elderly. Many burdened with such thoughts often exile themselves because there are no secrets among Cainites. In a society where vampires can sense intent through the hue of auras, spy on one another unseen and read minds, those with unbidden desires know that their fantasies are never safe. They can no longer protect their own thoughts, and they realize that isolation may be the only hope of true privacy. The tricky thing about Cainite society is that it is not often the passion that proves embarrassing, but the individual's shame in his own desires that is instrumental. Most Cainites do not give a second thought to same-sex lovers or addictions or fetishes. For a neonate who considers her lesbian attractions, foot fixation or need to be publicly humiliated an unwanted aspect of her personality, however, these secret activities now become her personal shame and an avenue into blackmail. It does not matter what other people think; it matters what they know. The majority of Cainites quickly move past their mortal preconceptions of acceptable behavior, but a few either cannot or they know that their sect will never condone their activities. There is nothing left to do then but sequester one's self from other vampires and pursue these desires on society's fringes.

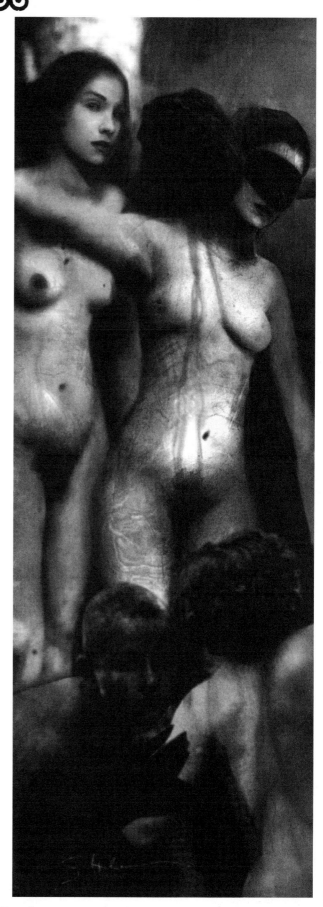

• **Envy** — Envy covers a gamut of desires, whether the Cainite covets the respected position of pack priest, the Ventrue's beautiful feeding vessel or the wealth of a dot-com success story. Of the deadly sins, this vice is generally directed toward a specific individual or target. Autarkis of this stripe saw something that was not theirs (be it a person, prestige, influence, power or capital), and they took every step to procure it for themselves regardless of the cost… and failed. The Cainite survived only because someone stopped him before he went too far, or because he fled destruction and is still running. In either case, his ambition is unfulfilled, but his desire remains enflamed. His very existence is a reminder of his failures, and he spends every passing night scheming and plotting with the hope of avenging himself. These autarkis are most dangerous, for they understand the benefits of patience and planning. They conceive intricate strategies, always with their eye on the prize. Of the autarkis, those cast out for this sin are most likely to monitor the activities of the local sect and make themselves indispensable to ambitious or oblivious neonates or fledglings. They want eyes, ears and hands to act as their proxies and move where they cannot. In return, the autarkis may offer wealth, information, secrets or even training in the gifts of the undead.

• **Gluttony** — Only in Camarilla society do such vices as sins of the blood exist; the Sabbat consider such activities a right of their superior existence. One of the many possibilities here is that the autarkis somehow endangered the herd too often by feeding to the vessel's death, feeding indiscriminately or maintaining overly large herds that risked breaching the Masquerade. When the news relates the story of a crack house raid, for example, it is possible that the sheriff or prince sanctioned the assault because a local vampire drew his herd from said crack house in squalid conditions and with little interest for his vessels' survival. No, the Camarilla is not universally so compassionate as to rescue "livestock," but it does care about the Masquerade. Such precarious herds invariably draw the attention of social services, child welfare, the police, DEA, FBI and a plague of news crews, so the prince steps in before the matter spirals beyond control and makes sure that someone quiets or kills the herd before the proper authorities can question them. Again, the Camarilla ostracizes the Kindred responsible for this "unpleasant situation," or he escapes.

Sometimes, though, the autarkis is not directly responsible for the gluttony. Recently, in New York, the Camarilla victory and a few Sabbat defections brought a surfeit of Kindred into the city. The ad hoc prince, the Nosferatu Calebros, feared that the influx would breach the 100,000:1 ratio of mortals to vampires for safe feeding practices, and he created scourge patrols to kick undesirables out of the city. At the top of the list were Sabbat defectors of lesser rank who knew that leaving the safety of New York would mean their destruction. Instead, they vanished into the New York underground, becoming autarkis.

Under some circumstances, the so-called "glutton" endures self-expatriation because he engages in the loathsome act of diablerie. Whether he committed it once and waits for the telltale black veins to vanish from his aura, or if the act has become addiction and the diablerist can no longer stop himself, becoming autarkis is often the only way to protect the truth. Unfortunately, turning autarkis means retreating from undead society, sometimes permanently and completely, lest former allies and acquaintances investigate the Kindred's whereabouts. Sabbat Cainites, however, enjoy some freedom with the Amaranth since it is one of the spoils of Monomancy. The Sabbat does question the loyalties of members who engage in such activities too readily, though. Diablerie is addictive, and the Sabbat wants Cainites servile to nobody's blood but their pack's.

• **Wrath** — Wrath involves crimes of the moment, often closest to the Beast in nature. While the Camarilla and Sabbat point to the autarkis as loathsome, self-involved creatures who prize themselves above all others, the fact is that anyone can become autarkis. It rarely requires a specific predisposition; it needs merely a moment of anger in the wrong place, at the wrong time. Wrath in context to Cainites implies an explosive, overwhelming rage, even frenzy, for a variety of reasons. While certainly embarrassing, it is rare, but not unheard of, for the enraged vampire to claw the face off the pack priest or a peer amid shocked Kindred at Elysium. In the second it takes to lose control, the Beast is supreme and the Cainite is marked forever by his actions. Sometimes, the powers that be inflict swift and decisive punishment because the Cainite attacked someone of importance. Other times, the vampire becomes autarkis after several displays of low self-control.

Unfortunately, Kindred who are banished because of their ill tempers are never truly alone. Camarilla authorities may use this vampire as an object lesson, but they also keep a watchful eye on the autarkis. Something about their fall from grace (such as an influential sire, a lenient prince or an ally among the primogen) did not warrant their destruction, but the Camarilla may well sanction destruction if the autarkis frenzies again — all in the name of protecting the Masquerade. Many autarkis who are exiled in this manner know that they are under surveillance. Someone watches them, waiting for them to frenzy so they can justify their murder. Someone may even try to provoke the autarkis, or just kill him and lie about the circumstances.

• **Sloth** — Ignoring the obvious connotation of laziness for a moment, accusations of sloth against Cainites imply that they are not "toeing the sect line" or "furthering its goals." This holds truer among Sabbat packs, which actively encourage their members to participate in sect rites and in the holy cause. Despite the Creation Rites, membership within the Sabbat still produces its share of "unworthy" Cainites (according to sect perception). Backing out of a War Party or legitimate Monomancy duel, allowing a traitor to escape during a Wild Hunt, fraternizing with the enemy once too often and consistently losing in Games of Instinct are all punishable failings. Regardless of the cause, there are fewer Sabbat autarkis running around because the sect destroys its mistakes or allows them to bring about their own destruction. Unlike the Camarilla, which turns failures into examples, the Sabbat is far less forgiving.

For Camarilla Kindred, instances in which someone becomes autarkis through "sloth" are rare, but they do happen. The Camarilla recently issued a blood hunt against a prominent ex-primogen and Nosferatu elder, after it was revealed that she knew about a coven of Sabbat amassing within the city. The Nosferatu understandably vanished. Several other Sewer Rats came to her defense claiming that the elder probably received the information in confidence and could not reveal it without betraying some code of silence or word of honor. Some Camarilla Nosferatu even hinted that they would not help destroy one of their own over a question of ethics. The Inner Circle dealt with the problem immediately by sending Nosferatu Justicar Cock Robin and Archon Federico DiPadua to handle the matter. The two accused several Nosferatu of being accomplices to the elder, and they allowed the accused to become autarkis (rather than suffer the Final Death) to stem any internal dissent. The ploy worked, and the Camarilla Nosferatu are now playing along.

Other Considerations

While the seven-Ds might seem like an easy way to quantify autarkis, most Cainites have dozens of other reasons why they might become an outcast. Some are Embraced into such an existence, with their sire already loathed by a sect (normally the Camarilla). The Sabbat believes in the pack over the sire, with loyalty offered to the whole first and the individual last. They are less likely to damn the childer of a particular Cainite unless she follows in her sire's footsteps. Camarilla Kindred, on the other hand, place the onus on the sire through the Fourth Tradition. Therefore, while the sire is responsible for his childe's actions, some Kindred also believe that the progeny carries the burden of their sire's mistakes — again bringing new definition to sins of the blood.

Other autarkis are the bastard childer of illegal Embraces (those committed against the Third Tradition, or done without the recognition or the sanctity of a Creation Rite). For whatever reason, the sire abandons these "orphaned whelps," leaving them to fend for themselves. Panders, some Caitiff coteries or anarchs occasionally adopt these autarkis and introduce them to one faction or another. Only the rare orphaned vampire is strong, smart or lucky enough to remain autarkis for any length of time. Both the Camarilla and Sabbat fear these strong individuals, however, for among them may lie the next Vlad Tepes, the most reviled of all autarkis.

Another sub-segment of autarkis includes the traitors, those Kindred or Cainites who switched sides before their city fell to anther sect's incursion or under some other dire circumstance. While both sects appreciate high-ranking or ideological defections for their propaganda machine, they rarely trust someone who betrayed their compatriots and ideals because their survival was in jeopardy. These traitors are momentary heroes for the night it takes either sect to parade them around, then oft forgotten and ignored. Few packs or coteries want these individuals as members, and some make it a point of beating that lesson into the defector. In some cases, such a Cainite becomes autarkis by circumstance, drifting far enough outside sect activity to avoid attention, but not far enough that the other side can easily deal with the traitor. These orbiting autarkis rarely survive beyond a few years, whether because they commit suicide from the isolation or because someone finally destroys them. For more information, see "Switching Sects."

Never forget that while some Cainites simply fall between the cracks, others jump. Both sects have their merits, but unlife with either includes some ugly possibilities. The Sabbat renounces its mortal ties and focuses on its holy struggle against the Antediluvians, while the Camarilla is a nest of Byzantine power ploys and political back-stabbing on scales undreamed of by kine minds. Some Cainites want part of neither world for whatever reason, and they forge their own way. This decision is a difficult one, for the sects do not believe in true neutrality when it comes to individuals. One is either a potential ally or a potential enemy. Unfortunately for these autarkis, their preferences and practices ostracize them automatically, and joining either side entails their destruction. Some Cainites are purely mercenary, with no interest in any war or cause that forces them to break their neutrality. Others are still strongly tied to the mortal world: a Malkavian who plays messiah to her kine community to atone for her "condition," a Tzimisce who looks and acts like a child because he can only relate to children (mentally and physically), a Brujah detective who has ghoul spies among the department to help him stem local crime. All these autarkis cannot surrender some facet of their mortal existence, so they remain a strong part of it regardless of the dictates of either sect. Many Cainites mistakenly believe that becoming a vampire washes all mortal concerns away. The truth, however, is that the first few years (or decades…) are a period of adjustment. A Cainite does not recognize the weight of undeath until she sees her friends and family grow old and die. A Cainite does not suddenly stop loving or hating everything she did in her mortal years. Everything simply pales in comparison to blood, but the ties are strong enough that some Cainites become autarkis because they can never abandon their former lives and loved ones (at least not yet). It is their weak anchor in a truly frightening world.

Although certainly not the last word on the matter, a growing body of self-exiled autarkis has turned away from the sects because Gehenna looms. Gathering around the campfires of Gehenna cults, they pursue a variety of actions. Some fear the apocalypse and worship these elder Cainites in the hopes of surviving the end times. Others hunt the Antediluvians and their "servants" in hopes of preventing their rise. At the spectrum's extremes lie suicide pact cults, Golconda-quest groups (to save their souls before it is too late) and Cainite survivalists. The Jyhad is reaching its endgame, and they all know it. How they conduct themselves, however, is the issue.

Whiling the Nights Away

With the longevity of many mortal lifetimes, it is perhaps a tragic reality that autarkis spend their unlives simply surviving. The Kindred have no support groups or mentors ready to guide the autarkis past the sharp rock rapids of their existence. They have only trial, error, pain and the constant threat of destruction to play teacher. These outcasts learn their lessons quickly, because there is no such thing as a slow-witted autarkis… or at least none have survived thus far. Instead the autarkis must adapt and become cunning. More importantly, they know when to obey the rules of the game and when to throw them out the window.

Whatever made the Cainite an outcast also turned him into someone's enemy; it is an inevitability of living among monsters. Few vampires simply vanish into the world without causing ripples somewhere. On the most immediate level, the enemy might be a specific person or creature whom the autarkis wronged. On a grander scale, the outcast is antagonist to an entire sect by often nothing more than reason of suspicion. Regardless of whether the autarkis knows of such adversaries or not, he should always believe that someone is out to destroy him. It is the only way to continue existing.

The first rule one realizes upon becoming autarkis is that she is immediately *persona non grata*, the same way India's old caste system treated *Harijan* (Untouchables), and Westerners ignore their homeless. These Cainites are an unfortunate embarrassment to anyone of greater station, and few individuals are lower than autarkis, except perhaps for the subject of a blood hunt. Even the Camarilla's view of the Nosferatu shines in comparison to its treatment of these outcasts.

In the best of cases, *persona non grata* is an accurate term, and the autarkis enjoys — if such is the proper word — relative privacy outside occasional harassment at the hands of fledglings and neonates. This luxury exists only for Cainites who were once important to the local sect scene. Their fall from grace warranted their sentence, but the regional elders bear the autarkis no ill will or hatred, only pity. Other autarkis, however, are not so fortunate. Benjamin Crayshaw, a repatriated Toreador pariah once existing on the fringes of San

Diego, described his experiences as akin to the Nazi's treatment of Jews in the 1930s, before the "Final Solution." The Camarilla and Sabbat rarely advocate open violence against autarkis (or else they would have destroyed the outcast themselves), but neither do they often reprimand any Cainite who wrongs them. Autarkis have seen their havens burned, their finances and assets suddenly evaporate, found their mortal loved ones drained (or worse, Embraced), received destruction threats and barely escaped ambushes.

Autarkis are often convenient scapegoats for whatever ails the sect. When it finds a member destroyed or someone cries traitor or a Cainite robs the communal haven, or the prince wakes in a foul mood, the autarkis make convenient (and politically impotent) victims. They can call upon no one. The only vampires who play at fostering relations with the autarkis know that they are the perfect patsies if anything goes wrong. Even sadder, the autarkis realize their true worth, but what choice do they have? Nobody else will talk to them, and regardless of the "lone creature of the night" routine, Cainites need some — any — companionship. Many willingly entertain alliances that might work against them because three years have passed since anyone spoke to them, or more importantly, listened.

Some autarkis exist as nomads because it is the only way to stay sane, to continue existing. Others are hunted. Remaining in one place means everyone knows where the outcast makes her haven; one night someone will destroy or stake him. Staying in one place limits a Cainite's options for escape and retreat. It is just another anchor slowing him down. Like Emmet of Clan Nosferatu, nomadic autarkis travel to cities where nobody knows them, taking melancholy comfort in the company of others, if only temporarily. It offers them a sense of control over their own unlives, even if it is tenuous. The risk of this practice is if a Cainite discovers that the autarkis deceived him into sheltering her. A duped host may become hostile at being played for a fool by such a vagrant, or he may even stake or destroy the pariah. After all, who will miss the autarkis or even protest her disappearance? Other risks include encountering Lupines, or even falling to the proliferating number of hunters crawling out of the woodwork. Therefore, the autarkis seeks refuge in temporary havens and travels to different cities until knowledge of her legacy dies down enough to settle somewhere in obscurity. Although she is no closer to making allies or finding comfort, the autarkis holds at least some control over her existence, no matter how transient.

Many vampires harbor the misconception that autarkis exist in a withdrawn, almost monastic unlifestyle. Somehow their seclusion from the sect offers them time to contemplate personal matters. Their lack of responsibility allows them to pursue a simple, almost idyllic existence. This assumption is as far from fact as the Cainite's own living heartbeat. Becoming autarkis is a nightly contest for survival against xenophobia, against denigration, and against the possibility of destruction. Even those left to their own devices struggle against the decaying spiral of their sanity and humanity. Cainites claim to be solitary creatures, but it is the Beast that is solitary in nature. Cainites still bear some shred of humanity — enough to instill them with need for community and fraternity. Autarkis possess no such anchor. Whether robbed of this companionship or enduring the lack of it because of self-inflicted isolation, the outcast has more time to contemplate the whispers of the Beast and endure its hunger. Few emerge from this continued harrowing intact.

Slings and Arrows of Outrageous Fortune

Given the loneliness and isolation endured by autarkis, is difficult to believe that they pose a threat to either sect. Yet, the Sabbat and Camarilla are very wary of these pariahs. They represent unknown quantities, seditious elements, a sect's weakness, and sometimes, they even represent personal fears. The sects have their reasons — some valid, some baseless — but the very fact that the fears exist is enough to elicit their general suspicion against the autarkis.

On a fundamental level, both the Sabbat and Camarilla distrust the autarkis because of their potential for sedition. The sects' example in illustrating this fear? Son of the Dragon, Vlad Tepes, Dracula. The feats of this legendary Cainite are well accounted for by other sources; suffice to say his actions and very existence worry both the Camarilla and the Sabbat. They fear him, and they fear that another like him could rise up from among the ranks of the autarkis (that is to say, a potent Cainite outside their jurisdiction and influence). In these Final Nights, the Sabbat needs more than just powerful allies. This sect must make sure that the Antediluvians cannot manipulate someone like Dracula. The Camarilla, however, fears the rise of yet another potent or directed force countering them. Dracula represents the ultimate in ego, casting aside the Camarilla Traditions for his own pleasures. The war against the Sabbat is taking its toll, and the Camarilla cannot afford to fight on two fronts simultaneously. Already the proliferation of Gehenna cults worries them, and it taxes their resources and manpower. The appearance of a charismatic "messiah" could easily weaken their power base at this crucial time. Yet, if either side wantonly slaughters the autarkis out of fear, it runs the risk of alienating some of the independent clans, making a martyr out of a small-time cult leader or galvanizing the autarkis against it.

The sects also fear traitors in light of recent events (the fall of New York and Atlanta, the destruction of the Tremere *antitribu* and Ravnos, the bloom of Gehenna cults, etc.). Many autarkis are former members of one or both sects, and they may carry with them unaccounted secrets. Both the Camarilla and Sabbat walk a fine line between diligence and paranoia, but even they cannot destroy everyone who crosses the line. The sects reserve the Wild Hunt and the Lextalionis for the most grievous offenses. All others endure corporal punishment, censure and, rarely, excommunication — abandonment by the sect or a declaration of anathema. Given recent losses for either side, however, the Camarilla and Sabbat do advocate harsher punishments over banishment to prevent secrets from falling into the enemy's hands. This policy may decrease the number of existing autarkis, but neither sect can account for those Cainites who abandon camp willingly.

Beyond the sect itself, individual vampires loathe and abuse autarkis for very personal reasons: fear and ignorance. Part of it is the cliquish nature of the sects, packs and coteries, all of which encourage the xenophobic treatment of outsiders or those deemed different. The real reason why some Cainites treat autarkis harshly, however, is that ever-present fear that they themselves could share the autarkis' fate. Many autarkis are victims of simple mistakes and failings that everyone commits. Every Cainite frenzies at some point in his existence; every Kindred invariably offends another vampire of greater or lesser station. The difference between a sect vampire and an autarkis, however, is that the circumstances were somehow different, and one managed to walk away from his encounter while the other paid for it. Knowing that unlife can be that random, that brutal, in its finality is a scary lesson. Unfortunately for such outcasts, the autarkis is constant proof of this inequity, and Cainites would rather lash out at that image than address it. Autarkis are a warning that anyone can fall far and fast, and nobody wants that truth waved in his face.

Of course, few autarkis deserve this justification or pity. Some Cainites endure this existence because they earned their punishment. They injured, stole, raped or committed some other act of violence or malice against their own community, and they received proper sentencing. If the individual is autarkis by choice, however, this arouses even greater suspicion. What is she hiding? What does she fear? Is she actually a spy or traitor? In this case, Camarilla and Sabbat alike feel fully justified in unraveling this mystery, all in the name of protecting their sect. Since autarkis rarely possess any recourse to protest their treatment or bring their attacker to "justice" outside of destroying them, sect vampires rarely worry about retribution for victimizing the autarkis.

Yet, not all autarkis are helpless targets of sect harassment. Occasionally, a Camarilla prince or Sabbat bishop hires able-bodied and skilled autarkis to perform his sordid deeds. With Clan Assamite's recent "liberation," many elders need Cainites to perform thefts, assassinations and other duties with no questions asked. Autarkis are obvious choices for such assignments because they hold no affiliation with the local sect, they have more to gain by cooperating, and if caught, their employer can deny all affiliation. The autarkis know that they are expendable, but some opportunities are too lucrative to ignore. In fact, some pariahs manage to survive through these ventures, preferring the autonomy of contract work to swearing fealty to a particular sect. All autarkis-for-hire, however, recognize the risk of betrayal that they run, but most believe that they can avoid such fates… or else they are truly desperate.

Anarchs

Equality, redistribution of wealth, freedom from the shackles of elder rule… all these slogans sound egalitarian and even noble to mortal sentiment, but Cainite society views such maxims with the same virulence that Senator McCarthy displayed pursuing so-called "subversives." These are dangerous ideologies in dangerous times, but for the anarchs, change must come now, regardless of the cost. In many ways, their demands echo different equality movements, including their failing impatience and dismissal of the potential backlash. On the surface such friction invariably boils down to generational conflicts between the status quo and the childer who envy the wealth of their elders (at least to the elders' perceptions). With the anarchs and the sects, however, these fears are more deep-rooted in experience and modern fears. To the Sabbat, the anarchs are an undirected and unruly mob, ripe for a cagey elder to direct at her whim, while the Camarilla believes that they endanger the very Traditions. Unfortunately, such conflicts are never about right or wrong; they are always about who brays the loudest. Right now, the Sabbat and Camarilla appear to be winning the match, but some conservative factions within the sects also wonder if the elders of the great clans felt as confident before the Anarch Revolt upended the Middle Ages.

Camarilla Views

The Camarilla bases its concerns of anarchs on present anxieties, but it backs its arguments with experience. Fortunately, those experiences serve as a form of hindsight given the Camarilla's encounters with the Sabbat, but it blinds them to the present agendas and capabilities of the more modern anarchs.

Two major events in Cainite history revolve around generation-based conflicts, beginning with the Second Generation's destruction at the hands of their Antediluvian childer, and continuing through to the Anarch Revolt that eventually saw the extermination of several Methuselahs, two Antediluvians and hundreds (if not thousands) of Cainites. Granted, such things as Antediluvians are largely discounted by the Camarilla, but stories about them are understood to be metaphorical at least. In these cases, the metaphor represents a significant upheaval in Kindred history, probably embodying the death of many vampires or the destruction of a brood's founder. The latter event's baptism in blood gave rise to the nascent Sabbat, a constant thorn in the Camarilla's flanks for over 500 years. Given that the contemporary Anarch Movement bears some similarities with the formation of the Sabbat, it is safe to say that the Camarilla does not want a repeat of that historical incident.

Currently, the anarchs represent the second strongest threat to the Camarilla's manifest destiny (outside the Sabbat). Knowing that old Clans Lasombra and Tzimisce fell when they failed to acknowledge their internal problems, the Camarilla is trying desperately to avoid another Anarch Revolt and Convention of Thorns fiasco. Additionally, the anarchs are slowly losing ground in their strongholds along the Pacific seaboard thanks to the Cathayans, prompting some within the Inner Council to declare the anarchs a fading threat. Others, however, fear an anarch resurgence, a final push, as it were, to restore their political struggle. If such a thing occurs, these young rabble-rousers may well prove the cornered animal fighting for its very survival.

Beyond historical bias, and on the surface, the Camarilla's central grievance with the anarchs' policies is the redistribution of finances, power and assets — or the opportunity for such, to hear the anarchs tell it. Such a redistribution might work out if everyone had been Embraced at the same time, but the fact remains that the Kindred in power took centuries to accrue their wealth and influence, and they are not willing to surrender all that hard work. Why should they advocate equality for everyone when their entire existence followed a harsh pecking order and centuries of slaving toward one goal? There is no parity in this existence, and only mortals believe that everyone is born equal. Cainites enter this existence with automatic advantages and disadvantages. It is the nature of the Beast. The difference in the potency of vitae alone sets one generation apart from the next and establishes a perceived order of rightful supremacy. Age is the second factor distancing sire from childe.

To Kindred, the anarchs are their jealous and unruly offspring who throw tantrums when they cannot have what they want. The Camarilla argues that power and wealth come to those who work and struggle for their position. They deserve their keep, and they appreciate their status all the more for it. Earning something for nothing creates a weaker society ignorant of its accomplishments. It rewards the lazy. Amusingly, these arguments are merely window dressing and misdirection for the Camarilla's true, but unspoken concern: the threat to the very Traditions that founded the sect. The anarch's call for equality and an end to the "tyranny of the elders" flies in the face of the Tradition of Domain, the Tradition of Progeny, the Tradition of Accounting and the Tradition of Hospitality. The Anarch Movement is a menace to the Camarilla by virtue of its demands, and the sect knows that the anarchs will accept nothing else. Therefore, there is no negotiation to be done or alliance to be made. The anarchs pursue a path and unlifestyle that the Camarilla does not and cannot condone because it counters everything upon which the sect prides itself. Their struggle for equality, as far as the Camarilla believes, is a return to the Dark Ages, during which injustices against Cainite and kine alike went uncounted. The Camarilla refuses to return to these unruly times, and it simply refuses to surrender its accomplishments and gains.

Fortunately for the anarchs, two issues are currently in their favor. The first is their loose relationship with the Gangrel, and the second is their adherence to portions of the Masquerade. First, the Camarilla lost potent allies when the Gangrel walked, and it wants them back for obvious reasons. The Gangrel, however, intermingle with the anarchs freely given their shared tastes for freedom and the opportunity to determine their own fates, and that means the Camarilla must treat either faction with kid gloves. Many accounts figure that the Gangrel are the most numerous clan among the anarchs, and no doubt contribute to the Caitiff population among the Gangrel as well. The Inner Council knows that it cannot risk subduing the anarchs openly without inadvertently injuring or drawing the Gangrel into the fight. The risk is currently too great, and the split between the Gangrel and Camarilla is too fresh. Second, the anarchs observe certain principles of the Masquerade including the need to remain hidden, and demonstrating self-control when feeding by not killing mortals. This reserve alone makes the anarchs far more tolerable than the Sabbat, and more sympathetic to some Camarilla elders. Therefore, the Camarilla currently advocates a grudging *laissez faire* policy until the situation either changes with the Gangrel, or the anarchs abandon their more tolerable practices.

Sabbat Views

All the freedom; none of the responsibility. To the Sabbat, this mixture is a dangerous one, perhaps more dangerous than the Camarilla's naivete. The anarchs are undisciplined, undirected and perfect for manipulation at the hands of the Antediluvians. The sect's fears, however, go far beyond this simplistic rationale. Yes, the Third Generation are a looming threat, and yes, too many vampires are unprepared for the impending conflict, but the anarchs are also an affront to the Sabbat's principal tenets. The Camarilla fears a potential alliance between the two factions, but the truth is that many within the Sabbat do not respect the anarchs' manifesto. Some Brothers and Sisters in Caine even consider the rebels' name an insult to the spirit of their own struggle for freedom.

The Sabbat agrees with some of the Camarilla's grievances against the anarchs, though certainly not publicly. Equality cannot exist when blood potency automatically differentiates one Cainite from another, and anything taken without sacrifice is not worth the effort. Beyond that, the Sabbat's grievances against anarchs diverge wildly. What the Camarilla calls "earning your keep," for example, the Sabbat calls survival of the fittest. The two may sound similar, but their approach to the matter differs drastically.

Chief among the Sabbat's tenets is the precept that only the strong survive. Everything in their existence involves winnowing the weak and strengthening the whole. The Creation Rite ensures that only the intrepid emerge from the Embrace, but it also hardens the mind and heart of the fledgling. Subsequently, unlife is a series of *ritae*, challenges and contests continually weeding the Cainite garden while training the packs to respond fearlessly. The Sabbat's eldest already faced down legendary Antediluvians and hoary Methuselahs, so they have an inkling of what to expect of the Final Nights. The new Sabbat, however, do not, so the eldest take it upon themselves to educate, discipline and train their younger pack mates for Gehenna — or for the battles that will prevent this cruel night. The anarchs, however, are an affront to this rigorous discipline and training. To the Sabbat, the anarchs are lazy, weak, and mostly undeserving of the Embrace. They do not challenge themselves to improve and become stronger. They insult Caine's gift and their obvious superiority in favor of pursuing mortal desires of equity.

More so, some of the more radical elements of the Black Hand fear that the new Anarch Movement is an attempt to weaken Cainites in preparation for the arrival of the Antediluvians. The anarchs' manifesto turns vampires soft and docile by eliminating the need for struggle. The Black Hand accuses the anarchs of serving the Ancients by attempting to de-fang and de-claw Cainites, turning them into sheep for the slaughter. The Ultra-Conservative faction, while supporting the Black Hand's assertions, also uses the anarchs to illustrate the dangers of decentralized rule. Moderates, however, counter the Ultra-Conservatives by saying that the anarchs represent the fighting spirit for independence that fostered the original Anarch Revolt. The Moderates recognize the current anarchs' deficiencies, but they believe that the Sabbat can convert them to the Sword of Caine. Some Loyalists agree, and they advocate bringing these revolutionaries into the sect in order to create a fifth column within the Camarilla that will undermine that sect and sunder it from within. Naturally some Loyalist packs specializing in "field conversions" are at the forefront in Los Angeles and Las Vegas, recruiting those anarchs who orbit too far outside the protective nucleus of a coterie or gang.

Regardless of the heated debates concerning the anarchs, the Sabbat, as a whole, seemingly frowns upon the movement's undirected and undisciplined methods. Like the Camarilla, the Sabbat draws its arguments from history as well. It cites Caine's failure to establish a peaceful kingdom as the reason why the anarchs' attempts at equality will fail, and it uses the Anarch Revolt as proof that survival of the fittest holds true. A side-argument to this point is the Sabbat's reverential use of the Vaulderie and the bonding through the Vinculum, a practice created during the Anarch Revolt to break the shackles of the elders and unify the Sabbat in strength of purpose. Anarchs, many of whom are already fleeing from blood bonds and menial service to their sires or erstwhile masters, abhor the Vaulderie unless it is the only way to escape their present obligations. The Vinculum is an infringement on the anarchs' vaunted personal freedoms, and this resentment offends the Sabbat's sense of faith. The sect does not consider the Vinculum a fetter. Instead, it believes that the ritual strengthens the sect's cause. The anarchs' unwillingness to join in the Vaulderie is an affront to the sect's faith and further proof that the anarchs are weak and misdirected.

Switching Sects

In the unlife of a vampire, it is difficult to know where to stand and whom to trust. But vampires have their own societies, their own political structures and their own ideological factions. Two sects, the Camarilla and the Sabbat, dominate Kindred culture, and only the powerful, the reckless and the lucky can avoid belonging to either. Most Kindred must choose one just to survive, and sometimes they make a choice that doesn't suit them. For almost all Kindred, however, it's not a choice at all, at least initially following the Embrace.

It is not impossible to switch sides at some later point — indeed, in some ways, the switch is very easy. The Camarilla claims that every Kindred is already a member, and joining requires little more than announcing interest and willingness to participate. The Sabbat is less presumptuous, but it also accepts most Cainites — once they've passed certain initiation rites.

Of course, unlife is never truly that simple, particularly for a vampire who was once part of the opposing sect. A fledgling's "default" desire to join the Camarilla is seen as genuine self-preservation, and sometimes as a true interest in joining and upholding vampiric "society." For an established Sabbat member, however, even such a simple act is treated with suspicion. What is the Sabbat up to? Why is it sending one of its own to spy on the Camarilla? What does the Sabbat stand to gain from this? How and when will this lead to carnage, and who is the target? After all, the Cainites of the Sabbat are blood-sucking fiends in the worst sense — they have no interest in the Traditions that protect the Kindred from destruction at the hands of righteous mortals.

Out of the Frying Pan...

Why would a Sabbat member choose to join the Camarilla? Several reasons come to mind. First and foremost, the Camarilla offers protection. If a vampire is in a Camarilla-dominated city, or even just one where that sect is strong, he can present himself to the prince. If the prince accepts him, that vampire should be safe from attacks by Camarilla vampires (at least in theory), and he can call upon his new prince and other members of the city for aid in repulsing Sabbat treachery as well. This is all assuming that the prince accepts the Kindred, of course. By presenting himself, the fugitive may be calling down a blood hunt on his own head and saving Camarilla agents the trouble of having to look for him. Or, if the prince chooses to keep his hands clean, he can simply turn away the Kindred. What happens to an unaligned intruder caught within Camarilla territory is considered self-defense, a justified response in an ongoing Jyhad, and if he is denied protection or asylum, the victim becomes fair game. Most Camarilla members will wait until they are away from an assembly of the undead before acting on this unwritten rule, though, for civility's sake.

A second reason to join the Camarilla is freedom. In the Sabbat, Cainites are part of a pack, and they do almost everything with their packmates. No secrets are allowed, and personal interests are subjugated to the interests of the pack as a whole (again, in theory). Sabbat members are also expected to take part in various rituals, rites and outings. Participation is not open for discussion — packs have been known to drag reluctant members along and force them to take part, in order to maintain their own standing. Ironically, although the Camarilla has more rules, it is more open. Camarilla members are rarely required to attend meetings or participate in activities, barring the occasional blood hunt or convocation. Provided they pay respects to the prince upon entering the city and they obey the Traditions (which often means simply upholding the Masquerade, not killing other vampires and not making a spectacle of oneself), Camarilla members are left to their own devices. For a Sabbat member, this can look like heaven, particularly if he or she has interests outside those of the pack and ambitions that do not follow the pack's plans and actions. Clever Sabbat may even see through their own sect's backhanded notion of freedom and elect to join the Camarilla to taste freedom that isn't so inextricably tied to constant conflict.

Another reason to join the Camarilla is ideology. The Sabbat disapproves of the Antediluvians, and it claims that the Camarilla is merely a puppet show doing those ancients' bidding. Many Sabbat members also believe in separating from humanity, not hiding from it. The Camarilla believes in a quiet coexistence with humanity. Switching from the Sabbat to the Camarilla states without words that the Camarilla's goals are more valuable and viable than the Sabbat's, and that the future of vampiric society lies in peace and cooperation (and secrecy). Saying that it is wrong is an obvious slap in the face of the Sabbat. It is also a direct insult to the Cainite's packmates and sire; one that is difficult to hide or ignore.

(It is important to note that joining the Inconnu is not considered an act of defection by many Kindred. The Inconnu is not an opposing side, it is assumed to be a loose collection of vampires who have opted out of the political games and power struggles. Whether this withdrawal is an act of courage, cowardice or foolishness is not important. Becoming an Inconnu is a step laterally rather than an about-face. But few can join the Inconnu.

Their numbers are few, their invitations are rare, and their methods are secretive. Only rarely do individual vampires earn their attention and the opportunity to join them.)

Politics is also a question. The Sabbat has political games of its own, of course — no large society can exist without them. But in the Sabbat, most games are overt, contests of will and strength and determination, and they tend to end quickly and violently. In the Camarilla, politics is long and drawn out, and occasionally even bloodless (in every possible sense of the word). Sabbat members who are tired of the constant physical challenges might long for a more cerebral challenge, and the Camarilla can certainly offer that, with its twisted, tangled schemes and hierarchies and alliances.

In point of fact, Sabbat elders engage in intricate plots just as Camarilla elders do. Some even see the Sabbat-Camarilla conflict as an elaborate chess game, with elders on both sides committing pawns and rooks to battle. The difference is that many Camarilla members play at politics, if only to survive. Within the Sabbat, it is usually only the elders who have the luxury and the security to play such games, and few survive long enough to achieve that age and power.

...Into the Fire

Why would a Camarilla member choose to join the Sabbat? Again, one answer is freedom, although of a different sort. Kindred in the Camarilla spend much of their unlives hiding what they are, concealing their abilities to avoid disturbing the potentially deadly rabble that is mortal kind. The Sabbat sees little point in this deception. They are what they are, supernatural night predators, and they take pride in that. After years or even decades of hiding, it feels good to get out and stretch, to openly acknowledge the truth of one's undead existence and to proudly display one's abilities. This is a seductive lure, and the Sabbat uses it to tempt members of the Camarilla, offering them the chance to set pretense aside — to finally reject the lie that they are still human, and accept the Beast inside.

This is not to say that the Sabbat announces its presence and nature to the world. Far from it. The Sabbat is crafty and well aware that sheer numbers are against it. But many Sabbat consider the Masquerade outdated and far too restrictive. Packs are expected to avoid massive exposure, but they are given far more leeway with individuals, particularly since they may choose to kill any witnesses afterward.

Another lure of the Sabbat is power. The Camarilla frowns upon open use of vampiric abilities, since that could alert humanity to their existence and presence. The Sabbat has no such qualms. Why not use one's abilities openly? Such abilities are part of their existence, and they were obviously granted to make their unlife easier (and more enjoyable). And why hide from the humans when Cainites have the potential to subjugate them instead? Humans are sheep, sources of food and entertainment, but nothing more — why care what they think, and what they might do? Humans do outnumber the Cainites, but they are weak and frail and mortal, and if it ever became plausible to even up the battlefield, the Childer of Caine would have a significant advantage.

Another attraction of the Sabbat is politics — or the lack thereof. The Camarilla is riddled with politics of the worst sort, intricate plots created by centuries-old creatures who are willing to wait centuries more for their plans to reach fruition. It seems the Kindred of the Camarilla cannot take a single step without running afoul of some scheme or plan, and they must weigh every word and action carefully, lest they offend the wrong elder or ruin the plans of the wrong coterie. In the Sabbat, everything is more straightforward. The pack is first and foremost, and the politics within each pack tend to be a simple matter of who leads the group and who follows orders. The Sabbat itself has certain goals, but they are open goals, not subtle and hidden, and less time is spent plotting and scheming than pursuing their objectives actively. For those Kindred who have spent years enmeshed in detailed plans, hemmed in on every side by careful considerations and counterbalances, it is good to be able to concentrate only on the wind, the night sky, the blood and the scent of mortals' fear. In the Sabbat, Cainites know who their enemies are, and such enmities do not last long — usually because one or the other is destroyed shortly thereafter. But at least it is open, and quick, and not something to worry about for centuries on end. Again, this is more true for neonates than for elders, but few Sabbat survive that long, so they have little reason to concern themselves with those unpleasantries.

Mutual Enmity

One reason that holds true for both camps is power. Different clans and bloodlines have different abilities, different potential and different secrets. Certain clans are traditionally Sabbat, and others are traditionally Camarilla. A handful may go *antitribu*, but they are certainly difficult to locate. By switching to the other side, a vampire can gain proximity to new powers, powers not available to them before. They can study these powers and attempt to master them, thus increasing their own personal strength. Many vampires exist for nothing more than power, and to them, the opportunity to grow in strength is worth any risk. Also, after a few centuries, most vampires become mired at a certain political level as those around them relegate them to certain roles and tasks. Without major upheaval, they may never rise above that level. It is not unlike the mortal "glass ceiling," with one major difference — it lasts *forever*. By switching to the other sect, those vampires step outside their rut and gain the possibility of advancing further because they are no longer locked into the same place as before and no longer held back by others' expectations. Even if they have to rise up to their former level again, it should be much easier the second time around, given that their strength and experience is much greater than it once was.

But if existence is so good on the other side, why do so few vampires switch? Several reasons prevent large-scale defections. First and foremost, escape is necessary. Although the Camarilla grants its members a large amount of autonomy, it draws the line at breaking the Traditions — and joining the Sabbat is tantamount to breaking them all, since if the Cainite has not yet violated the Masquerade, he will before becoming a full-fledged Sabbat member. (At least, so neonates are told, in order to increase their hostility toward the Sabbat.) Openly stating the desire to defect to the Sabbat is foolish and self-destructive. The Kindred may well find herself taken into custody and "helped" to see the error of such a path. Such treatment may result in the Final Death of the Kindred in question, or in the destruction of her personality, but for the Camarilla, that is preferable to the alternative. Fleeing Camarilla members often take secrets, as well — blackmail information that could come in handy later, if they need to deal with their former allies again. It is far safer to kill the fugitives and bury that material forever, rather than continually watching over one's shoulder.

Defecting from the Sabbat has its own problems. The major difficulty is the pack. Each Sabbat member is part of a small pack, and each regularly drinks of the others' blood to strengthen their bond. This bond is more than symbolic, it is mystical, and it can be used to call the errant member back. If a Sabbat member manages to break his bond with the pack, he is veritably an outcast, and he may even be hunted at will. His former packmates will be the first to seek him out, and they will be the most rabid at tracking him down, to assuage their own betrayal. Sabbat members outside a pack are also vulnerable. They band together for mutual protection, and a lone Sabbat might find himself preyed upon not only by strangers but even by other Sabbat, who will may taunt and attack a perceived loner. Since Sabbat-dominant cities are often home to a large number of packs both founded and nomadic, escaping that

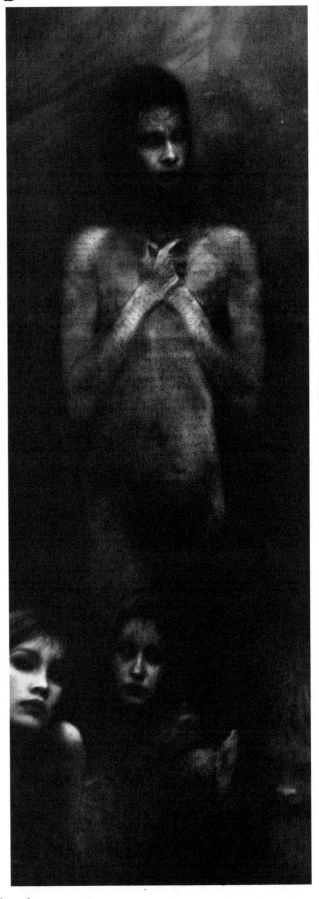

CHAPTER TWO: SINS OF SOCIETY

environment with one's unlife intact can take a good deal of daring, luck and skill.

Doing the Deed

What if a vampire does escape his old sect?

In some cases, the next step is seeking out the other side, which is dangerous in and of itself. It would be wiser to seek out and join the opposition before leaving, but because defection is a matter of courage, many Kindred — although they may spend decades considering the move — finally act in a moment of undead passion. They simply gather their courage and run blindly into the unknown. Even elders have been known to lay down elaborate plans for their defection, only to toss them aside in a moment of panic and trust to their wits and strength to survive.

For those who do think ahead, plotting an unlife with "the enemy" must be done with utmost delicacy. Initial research into the matter is nothing less than exploring heresy. If one's allies or rivals find out about the vampire's considerations, she may find herself without a choice, or at least without an appealing one. For this reason, few vampires undertake such matters casually. Renouncing one's sect is not unlike renouncing one's mortal citizenship — it is a grave affair, and it must be done with utmost certainty.

Locating the opposing sect is not particularly hard — both sides tend to claim territory, and Kindred in an area know who claims which domains, neighborhoods and cities. Once in the appropriate territory, a Kindred can draw attention to himself. Doing so becomes dangerous, however. Both Sabbat and Camarilla Cainites are wary of newcomers, and they tend to question strangers as to their affiliation and intentions. Sabbat members may attack strangers on sight, assuming that anyone unfamiliar must be an enemy. Camarilla vampires are more cautious, but they may visit their own brand of suspicion or hostility upon a stranger if they consider that stranger a threat. Such is especially true if they decide that the visitor is Sabbat, and thus may be undone without angering the prince.

A fleeing Sabbat member must reach the city's prince, which can mean navigating a gauntlet of retainers, bodyguards and officials. Sometimes a defector can do so through bribery or diplomacy, but more often, it will require stealth and often brute force. Once granted an audience (perhaps unwillingly), the vampire must convince the prince to accept her plea to become a member of the Camarilla and a recognized Kindred of the prince's domain. Of course, the aspiring Kindred doesn't *have* to do this, but unacknowledged Kindred in any but the most lax domain are seen as autarkis at best…. Many princes have faced the agents of the Sabbat at some point or another, and they may be disinclined to welcome such monsters into their realm. It is far safer to kill a rabid dog than to house it and attempt to tame it. Of course, defectors can also find themselves subjected to torture. Information about the enemy is always useful, and freely volunteered details are less reliable than those extracted by force.

Kindred still tell of one Cainite who defected from the Sabbat. She slaughtered her own packmates and two other packs as well, fought her way out of Sabbat domain and into Camarilla territory, battled a path into the prince's haven, killing a handful of Camarilla members in the process. When she arrived, she bludgeoned the prince into granting her an audience, only to vow eternal pacifism if he accepted her into his domain. According to some, she has since claimed that prince's title and domain. According to others, her remains were scattered to the corners of the prince's domain, and her fingers were given to the childer of each Kindred she had slain.

In some ways, fleeing to the Sabbat is safer, but in other ways, it is more dangerous. The Sabbat doesn't have princes, so those running to the Sabbat do not need to fight their way through to a central figure. A bishop or archbishop's support is preferable and can smooth many difficulties, but initially any pack leader will do. However, packs do not have to restrain themselves until their leader has accepted a new member. Each pack can decide for itself how to treat a "visitor," and if they choose to destroy their would-be peer, no one need be the wiser. If the newcomer is a vampire of age, power and/ or reputation, such a coup might become public, boosting the reputation of the pack. In cases of particularly potent or high-profile Cainites, the defecting vampire might not join a pack at all, as is the situation with many elders of the Sword of Caine. Although a defector is unlikely to assume a place among the prisci (or even the bishops after such an unproven development), she may find herself made a consultant to a cardinal or templar to an archbishop. Few Camarilla Kindred of advanced age would even consider joining the Sabbat if it were such a blow to their dignity as to see them cleaning up a fledgling pack's haven. Packs might torture younger Kindred for useful information and then diablerize him to steal his strength. If a pack does decide to spare a newcomer, its members may choose to initiate him themselves, which may take a Camarilla refugee by surprise. The Camarilla is a social institution, and initiations are usually a formality, based on words and traditional gestures. The Sabbat is a religious war party, with each pack a dedicated fighting unit, and initiation is very real. Prospective members, even fledglings Embraced by members of the pack, might be subjected to torture and degradation. But a former Camarilla member might have to undergo far more, because he has more to prove. Provided they survive the initiation, such Cainites become full-fledged members of the pack, afforded all the protection and rights of every other pack member.

At least, that is the theory. The reality is often quite different. Sabbat packs are tight-knit like families, and most are wise to distrust strangers. Any new member would be treated with distrust until that member has proven himself. But the Camarilla is the enemy, the antithesis of the Sabbat. Its members are puppets of the elders at best and deadly fiends determined to weaken the Cainites for Gehenna itself at worst. Having a reformed Camarilla member in the pack is a mark of distinction (for having "turned" the enemy), which means that packs may covet that honor, but if the new member is in fact a double-agent, a spy or saboteur, the entire pack could suffer for it. The best response is to push the new member mercilessly, break him completely, and then subjugate him utterly. If he has no will but that of the pack, and no identity but that of the pack, he cannot betray the pack. Therefore, many defecting vampires can find existence in a Sabbat pack much more difficult than any other pack member. They will get no breaks, no leeway and no leniency, and when faced with danger, they may find the rest of the pack standing back and watching to see what they do. And if the new member dies the Final Death because the pack held back from his defense? Then perhaps he was sincere after all, and his memory may even be honored.

The newly reformed are treated much the same way in the Camarilla, only the treatment is subtler. A Kindred who has been recognized by the prince must often endure gossip, taunts, insults, slights of all sorts and obstacles in every direction. The haven she's chosen is suddenly unavailable, or uninhabitable, the prey she was stalking is suddenly frightened off, someone resembling her is now wanted by the police, Kindred-only affairs fill up just before she reaches the door, and other such blatant social snubbing occurs. In short, a defector is usually treated as a second-class citizen, looked down upon and typically suffering the worst of any bargain. She has to work harder to prove herself, and even a single mistake is justification enough that she is unreliable and untrustworthy.

Some Kindred have little in the way of possessions — material things break and turn to dust, just as mortals do, while vampires still remain. Therefore, vampires tend to value those things that cannot turn to dust, such as experience, power, wisdom and honor. Strangely enough, in a society of predators and killers, personal honor means a great deal. A vampire whose word is good is treated with respect and admiration, and that is worth more than a faded painting or a warped piece of masterwork furniture. But when a vampire switches sides, his honor is gone. After all, by initially joining a sect he had pledged himself to follow the ideals and procedures of that sect, and by leaving, he has broken his word. Worse, he has not simply left that sect, but actively sought out and joined the opposing sect, which makes him not only dishonorable but traitorous. Younger Kindred may not see any significance in this, but older vampires recognize it as a major blow, a vicious attack against one's self-image, and a loss of incalculable value. It is also impossible to regain fully. Just as a shattered sculpture can be repaired but will always have cracks, a defector will always have broken a major promise, and thus he can never fully be relied upon.

In many ways, this loss is worse at higher levels of rank and power. Fledglings can be considered lost children who were swayed into taking the wrong path and have now grown wise enough to see the truth. They may be punished for their mistake and ridiculed for their weakness, but at the same time, they may be honored for coming to their senses. Even neonates can say that, once they were allowed to stand without their sire and make their own decisions, they realized that the other side did not appeal to them and so chose to leave. Older vampires have no such excuse. It is difficult to claim that the last 200 years were all a careless error that could not have been rectified more quickly. Elders are also treated with more fear, and thus more distrust. A fledgling cannot cause much damage alone, but a powerful elder could wreak havoc and even endanger the sect's leaders. It is also harder for an elder to escape in the first place. In all but the most irreconcilable situations, her original sect will use every means to convince her to stay, or, failing that, to destroy her, rather than let her power, experience and knowledge go to the enemy.

One drawback to defection is that it never wears off. Vampires can survive for millennia, and they remember slights and attacks clearly even after centuries. A vampire who defects from one sect to the other should not hope to have the deed forgotten over time. The only way for that to happen is if everyone who knew the situation no longer exists — which may explain why vampires do not trust defectors. As long as even one witness remains, the defector can always carry that label, and it will often be the first thing anyone hears of him, before any strengths or deeds or lineage. The badge of the defector never fades, and it cannot be hidden from view unless the vampire is willing to create a new identity or start over again some place where his name has not been heard.

Another issue with defecting is the cost in status. A fledgling has no rank to lose — he is on the bottom rung regardless. A neonate may have to start over, but that is a small price to pay, as it is not a major step back. It is also reasonable for a vampire who is still young and barely self-sufficient, to adjust from the beginning so that she has a better understanding of and appreciation for her new situation. But for ancillae and elders, going to the opposing sect can have major consequences. Some rank may be bestowed upon joining their new sect, but most ancillae and even some elders are stripped of esteem and are forced to advance from the bottom once more. This is embarrassing and humiliating for ancillae, but it is almost unspeakable for elders. A fifth-generation Kindred could find himself consulted after a two-years-undead fledgling. The elder may still have his personal power and resources, and even some continued contact with old allies, but ties may become more tenuous. Connections made through the other sect could certainly be strained, if not severed completely. This drastic fall from favor and importance is often a deliberate test of the vampire's willpower and self-control, but it also serves as a reminder that past honors and titles mean nothing in the new sect, and that every bit of respect must be earned.

One thing that must also be considered is the social network. For all their claims of inhumanity and solitary ways, vampires still socialize. They still interact with one another, and they still form acquaintances. These may all start out as alliances, strategic partnerships and agreements, but in many cases they evolve into true companionships, particularly since vampires cannot share their nature and their concerns with many others. Two elders can be acquaintances for centuries, meeting every few decades to catch up, compare notes, and simply enjoy the presence of a like-minded individual who values the other's opinions. But everything can vanish in an instant if the vampire changes sides. Old comrades no longer speak to one another, no longer trust one another, and the oldest, most trusted peer may suddenly be the most feared rival, the one who knows every hidden haven and every back-up plan. Why would old acquaintances turn on one another in this way? Because choosing a sect is stating an attitude toward the world, toward existence and toward humanity, and changing that attitude suddenly means changing the person as well, becoming a new personality with new interests and new attitudes.

Of course, it can take decades to build relationships with other vampires, and even longer if one is treated as an outsider and a possible spy. Particularly since each defector brings a new list of enemies, vampires who did not bother with the sect conflict before but who now have a personal reason to oppose the defector and any who stand with him. Small wonder that these Kindred often find themselves alone, isolated from the very group that they gave up so much to join.

Most vampires belong to a clan, and the clan is an extended family, which means that it can sometimes be a source of information, advice or aid. Unfortunately, even this is not true for defectors. Most clans have *antitribu*, mirror versions in the opposing sect, and clan and *antitribu* usually despise one another. By leaving one sect and joining another, vampires find themselves either facing their *antitribu* or one of the rare *antitribu* reconciled with the original clan. Either way, the defector is yet again an outcast, not wholly understood by those semi-clanmates and branded an outcast from still another direction. The vampire is also cut off from one more possible avenue of support, leaving him few other places to turn.

Sometimes vampires defect in a group. Doing so provides a built-in support network — allies and packmates still have a common lot, and they still have a like mind. With Cainites to watch each other's back, physical threats are less of a problem, and challenges can be met in a group. Groups do have a disadvantage, however — visibility. A prince or a Sabbat bishop may not notice the departure of a single fledgling or neonate, but neither is likely to miss the departure of a group of six acknowledged vampires, and both may feel that an example is necessary before other coteries get ideas. And, since defection is usually a personal choice, when an entire group defects together, others suspect that something more is at work. Perhaps the group fears that something terrible is coming and it is running from a certain danger, or perhaps it has valuable information on someone and is cashing it in. It may be that the group members have a plan of some sort to damage their former allies. Regardless, the movement of an entire group is enough to attract attention, and suddenly the group may find itself surrounded on all sides by "curious parties."

The Price of Choice

The most significant problem with defecting is burning bridges. Not only are old allies now unlikely to consort with the vampire, but his old contacts may also be gone, and all of his prior plans must be rebuilt using his new framework. The Sabbat often requires that a defector sever all ties to the mortal world, including trusted aides and allies, to demonstrate sincerity and commitment. Defectors can almost never go back. A vampire who left the Camarilla, joined the Sabbat, and then returned to the Camarilla would be assumed to be a spy or a saboteur and would probably become the subject of a Wild Hunt *and* a blood hunt. Similarly, someone returning to the Sabbat after having joined and then left the Camarilla might find his old pack waiting to exact revenge for leaving at all, and several disapproving elders waiting for when it has finished. Most vampires can adopt a new sect only once, if that. Most will not survive switching a second time, assuming that they survive the first one, for by then, their treachery will be known.

One reason both sides are so cautious is the Jyhad itself. The Camarilla denies the existence of such things as Antediluvians, regarding them as only metaphors for the Kindred's creation myth, but the Sabbat both fears and loathes them. Some fledglings and even a few neonates claim that the Antediluvians no longer exist, that they are merely legends and folk tales. Elders, however, believe strongly, and some have even seen the monstrous old beings. If the elders spin plans that span centuries, the Antediluvians' plots can cover millennia, and anyone can be trapped in strands of those schemes. Defecting to a new sect, leaving behind one's entire world and network and history, is an enormous step, and surely a radical departure from previous behavior. Why would a vampire suddenly behave in such a manner?

Perhaps he is under the influence of the Antediluvians, caught up in the eternal Jyhad, and this drastic action is ultimately a chess move on some enormous board. But if that is the case, the vampire is a pawn, and he probably has several more actions in the future. The Sabbat would sooner burn its own members than allow an Antediluvian to gain the tiniest influence or insight into them, and if a former Camarilla member appears at the door, it is safer and easier to destroy the intruder than to risk being dragged into that chess game. The savvy Kindred sees every action of his fellow Kindred as part of a greater Jyhad to begin with, but if the scheme's author is an Antediluvian, even elders quake in fear. It would be suitably twisted for one of those ancients to use Sabbat monsters as their tools and their minions. The worst part about this consideration is that it is unverifiable. Who knows what moves the Ancients truly make? Regardless, the paranoia many vampires feel with regard to the Jyhad is very real, even if the sources that stir it might not be.

So why defect? The reasons already listed are technically true, but mistrust and suspicion and outright hatred color them. Ultimately, a vampire changes sides for only three reasons. First, he is deluded. He actually believes the hype he's been told by the opposition, and he switches sides thinking that his existence will become better immediately, and that he will be welcomed with open arms by his new allies and sectmates. This vampire often receives a rude awakening, as he learns that traitors are rarely welcome, even by the sect to which they have defected. Second, a vampire may have no choice but to leave. He has done things so terrible that it is no longer safe for him to stay in his old sect. Yet he fears being alone, so he switches to the other side. This vampire discovers that he is just as alone as ever, perhaps more so. Now he is surrounded by "allies" who eye him constantly, waiting for a single error, and he is distrusted and avoided at every turn, until whatever punishment he escaped begins to look more appealing simply for being familiar and finite.

The most common reason that a vampire defects is moral or political — he simply feels that his old sect is wrong in its approach, and he decides to join the "right" team immediately. This vampire is also in for unpleasant revelations. Neither the Camarilla nor the Sabbat have a clear, universal attitude toward the world, and each one has hundreds of variations, with new versions appearing every time a new vampire joins the ranks, whether through Embrace or otherwise. While each sect claims an ideology that it idealizes, such philosophies go only as far as the individual member upholds them. A vampire may discover Camarilla coteries more bloodthirsty than any Sabbat pack, or Sword of Caine political maneuvering that surpasses any Camarilla web of prestation for conspiracy in intricacy, duplicity and sheer egotism. Neither side has a unified opinion, being instead a wide array of similar-minded undead. Those Kindred who join seeking clarity are confused by the sheer number of different opinions and approaches within their new sect, and dismayed to learn that it is just as difficult and just as violent navigating their new side as navigating their old one. While it is not impossible to rally behind a given sect's cause, it is exceedingly difficult to become a paragon of that cause, even for the most principled of the Damned.

One thought is that defectors can at least find solace and support with other defectors. After all, these are other Kindred who were originally on the other side and chose to switch allegiances. They understand what it is like to have that background and those former attitudes, what the defector sacrificed to make the transition, and how difficult it is to fit in and to build a new existence in a strange new environment. Therefore, they are the best people to speak with, and the ones most likely to show understanding and support.

Such is not always the case. In fact, it is quite often the opposite. Traitors are always under scrutiny, and any time two or more of them group together others might suspect that they are plotting against their new family, setting in motion whatever fiendish plan they hatched before leaving their true sect and pretending to switch sides.

Therefore, most defectors avoid one another in order to appear disinterested and to show loyalty for their new peers. Indeed, one of the best ways to show loyalty to their new home is to mock their old home, and to make existence miserable for anyone from there — including other defectors. Existence can become a large-scale "pissing match," with each vampire attempting to outdo the others and thus show his superiority and loyalty. This often results in the physical harm or even death of one or more defectors, but the elders rarely intervene. Perhaps they think the most sincere will triumph, or perhaps they simply feel that no one will miss a handful of traitors. Regardless, many allow such conflict, and some even seem to enjoy it, observing and remarking on every jab as if they were watching a gladiator's duel.

Defectors are often barred from holding offices or positions of power, at least initially, for fear that they may abuse those positions or run back to their old sect with compromising information. Their movements are sometimes monitored, as well, and any irregularities could result in questioning by cautious princes or bishops. In fact, defectors are often expected to make "social calls" upon those of rank, simply as a way to remind them of their subservient position and of the gravity of crossing their new sect. Ironically, most vampiric leaders know their defectors better than they do other less controversial vampires in their domains, if only because they rarely have cause to watch, threaten or torment their subjects.

Not every defection is real. Some Camarilla members do "defect" to the Sabbat to infiltrate that camp and acquire valuable information, which they can then bring back and use to advance themselves, their coterie and their sect. On rarer occasions, a Sabbat vampire will "turn" to the Camarilla merely to see how the other half operates, and perhaps to covertly interfere with as many plans as possible before running back to the safety of the pack. These vampires discover that defection is not a game, or a casual act — it is deadly serious. In order to survive defection, a vampire must have enormous mental and physical endurance, as well as tremendous self-control. Returning can also be a problem. In many cases, the vampire discovers that he cannot leave his new pack because the ruse has become real and the ties are binding. In others, the vampire learns that his old sect no longer wants him back. Who can ensure that the defection did not become genuine, and that the vampire is not returning now as a double (or even triple) agent? Even if the defection was arranged or suggested beforehand, the reality may prove very different, and leaders have a way of changing their minds. The other side may also become suspicious of any defector whose escape to them seemed too easy, so the old sect cannot spare the fugitive from difficulty — for the defection to appear real, the danger must be real. Is this elaborate ruse worth it? For those few who manage to defect, join the other side and return safely, yes. The information they provide can be invaluable, revealing many plans and weaknesses of the enemy, and the prestige and esteem they receive can alter the political arena dramatically. But this elevation comes with a price. Even "fake" traitors carry a stigma, and the better their deception, the more their old allies wonder how much of their current loyalty is real and how much is also fake. The sect they "defected" to can also be a danger. Nothing is worse than being played for a fool, and if that sect discovers the trick, the vampire may well find himself hunted for centuries by vengeful Cainites. He also may not find as much protection as he had hoped, from his true sect. After all, once the information is acquired that vampire is no longer useful, and potential liabilities should be removed before they cause additional problems.

Unlife Anew?

Leaders are often deliberately cruel to defectors, testing their loyalty and their resolve. Some iron-fisted princes require an immediate blood bond of all fugitive Sabbat, and only part of the reason is the corresponding influence over the fugitive. The other reason is to see whether the supplicant defector will sit still for such treatment. Princes frequently engineer situations to enrage their new subjects, so that they can see whether or not the new vampire can remain calm. After all, maintaining the Masquerade requires willpower and self-control, and the Sabbat is notoriously weak on both fronts. Therefore, former Sabbat often find themselves the butt of jokes and the target of pranks and even insults, in an effort to goad them into betraying themselves.

The Sabbat often takes the opposite tack. A local Sabbat leader may also require a blood bond, but the new member is supposed to be bonding with his pack regardless. Some Sabbat leaders may engineer situations for the new members, but with a very different goal in mind. The Sabbat wants to know that the vampire asking for admission is in touch with his inner Beast, and has learned how to release that Beast and "ride the wave" of its frenzies. Former Camarilla Cainites often have difficulty with this abandon, and they may object to the pressure toward violence, but ultimately it is a question that must be answered for each vampire. Has the Cainite fully accepted the Beast within, and accepted existence as an undead? Vampires showing too much reluctance do not belong in the Sabbat, while vampires with no restraint are prohibited from the Camarilla in order to protect the Masquerade. It is also a question of danger and safety, both the new member's and those around him. A Camarilla member who fights constantly risks drawing attention from outsiders, while a Sabbat member who will not fight risks dragging her pack down and leaving the pack without full support. Leaders wisely consider these dangers first, before introducing the new member to his or her new packmates.

In some Sabbat domains, it is common practice to starve a new defector. A vampire's true personality shows through after several nights of hunger. His pretenses are stripped away, and a clear chain of priorities appears. A few Sabbat members claim that they never use trickery, preferring the direct approach at all times. Most Camarillists maintain at least a veneer of civility, so forcing the veneer to drop is a rare but valuable occasion. This tactic gives the bishop or pack a chance to study the newcomer, to see the person beneath the finery and fangs and to decide if that person is worth the effort and risk involved. It also allows the bishop to dole out sustenance as a reward, providing yet another tool for establishing the defector's respect for and understanding of the power hierarchy. This is especially true because most vampires have established feeding grounds, and if the defector is barred from those private areas, the need for vitae increases drastically.

Defectors run a very real risk of becoming lapdogs, especially if they are old and powerful. A prince can command that all other Kindred avoid the defector, and that no other sources of blood be allowed (even to the point of "deputizing" Kindred who actively prevent the defector from reaching or partaking in vitae), then blood bond the defector to him, ensuring his loyalty and compliance. Thus a Sabbat member of great power and influence can be reduced to little more than a Camarilla lick-spittle, devoted to a cruel prince and unable to act against him. Many defectors destroy themselves to avoid such a fate. The old line about serving in Heaven versus ruling in Hell definitely applies, but that realization sometimes comes too late.

Why, then, do defectors never learn? If existence on the other side is so difficult, why do vampires continue to defect? And why do the sects continue to allow it? The defections continue because such matters are kept quiet. No one likes to admit that they have lost the faith and support of a once-loyal member, and once a vampire leaves a group, she is usually considered nonexistent, and any talk of her is quelled immediately or conducted in hushed tones. On the receiving end, the sects often resist the urge to brag of their new acquisitions (particularly to the opposing sect). For the Camarilla this is to derail any plans made by the Sabbat, as it is difficult to proceed with an infiltration without being certain the spy entered the premises successfully. Not announcing the fate of the defector can stall or even demolish a Sabbat plot, and that confusion allows the Camarilla to build counter-tactics of its own. The Sabbat rarely brings attention to such matters because of the risk of reprisals. If the Camarilla wants that defector badly enough, it may attack, and the Sabbat prefers to choose its own battles. Even if the defector is a vampire of no real status, the risk remains that he could be used as an example (either for the side that "won" him or for the side that "reclaims" him), so the best course of action is to keep quiet. The other reason defections continue is that the lures still exist. The blood always seems more red in the other victim, and disgruntled members of a sect will always wonder if the rumors are true about the other side, and if their chances there would be better. As always, the final and most compelling reason remains that, despite the difficulties, some vampires truly come to embrace the philosophies of the other sect — in whatever capacity they actually observe them — and make the transition out of commitment to the ideology.

The reason both sects allow defections to continue, or at least allow defectors to approach them, is twofold. First, doing so reminds their own members that they have chosen the correct side. (After all, members of the opposition keep asking to join!) This boosts morale and suggests that the other sect is weak-willed and ineffectual; the "wrong" party in the ideological war. The second reason is that defectors provide a useful source of information, because even if they arrive without secrets, they still know about their former sect's size, location and recent activities, and any information can be used against the sect. The third reason is to set an example. The Sabbat allows Camarilla defectors in to show the Camarilla that the door is always open — any Cainite who survives initiation can become Sabbat and join the fight. Similarly, the Camarilla wishes to show that any Sabbat member can be redeemed and returned to the fold — all Kindred are members, if they only wish to admit it. But the sects also set examples for their members through the way they actually treat fugitives. The Jyhad rages nightly, and traitors are treated as such, so it is dangerous to let loyalty flag or suggest deviation from the established party lines. After all, no Camarilla member wants to be treated as badly as they treat former Sabbat, and surely the Sabbat with its violence and anarchy must be even worse. And no Sabbat member wants to be treated the way they handle former Kindred, especially in such a manipulative and Antediluvian-enthralled maze as the Camarilla.

Foul Diablerie

The Amaranth, better known as diablerie, is one of the few words in Cainite vocabulary that will stop conversations and silence entire rooms. It fills elders with understandable dread, and neonates and fledglings with morbid curiosity. It is an act beyond simple murder from which there is no return or reprieve. It is the desecration of humanity for both victim and aggressor — the wanton and malicious condemnation of someone's spirit forever after.

Diablerie is an inherited fear from the nights when the Assamites followed the Mongol hordes to the gates of Eastern Europe, and the Anarch Revolt felled sires, masters and lords of numerous manors. The "noble" practice of giving an amaranth to the victim a week before his destruction fell to the more barbaric practice of descending upon a victim like a horde of dogs and ripping him to tatters. Many elders from both sects remember these bestial nights well, whether they participated in the carnage or eluded it. They fear it, remembering how those depraved times were almost Gehenna-like in scope. They also notice how diablerie is on the rise again, given the recent liberation of the Assamites and the wanton fatalism that some Cainites have adopted in face of the Final Nights.

The Camarilla denounces such action for obvious reasons, and even the Sabbat advises its pursuit only "in moderation." Topping the list of reasons why the sects fear, or are at least wary of, the Amaranth are the concerns of elders and those of potent vitae. Further down the list, however, the argument against diablerie borders on oral Cainite legends and myths. Nobody can say for sure whether some rationales are even true or not, but the elders of either sect undoubtedly help propagate these fables for their own benefit.

The most obvious opponents of the Amaranth are the Camarilla elders, ancillae and even low-generation neonates who realize that there is little they can do against a coterie of diablerists intent on draining them of their blood. The sect agrees, for with Assamites and Sabbat packs on the prowl, the Camarilla can ill afford to lose the strong-blooded to its own hungry childer. So the sect enacts various measures to stem diablerie. Foremost are harsher punishments imposed under the aegis of the Tradition of Destruction, in which the prince, sheriff and scourge may pursue any means necessary to destroy diablerists. Such is not always the case, however. Some princes realize that if they cannot stop the practice of the Amaranth, they can certainly direct it elsewhere, such as against autarkis, Sabbat targets or anyone under a blood hunt. This subtle direction swells the scourge's ranks with would-be diablerists hoping to notch their way "closer to Caine." Such enthusiasm serves the prince in a twofold manner by first putting potential agitators in the line of fire, and second redirecting these rogues away from local elders. The Camarilla may frown upon such practices, but it currently has bigger problems to worry about.

Beyond the fears of elders and ancillae rests a number of valid, quantifiable fears concerning the Amaranth outside, "Please, don't hurt me." The Camarilla is rightly leery of the addictive nature of this act given the already powerful hold their vitae has over all Kindred and their eventual slide toward the Beast. Many can sample of diablerie once and simply walk away, but each indulgence of the Amaranth after the first grows more intoxicating. Mortal junkies claim that the first high is always the most intense, and that they become addicted trying to recapture that initial rush. With the Amaranth, the opposite is true. The sensation of draining another is so intense that memory does it no justice. It is a moment of absolute bliss that leaves an aching longing behind, an emptiness that the Beast screams to have filled. The Cainite remembers that moment, even tastes his victim, but the sensation is fleeting. If the diablerist ever wishes to recapture the initial rush, he must partake of the Amaranth again, and each time he does, he is unprepared for the intensity of the experience. The danger in this rush is that the vampire eventually exists to destroy others. The Beast exerts greater control over the rogue, robbing him of humanity, hope and even direction. Without these three anchors, any conceivable sin, any conceivable evil, is possible.

Even more dangerous, diablerie is the quickest way into the clutches of the Beast. Vampiric philosophers wonder if this is so because the act not only steals another's damned soul, weighing down the hope of redemption, but because it amplifies the Beast's roar by

absorbing the victim's savage nature as well. Regardless, each act of diablerie punches another hole in the Kindred's moral center, destabilizing the vampire's already faded seat of consciousness. In short, the undead fool becomes more bestial and threatens the Masquerade with an inevitable rampage. Ego surrenders to urge, and both frenzy and depravity become easier, even comfortable and familiar. Soon insanity steps in and, again, the Camarilla must deal with its deleterious effects on Cainite society and the Masquerade. In short, diablerie is akin to committing suicide by driving a car rigged with explosives into a building. The diablerist will eventually destroy himself, and he will hurt or kill others around him. At the very least, the Camarilla justifies its concerns thus.

On a political and purely selfish level, the Camarilla prohibits diablerie because it gives the sect greater sway over who comes into power and who stays on the bottom rungs. It protects the sect's status in the world. Diablerie is a quick fix, a means of achieving unspoken station in a society where blood makes the world go round. It increases a Kindred's access to powers best exercised with a modicum of experience and common sense, meaning that the Camarilla does not trust certain Kindred with certain abilities. Each successive jump in generation also limits the number of Kindred who can influence the rogue through Disciplines like Dominate, meaning that the Camarilla has fewer people who can keep the diablerist in line. In short, diablerie threatens the status quo of the existing power structure. The Camarilla is socially and politically conservative. The Kindred in power like to know who is gaining influence, assets or allies, and they sabotage anyone who does not conform to their standards or beliefs. It is all part of the Jyhad, and the reason why anarchs can only find political expression through rebellion. Diablerie is a shortcut, however, affording the vampire power that the Camarilla's elders never had a chance to grant themselves (through the Embrace, blood hunts, etc.). It is an affront to their sense of integrity if only because they cannot control the situation. Vampires do not adapt well to sudden change. It deprives them of authority, and being Kindred is all about holding the reins. More importantly, the Camarilla fears that diablerie offers neonates the chance of usurping and destroying the elders themselves. That must never happen again.

Even the Sabbat recognizes the dangers of overindulging in diablerie given its expertise with vitae, but any such warnings appear more strongly rooted in superstition and urban legend. To understand why the Sabbat fears diablerie on some levels, one has to understand why the sect approves of its usage first. The Sabbat treats diablerie as a right of warfare and a privilege of superiority. Diablerie not only ensures survival of the fittest, but it rewards the victor with the ultimate fruit of conquest. The Sword of Caine also believes in a practicality behind diablerie, to bridge the potential for a weakened generation. Every Cainite who perishes creates a loss, a gap between the sect's veterans and potential fledglings, the latter of whom are now one generation weaker than they might have been. Diablerie in a pragmatic sense ensures that the Sabbat does not lose a link in the chain of generations. This is hardly a threat among those of thinner blood, but it is a concern for vampires of more powerful vitae. Following the loss of New York and the renewed aggression from Assamites, the Sabbat fears a thinning of its ranks among the middle and upper echelons. Therefore, if they are to fall, then let their blood fall to the Sabbat and strengthen it.

That said, a growing stigma against those Cainites who diablerize opponents twice or more removed in generation has arisen in the sect. The Sabbat considers the limited advancement in blood potency wasteful when compared to the potential gain, and instead, it advocates a new solution. In some Monomancy duels, the Cainites fight as normal, but each person picks a "champion" who can most effectively benefit from the change in generation (from diablerizing the opponent) more efficiently. Upon the killing blow, the surrogate commits Amaranth. Some later use this improved generation to Embrace a (doomed) childe, whom the victor of the Monomancy duel then diablerizes. No generations are lost, and two Sons and Daughters in Caine benefit from the experience. Many fledglings, however, find this method distasteful and even cowardly, preferring the thrill of inflicting Final Death themselves. Regardless of the individual Cainite's opinion, however, this is an almost certain one-way ticket into the talons of the Beast via degeneration. The Sabbat currently has no restrictions on Monomancy, and it cannot pursue this suggestion with any real force.

Another reason why diablerie is common and even expected from sect members is actually in response to the *Book of Nod*'s vaunted "time of thin blood." The Sabbat prides itself on its self-anointed image as a holy army struggling against the Final Nights, and it excises any hint that it might be contributing to the end prophecies. Therefore, Cainites consider being of weaker blood a disgrace, even if the vampire is 10th or 11th generation. This state is uncomfortably close to those pariahs unbelievably removed from the progenitor. Many within the Sword of Caine therefore strive to strengthen their vitae, to prove that they are not carriers of thin blood through their offspring and grandchilder.

Some theorize that this is why the Sabbat has not exploded numerically. Many of the weaker generations do not Embrace until their blood is stronger.

Nothing is unanimous among vampires, however, and some Sabbat including a few who rank among the Inquisition, Status Quo, Ultra-Conservatives, and Old World Tzimisce are slowly speaking out against the undisciplined use of the Amaranth. The arguments vary, but the sect believes that the Status Quo and Old World Tzimisce argue against diablerie for much the same reason why the Camarilla abhors its usage: It threatens the existing power structure. The Inquisition's objections, however, are a recent event, as are those of the Ultra-Conservatives. Their reasons are potentially more horrifying, but less academic than speculative fears. The Inquisition and Ultra-Conservatives claim the practice may adversely affect certain Paths of Enlightenment, again citing the inevitable slide toward the Beast for followers of most Paths.

The Inquisition argues that diablerie is acceptable through Monomancy, but repeated observance of the Amaranth creates addiction. While any substance dependency weakens the vampire, diablerie erodes a Cainite's ethics and often becomes a driving force behind his actions. The cause no longer matters so long as the violence serves his thirst. The Inquisition's fear is not with this course of action, but in the worry that once the Cainite abandons all concerns save sating his desires, then infernalism is rarely far behind. The Inquisition backs this claim up with the dubious argument that all destroyed infernalists uncovered thus far were habitual diablerists. The Inquisition questions whether infernalism resulted in increased usage of diablerie, or if constant engagement in diablerie brought on infernalism. Other Sabbat, particularly those of the Black Hand, are quick to dismiss this attack on one of their principal conventions as typically overzealous. The Inquisition, however, promises to study the matter closely, and they are not the first to state their misgivings concerning diablerie.

The Paths of Enlightenment are methods of harmonizing one's existence with the reality of the Beast. They are more than methods of conduct; they are anchors of the soul and intrinsic to a Cainite's very being. The Ultra-Conservatives believe, and perhaps with some merit, that because diablerie is subsuming the victim's blood and soul, that victim's innate strengths and weaknesses also join with the Cainite committing the Amaranth. If the victor is weak in Path, or he is the victim of a stronger (or conflicting) ethic, then the diablerist suffers from doubts, hesitations and even inner disharmony. He may question his actions or suddenly switch Paths because his ego advocates one issue, but the consumed soul tries to follow the course of least resistance, its former Path. Some Paths are naturally resistant to this manipulation, including the Paths of Caine and of the Feral Heart, both of which advocate understanding and appreciating the Beast. There is acceptance of this cannibalism in both Paths by virtue of their ethics, so it proves a bulwark against "intrusion." Those following the Path of Power and the Inner Voice, however, rely on themselves alone. Yet, doing so proves difficult when whispers and suggestions taint one's inner dialogue. Those of the Path may not fall, but they can stumble or fail to reach higher levels of understanding and appreciation of the Path's truths.

Again, however, and like the Inquisition, the Ultra-Conservatives lack the proof to back their assertions if only because their suspicions are not quantifiable or easily proved.

All speculations relating to the Sabbat's use of diablerie has failed to convince the sect that a danger exists. The belief that it encourages infernalism, that it influences the Paths of Enlightenment, that powerful personalities can sometimes dominate the infernalist et cetera are not new claims. The Sabbat, however, refuses to listen if only because diablerie is as strong a heritage as the Kindred's own Traditions. More importantly, admitting that the Amaranth is potentially detrimental means that the Camarilla was right, and the Sabbat certainly refuses to lose its battles on the field of conviction.

Chapter Three: Sins of Discretion

I know but one freedom, and that is the freedom of the mind.
—Antoine de Saint-Exupery

> Mme.—
> I found this document in the possession of an anarch named Rose near Santa Ana. She insisted that it wasn't her who had written it, but that she'd picked it up "as a warning" from the ubiquitous Smiling Jack. If this is true, I don't believe he's written it either, as the tone is a little too petulant and not quite histrionic enough.
> I suspect this is the work of a young Kindred, or at least designed to look like such. The content seems at first informative, if a bit biased, but the connotations it provides are certainly less noble than that. Is this is a warning or a primer? It's certainly propaganda, but whether adolescent and sincere or experienced and deceitful, I can't tell.
> I await your instruction in my usual humour.
>
> Jarbeaux

What would you say if I told you the Kindred have an enemy that will, beyond a shadow of a doubt, bring them to their knees? What would you think if I suggested to you that no Kindred, no matter how powerful or old, could foresee this adversary's destructive superiority? Can you believe in a foe so wily and so powerful that it never suffers even the slightest wound? Does the thought frighten you?

"Top of the food chain," we label ourselves. Fifty years ago, I might have agreed wholeheartedly. Unfortunately, I have learned of another that sits higher. It gorges itself on us. It hungers for dead flesh. Although it also preys on the living, it consumes us more regularly. Us, the Kindred, the night's royalty. I suspect our very natures make us easy targets.

This monster, the Destroyer, exists whether you believe in it or not. Not unlike the monster under the bed or in the closet, it becomes a personal stalker of its victims. It takes the most insidious forms. It has patience. It waits and watches. It establishes its influence with the gentleness of a lover, cleverly placing bits and pieces of itself among the Kindred's belongings until nothing remains untouched. It moves in. It redecorates. It spreads its disease from liege to serf and from serf to serf. It rides the king like a demon Hell-bent on omnipotence. It leads the queen to believe she controls her own destiny. It lies.

Throughout the centuries, the monster has nurtured strong ties with insanity. You should take care, however, not to confuse the two. Few victims start out insane. That comes later, once the Destroyer has clawed through the hard shell to the softer parts inside. The Destroyer's insanity is akin to that felt by the schizophrenic æ an insanity so complete the victim never realizes anything has gone horribly wrong. With schizophrenia, the culprit eats the links to reality, one cell at a time. The Destroyer eats everything, one cell at a time. Don't expect, however, to look at the Destroyer's prey and see madness. Sometimes, you will. Most often, you won't.

The monster has many disguises. It particularly loves to surround itself with religion, ritual and pomp. It does so to sate its lust for righteousness. It wears its own brands of logic and common sense like war medals, well-earned and admirable. It struts out in the open, unafraid of repercussion or censure. Nothing can touch it. Only the best, the astute, recognize it for what it is.

So many of our kind believe they have evolved beyond humanity. Because we have achieved preternatural awareness, because we have greater power, and because we benefit from extended longevity, we most certainly are the higher beings. I find this amusing. In truth, we are nothing more than children who have stumbled upon an arsenal. We turn our weapons upon each other, upon ally and enemy both, before we even realize the power we hold in our hands. Our fingers squeeze the trigger, sometimes with easy grace, sometimes with violent twitches. The bullets fly. Our companions fall before our eyes and we wonder, "What happened?" Some of us children stare down at our traitorous hands, in disbelief. Some laugh and practice some more, careless of whom they harm.

Few of us ever truly achieve a state of peace with what we've become. We continue to seek the things we sought as mortals. We walk the night, looking back over our shoulders at everything we've lost. We yearn for love and for admiration æ just like living men. Why do we do anything we do but to acquire some form of approval from someone æ just like mortals? We still feel we have something to prove æ just like mortals. That need opens the door to the Destroyer.

Do you know outrage? If so, then you know the scent of the Destroyer. Do you have enemies? Do you support a cause? Would you meet the Final Death for it? Would you expect others to die with you? Do you extol your beliefs to others? Do you recruit fellow believers from among your allies? Do you recruit your companions from among your fellow believers? If so, then you know the scent of the Destroyer. It has, most assuredly, stalked you.

"But," you say. But what? But, everyone should have a cause they advance and support? But, everyone should have an agenda? But, everyone must stand for something lest they die for nothing?

Is that so? You may wish to reconsider.

The Destroyer births inside its victims, invisible and immaterial. It flourishes because people, dead and living, want to belong. It knows that people create their coteries and extend their families so they won't have to spend the balance of their eternities alone. They seek out and make followers, subordinates and audiences, so they can feel important. They flex their political and supernatural muscles so they don't have to face the fact that they're no better than anyone else, including, for Kindred, the mortals upon whom they feed.

I would suggest, for the sake of argument, that fundamentally Cainites are nothing more than mortals with fangs.

Ah, I bet that bothered you. You don't like to think that you're just like the cattle from which you take your sustenance? You believe the clothes make the man... or the Kindred? You're wrapped rather tightly in undead power, aren't you? Do you really think that makes you more emotionally and mentally balanced, gives you a higher intelligence, makes you spiritually superior or even improves your looks? You make me laugh. Look around at your fellow Cainites. Are *they* emotionally balanced? Mentally? Spiritually? Of course not. But then, you're better than they are, too, aren't you? Of course you are.

The Destroyer loves people filled with self-importance and sinful pride. The Destroyer has many different names, you know. Sometimes, people call it "megalomania." Is it making more sense to you now? Only by cutting out one's own heart can one destroy the Destroyer. We are our own worst enemies.

The Church of Ego

How far would you go to gain the adulation of your superiors, your peers or your subordinates? Do you ever smile and agree, even though you disagree, just to avoid conflict? Do you ever pretend to feel something you don't, just to fit in? Have you ever found your values changing to fit the people around you? We all do this. There's nothing wrong with you. Every single one of us comes up with the most extravagant justifications for the adaptations we make in order to blend with our comrades. Both mortals and the undead have grown quite adept at these rationalizations. Unfortunately, predators have learned to take advantage of this very human weakness in both populations.

In English, we have a word for this phenomenon, an often poorly defined and negatively weighted word: cult. Say it aloud. Cult. Sounds dirty, doesn't it? Does it come uncomfortably to your tongue? Cult.

This word has come to mean many things to many different people. Most associate it with Satanism, but this does cults an injustice. Not all cultists pray to Satan. Some revere even more destructive gods.

An Introduction to Cults

Mind-manipulating groups. Socio-psychological influences. Exploitive organizations, coercive persuaders, new religions… they're all cults. Many different terms define the same thing.

Of course, many factors differentiate cults from legitimate organizations. You'll learn soon enough how to tell them apart. For now, keep it in the back of your mind that perhaps the social entities you've come to trust, to understand and to take for granted might actually be the cement shoes that will drag you to the bottom of the proverbial river.

What Makes a Cult a Cult?

Some anti- and counter-cult organizations and academicians have pulled together lists of criteria for what determines a cult. You can find pamphlets about them all over the Internet and littering the end tables at counseling centers. No one seems ready, however, to commit to a definitive description of what makes a group a cult. The educators who write these things remind us throughout their dissertations that they provide these evidentially

An Eye on Cults

We've all seen the TV shows, the superbly dramatic and "unbiased" reports on the status of cults in the United States, Europe and rest of the world. If not, browse the World Wide Web or the backs of magazines a bit and find them. They're out there, everywhere æ for purchase on video, at least. Cults draw attention. Drop the words "secret" and "mysterious" and "cult," and you can draw the attention of an entire nation. "Is your child in danger?" The public gobbles it up and begs for more.

Some sociologists now dedicate their careers to studying what they call the "cult phenomenon." Not so long ago, "cult experts" began to appear, primarily as a result of media attention focused upon the Branch Davidian mess and the Heaven's Gate shocker. Legitimate news programs and yellow-journalism tabloids alike adore presenting the populace with expert witnesses. It lends them credibility and draws a clean line between them, the movie of the week and the sensationalism practiced by their competitors. These self-proclaimed experts, clumsy men and women with thick glasses and the best make-up job they'll have in their entire lives, love to coin multisyllabic phrases of psychobabble. Who can blame them? We all want our 15 minutes of fame. We all want to leave our mark. Shall we call it the cult of journalistic disintegrity? Perhaps the cult of ratings.

Cults appeal to the media and to scholars, not only because many cults display socially rebellious and shocking behavior, but also because they exude adventure. Adventure excites. Abnormal Psychology classes always have more students than Child Psychology classes. Who cares at what age children learn to walk or piss in a pot? We want to know about the serial killers, the sexual deviants and the cultists. We want the academic version of a freak show. Tell me again what they did to each other! What's that you say? They believed *what*? The pictures in the textbooks disturb us so profoundly that we can't quit turning the pages and looking… and looking… and looking….

We look at cults and, though we might never admit it, wonder what it would be like to live so single-mindedly, with such conviction and such all-encompassing faith. Yes, it takes commitment to walk away from the societal norm and practice a different "religion." Of course, it also takes commitment to walk into someone's Hollywood home and slice open an eight-months-pregnant actress.

Chapter Three: Sins of Discretion

unsupported lists only as guidelines. The term "cult," it seems, refers to a theoretical entity to which we compare actual groups. We take what information we have on an organization and hold it up beside the list to see how well they reflect one another. The "experts" further wax debatable by saying that you cannot draw conclusive stereotypes from the theoretical entity described by the list, because you will always find those cults that don't fit a stereotype. How convenient a loophole in their persecutory stance. Reminds me of the utility of the politically and socially arbitrary manners in which tyrannical princes interpret the Traditions.

Despite their unwillingness to commit, undoubtedly inspired by the threat of a lawsuit, these "experts" have actually produced something of value. The list of cult characteristics gives you a diving board for the first launch into examining an organization. Think about your own associations as you read through the list.

Charismatic and powerful leadership. Cults always have a single leader or cabal of co-leaders who drive the organization. Members give these leaders their unquestioning support. Although the faces may change, the existence of a figurehead does not. This leader inspires awe or fear in members of the cult. Followers line up to kiss this person's ass. They bow to him. They whisper the leader's name as a warning against misbehavior. "Better be good, or [insert authority figure's name] will get pissed." Sound familiar?

Most cults have a dictatorial organization, sometimes based on a revered document rather than an actual leader. For example, certain para-religions base their tenets upon religious documents. Other organizations may have bylaws or traditions handed down through numerous generations of members. Few simply follow a code of chivalry or a similarly broad behavioral guideline. Most have much more detailed rules that include the punishment meted out for breaches.

Isolation from family and friends. This requirement for membership in a cult eventually arises, although it may take some time. Through manipulation, threats and sometimes outright kidnapping, the organization removes you from all connection with your previous support structure. It cuts you off from your past. It tells you that you're different now and can never go back. It may convince you that you're a danger to your family and friends. It may even threaten you, your family or your friends if you don't cease all contact. Sound familiar?

Control. A cult immediately renders you powerless to control your own destiny. You enter a hierarchy at the lowest level. The cult makes sure you understand that it knows what's best for you. It tells you that you must learn to function according to its rules or flounder. In order to join, you must dedicate yourself to it for the first weekend, week, month or year. During that time, it tells you how and where to eat, what to think, what to feel, whom to love and when to sleep. It teaches you existence according to its tenets. It binds you to its best interests and leaves you no power to change your fate. It bullies you. It terrorizes you. It makes you weak. Sound familiar?

Mind-adjusting techniques. Certain cults use methods that suppress doubts among their followers. They may include psychologically damaging tactics such as meditation, isolation, forced discomfort, chanting, denunciation sessions, humiliation, exhausting work schedules, repetitive exercises, subliminal suggestion, behavioral modification, positive and negative reinforcement or hypnosis. When used in combination, these techniques — sometimes called brainwashing — change the victims' thought processes on a deep level. Sound familiar?

Increased suggestibility and subservience. A cult commonly uses psychological manipulation to weaken its members. It employs specific tactics to make you easier to handle. It teaches these tactics to its highest ranking members. It undoubtedly doesn't admit to its manipulation techniques, but it has an architecturally sound and ideologically convincing explanation for the necessity of the tactics. Sound familiar?

Powerful peer pressure. Guilt can be a powerful emotion. Cults rely on their members to reinforce their tenets. If your organization has a strong element of peer pressure, you may wish to re-examine your association with it. One voice alone doesn't carry the same power as many voices all raised together. Cults understand this. They encourage their members to "save" those who have not yet seen the light. Furthermore, people tend to shout the loudest when justifying their own actions. Cults also understand this and put it to excellent use. "Either you're with us, or against us. If you're against us, you must be criticizing me, in which case, I'll push my position even harder. I cannot be wrong. You are." The simplest psychology has the most power among the people hungriest for acceptance and love. Sound familiar?

Elitist attitude. In order for the group to justify itself to its members in a believable and lasting manner, it must touch the individual's need to feel special. Many people join an organization only because it makes them feel larger than life. It actively affirms for them that they are stronger, smarter or somehow better than the rest of the world's population. A cult carefully weaves its own identity into its members' egos. This way, in order for the member to tear down the cult, the member must shred her own ego.

Recruiting. Many cults encourage a process of recruiting that usually involves the approval of an authority figure. Especially in an era of awareness, where anti- and

counter-cults have focused negative attention on cults, these organizations realize the danger of accepting "a bad seed." They encourage recruitment, but within boundaries set by the leadership.

Information management. A layer of secrecy hangs over any cult. Perhaps those in charge don't reveal their identities or any personal information about themselves. They may have levels of disclosure. If you prove your loyalty to the organization, you earn access to different secrets. The cult may downplay the importance of the "mundane world." It may preach that nothing matters aside from what happens within the cult, and discourage or even forbid discussion of (or interest in) outside events. It may cut off access to information regarding health care, the repercussions of its actions as they manifest beyond the cult's metaphorical walls or information that would indicate to its members how to free themselves from the cult. Perhaps it filters information regarding other options and philosophies by forbidding its members to speak to anyone who disagrees with the cult's beliefs.

Suspension of individuality. In a cult, the individual represents the whole organization and must always act in the group's best interest. A cult will make it very clear that the individual is replaceable and even expendable, if the individual ceases to uphold the organization's goals and values. A cult encourages a sense of "family" among its members. It creates its us-against-them mentality as a means of reducing the importance of the individual and increasing solidarity. Most cults do not have a democratic structure, because each individual voice counts for nothing. The leader knows intuitively what the membership body needs (though perhaps not what it wants) and speaks for that body. A cult may even preach that, at some point, the member may have to sacrifice him- or herself for the greater good.

Total dependency. Without a shepherd, the sheep would undoubtedly fall victim to wolves, or so the shepherd tells his flock. They believe him. A cult makes a solid case for why a member would be doomed or damned without the shelter of the cult. The cult teaches that it alone can save the member from sure failure, unhappiness or even eternal Hell. As long as you're in the cult, you're one of God's chosen, one of another god's chosen, on the fast-track to wealth, on the fast-track to health, safe, the perfect mother, the perfect father, the perfect lover or the perfect whatever. Without the cult, you're nothing. You're a capital-L Loser.

Fear tactics. Sometimes, without the cult, you're not just a loser; you're dead. Some cults don't beat around the bush. You fuck up; you die. You leave them; you die. You betray them; you die. Sometimes, you die, your family dies, your friends die and your therapist dies.

Exalted ends justify any means. A cult teaches its members, either via instruction or example, that it can break any human or divine law in order to achieve its goals. Acts that a member would never have committed before joining the cult suddenly become acceptable in the new value structure. Looked in the mirror lately?

Daily Dogma

Now that you know the fundamental characteristics of a totalist or destructive cult, let's take a look at how these characteristics can apply, across the board, in many different types of cults. Not all cults have agendas that relate to God or to Gehenna. You may find it surprising that cults can have schemes anchored in politics, psychotherapy, commercial endeavors, racism or even belief in aliens. Belief in aliens? Yes, belief in aliens. Read on.

Cultic Currency

Every cult has something to sell. It must have a "product" in order to attract members. It must make a promise of some sort, usually related to providing the buyer with a better life. In some cases, it promises a better afterlife.

Not all cults set out to deceive their followers. Some cult leaders may sincerely believe in their products. They may mean no deceit when they make their promises. They may actually have something important to tell people, or they may just have lost their minds. Others purposefully seek to deceive. They know they're selling fiction, fantasy and pipe dreams. They want what they can get in exchange for their promises, whether empty or otherwise.

> ### Cult Statistics in America
> During the course of my research, I learned about more than 2,000 different organizations suspected of being cults. A cult may have anywhere from a handful to thousands of members. Research has shown that five to 10 million Americans have come in direct contact with a cult, and that many of these people have joined one. Nearly half of them never knew that anyone considered their organizations to practice cultic methods. I found an unsubstantiated reference to a study done with 1,000 high school students in San Francisco. According to the study, 3% of the students reported membership in a cult, and 54% had been approached by a cult recruiter. Another such study that focused on adults in Montreal and San Francisco reported that 20% of the adult respondents subscribed to a "new" religion or para-religious movement.

What *can* they get? That usually depends on what they want and how marketable their schemes are. In some circles, money takes a back seat. In others, it's all about raising the bottom line. Among the Kindred, we're often talking about vitae for the taking, but that's not always the case. Take a look at some of these cultic currencies and think back. Have you ever paid for the *right to belong* with one of these currencies?

Money. Many organizations use cultic methods for the sole purpose of wringing as much money as they can from their followers. The leaders of these groups may purposefully mislead and manipulate the membership in order to pad their own wallets, or they may be genuine about the cult's dogma, and any money they garner is icing on the cake.

How easily a fool and his money are parted. Promise him something he desperately wants, and he'll fork over everything he owns. Salvation makes a good product. Selling salvation doesn't require much. Package it in attractive dressings, give it an appealing slogan and find a charismatic spokesperson to tout it. The consumers will come in droves, credit cards in hand. The best part of selling salvation is that your customer has to die to discover that you sold him a lemon. Don't bother keeping the receipt.

Blood. We Kindred feed on blood. We need it to survive, as mortals need food or water or air. We need only blood. Mortals often define themselves based on their eating habits. Vegetarian, vegan, omnivorous, men and their red meat, women and their chocolate, kids and their cereals. They all have food plugged straight into their identities. Kindred do the same, only they have arguably less variety for their diversity.

Do you chow on children? Do you suck duck or cow or cat rather than touch human flesh? Do you feed on the freshly sexed or appreciate the esthetics of chemical additives flowing through the veins? Do you snub the dirty? Do you crave the unworthy? Do you kill when you feed? Do you cultivate your herd carefully? Do you take a moral stance each time you dip your fangs? Do you enjoy the hunt?

Who are you? Tell me how you feed, and I'll answer that question for you.

We can't take our succulent vitae, the blood that nourishes us, in the same quantities we once could. Cainite numbers continue to increase æ exponentially in some cases. Camarilla society designates feeding domains. It puts restrictions on where we can hunt, with the intent of controlling the number of deaths occurring in any one location. Too many dead bodies, too many attacks of "anemia" and the wise prince begins to take notice. Our Camarilla brethren, in typical anal-retentive fashion, organize and direct our feeding habits into a beautifully choreographed dance. Or so they would like to believe. Ventrue over here, Malkavians over there, Brujah down that-a-way, Nosferatu down below… and so on and so on. It never quite works as smoothly as they hope.

Even followers of the Sabbat understand the dangers of leaving behind an obvious trail of bodies. Despite their insouciant attitude toward the "herd of mortals" or whatever sneering slang they use, they know how to cover their asses. If they didn't, they'd have died out a long time ago. Like dogs that know better than to shit in their own dens, the Sabbat take their killing sprees to neighboring domains.

Anarch groups don't fit any mold. They're each unique. Those that fuck up and catch the attention of the local homicide division usually don't survive long enough to learn the lesson. More than likely, the Camarilla Justice Squad will hunt the anarchs down long before any detective can get anywhere near them. The Camarilla takes its self-imposed policing responsibilities to heart.

Supply and demand principles dictate that as demand goes up while supply remains the same or goes down, the value of the commodity goes up. Bottom line: Kindred traffic in blood. Blood has become a valuable commodity.

Blood cults have existed for thousands of years. Many ancient cultures believed they could steal a man's essence, power and wisdom, merely by drinking his blood.

Power. Who doesn't crave power? No one I know. We all carry within us the natural, *human* desire to maintain control over our own destinies, and sometimes even the destinies of others. The more of our environment we have at our disposal, the better we feel. Isn't that the case?

You'll find two kinds of control freaks in the world: the kind who have an addiction to that rush of sadism when others bow at their feet, and the kind who feel deeply insecure if they don't have complete dominance over their environments. Either kind goes to great lengths to acquire and maintain its power.

Hierarchies work because those at the top mete out power in ever-increasing portions. People climb the ladder, equating power with success. They lap up those portions as they rise through the ranks. Like wild dogs, they keep their eyes turned toward the source of their nutriment (power), watching for any dropped crumbs. When a succulent morsel falls, they lunge. Sometimes, fights break out. Competing beasts get injured. Some die.

Smart leaders hand out this power with care. They reward the loyalty of their followers with responsibility and trust. They create layers within the organization and define which layers have more power than others. Smart leaders, that is.

The Body of Christ

In a small Texas town, an old Mexican church stands amid oil drills and tumbleweeds. This church draws perhaps a hundred of the faithful every year. Believers make pilgrimages to the tiny church to pray at the feet of the Christ. In this church, which claims no particular denomination, a life-sized crucifix hangs on the wall. The sculptor had a remarkable, even divine talent. He created a work of art so realistic that the Christ figure looks as if it could turn its head. Indeed, it could and often does. Hung upon that cross once every year, a Kindred seeks his own personal salvation through penance to his Lord, God. Every year on the same night, his followers reverently nail him to the wood. His blood flows down upon the rocks at the base of the cross.

The Kindred doesn't move once crucified. For all intents and purposes, he appears dead or unreal. Still, many of the visitors to the church suspect that a live man plays the role of the Christ figure, breathing ever so shallowly like those living mannequins hired by department stores for their display windows. This doesn't keep the worshippers from coming to look, to pray, to gawk and shake their heads. They come, and later, they return with friends and family and fellow believers. Tourists, alone and on organized junkets, stop on their way to Las Vegas, to see the circus Christ.

Some stare because they think the model-Christ is insane, an oddity or an amusing fake. Others come truly to worship at his feet, having witnessed or heard of the miracles he performs. "He can see behind your eyes. He knows your darkest secrets and judges your heart as you kneel before him." Will he lead the righteous to Heaven? Many believe so.

What tithe does the church charge its flock for the right to kneel at the feet of a real crucifix? One pint of blood æ each pilgrim must donate one pint of blood. *Sign the appropriate release forms and take a seat in the chair; a nurse will be right with you.* Half the blood goes to the local hospital. The other half goes to the Christ figure.

I purposefully have not mentioned any particulars regarding location and name, not even clan, of the Kindred in question. Far be it from me to put his personal, religious pursuit at risk. The Camarilla has yet to notice him and how he dances at the edge of the Masquerade.

This Christ has acquired a dedicated body of followers. I do not doubt that Camarilla representatives would find themselves facing more than one faithful servant of the Lord if they were to attempt to steal or destroy the Christ figure. I've heard that insanity is contagious. In a little town in Texas, I think you'll find the proof that it's true.

Shit flows downhill. We all want to be as high on that hill as we can. Power exacts a high price, and many gladly pay that price.

Adulation. Do not underestimate the power of the ego. As children — and yes, every single Kindred in this world started in the womb, birthed from woman, had to learn toilet habits, and had to learn to walk and talk — as children, we crave love. Love me! Love me! Love me! Maybe we get it. Maybe we don't. The cravings never stop. They may evolve into something more adult, neurotic or psychotic, but it's all about love. You're nobody if nobody loves you, as Dean Martin used to sing.

Why do so many sports figures, businessmen, actors, politicians and other public figures give in so easily to rock-star syndrome? Because the adulation has an addictive clutch that takes hold and won't let go. Often, a cult leader wants nothing more than to become the center of his followers' worlds. In order to remain a member of the cult, you must adore your leader. Sounds so simple, doesn't it? So cheap a price without much consequence, yes? It is cheap, until you begin to consider that sometimes adoration equates to degradation and sacrifice.

Furthermore, in many of this type of cult, you can't always just file for separation and walk away. If you wake up one night and no longer *feel the love*, you could face persecution from your fellow cultists at best and "accidents" at worst.

Typecasting

You might find it surprising that cults come in such a variety of flavors. I've already mentioned that they vary according to what they demand in payment and what methods they use. Now, let's talk about what they're selling in greater detail. As I mentioned, all cults have something to sell.

Para-religion. It never ceases to amaze me what bullshit charismatic people can turn into a religion. Everyone asks certain things in their lives: Why am I? Who am I? Who is God? What should I do? How do I do it? When should I stop? Find an attractive, well-spoken leader who can present an even remotely plausible answer to these questions, and you have the formation of a cult. Hell, you don't even need the attractive part — look at Jim Bakker. People are so gullible. They don't want to think for themselves. They look to dogma for the level of guidance their parental figures gave to them when they were children. Responsibility sucks, so pass the buck to your god or to alien ancestors or to karma or to whatever you choose to worship. It's cool to believe.

Simultaneously, it's uncool to criticize someone else's beliefs. When you begin discussing and criticizing religions, you step into territory that makes some uncomfortable. How dare anyone slam another's religious beliefs? As a society, Americans have baggage left over from the country's youth, during which it had to fight for the right to worship as it pleased. The ideals held so righteously back then have turned into a societal catch-22. Where do you draw the line between allowing people to worship as they please and letting them get away with murder? Political correctness is next to godliness? Stand by and watch as a Christian Scientist allows her child to die for lack of a transfusion? Yes. Because we respect that parent's right to worship as she pleases.

America was founded on a principal of religious freedom. Do these cultic, new religions fall under the protective umbrella of the Constitution? Of course, they do — within reason. As long as they don't break the law... I mean, as long as they don't get caught breaking the law, they can worship Jeffrey Dahmer for all anyone cares. You'll find many people who vehemently defend a person's right to choose or invent their own religion.

The United States took a revolutionary stance with regard to freedom of religion, and it remained the only country to do so for a long time. Some nations tolerated minority religions, so long as the people took part in public ceremonies worshipping the accepted god. Other nations punished heresy and heterodoxy as treason. The First Amendment of the United States Constitution promises every man, woman and child the freedom to choose their own style, place and mode of worship, within the confines of the law. Specifically, it forbids the passage of laws "respecting the establishment of religion or prohibiting the free exercise thereof." The US and other countries that embrace philosophies of tolerance or separation of church and state have become protected gardens where neo-religious organizations can germinate and flourish.

Anti-cult and counter-cult movements complain that cults hide behind political correctness in order to practice inhumane and lawless behavior, all in the name of worshipping their gods. They snidely call those who defend the cults "cult apologists." They use the term to describe those sociologists and academics who examine new religious organizations, label the majority as harmless and advocate the organizations' rights to religious freedom.

Lest we forget, some Kindred are so far gone as to make their own religions. They get to play the role of messiah or prophet or even god. I can think of no better shelter from the law and the media than to proclaim a group "religious in nature." It excuses so many things, such as occult practices, so-called miracles, isolationism, survivalism, group housing and donations.

If the general public hears of a new religious organization that has grown up around a gifted psychic or a miracle-worker, it reacts in one of two ways. Either it believes and wants to join, or it discounts the veracity of the reports and thinks all the members of the church have lost their minds.

Centuries of exposure to a constant tide of potential saviors, during which any number of crackpot religions have come and gone, have desensitized the public. Religious organizations easily maneuver within modern society, picking and choosing their targets, because the bulk of the population ignores them. For our purposes, this equates to a natural Masquerade. No one, not the Camarilla and not any particular Kindred, can take credit for this phenomenon. Face it. Society has become numb to the freaks in the world. You think the Damned are nasty? Look at how people tolerate neo-Nazis. They have the right to parade and to gather, just like everyone else. Look at the BDSM clubs where "consenting adults" beat each other, cut each other, rape each other and stick six-inch-long needles through each other's fleshy parts. That's legal and accepted. Look at the consenting adults involved in bizarre cults that openly share blood and worship at altars that resemble a goth's wet dream. Even that's legal… and accepted. Various state laws require that you wear a seatbelt — for your own protection — but you're free to fuck up your life in a plethora of other ways, so long as you're a grown-up and so long as that's really what you want. I love it. One begins to wonder if the Camarilla isn't just a tad overprotective with the Masquerade, hm?

Psychotherapeutic. Prior to and during the 1950s, many of the cults in the world had a religious slant to them. The 1960s, however, saw the rise of self-help groups that focused more on modern philosophies of self-actualization, self-fulfillment and self-policing. Despite the "self" inherent in them all, these cults differed little from the abusive para-religions they resembled. Psychotherapeutic groups use buzzwords taken from psychology rather than religion. They cater to the self-indulgent and self-absorbed. As the rebellious spirit of the American 1960s spread, people began to question everything around them. They no longer trusted their government, the media, their doctors or their parents. None of those sources had any explanation for the world's craziness. So, people began to look inward for the answers to their questions.

Unhappy housewives nurtured Valium addictions. People read self-help books and went to weekend-long seminars. You've seen them on infomercials. For $700 and a weekend, you can learn to be more effective in your job, in bed and in life. Men are from Mars. Women are from Venus. Take charge of your life. Make more money than you ever dreamed possible. Practice the 12 steps to more perfect living. Recite the seven habits of highly effective people. Smile.

IDENTITY MOVEMENT

The name of this new religion, "Christian Identity movement," often confuses people into thinking it's just another Christian denomination, such as Methodist or Baptist. This confusion allows its leaders to pursue racial supremacist agendas behind a screen of religion. In actuality, their doctrines hold that Jews descended from Satan and the real Israelites are the English-speaking and Germanic tribes. They further believe that blacks, Asians and other minorities aside from Jews were pre-Adam, and thus, inferior creations, no more than animals, without souls.

According to followers of the Christian Identity theology, Satan seduced Eve, and Eve gave birth to Cain. From Cain came Jews. By their reckoning, Satan intends to destroy the pure, white race by enticing other races, which they call "mud people," to sexually pollute the white race.

The bloodsucker at the head of one Identity cell believes that other Kindred Embrace the pure white race in order to taint the blood. From Cain came, well, Cainites. The stain spreads. Few know of her connection with and support of the Christian Identity movement. However, she actively lobbies among her clanmates for greater discrimination when Embracing. Her own childer have "appropriate" Aryan genes.

SHRI MAHAJA

The yogi sits cross-legged and meditates with an audience of awe-struck, unquestioning followers. She preaches about how to raise children so they will have a place in the perfect afterlife. She teaches that you must slap the children in order to chase out the spirits that possess them. Misbehavior, of course, results from possession. Possessed adults require even greater violence, because their skin has grown tougher over the years. She oversees these exorcisms with pride and pleasure, proclaiming what a joy it is to free the innocents from their burdens. She uses her telepathic abilities to seek out doubters and their secrets. She looks them in the eyes and commands the *bhoots*, evil spirits, to reveal themselves by quaking. They obey her, every time. Her followers revere her all the more. She collects their worldly goods and gives them back their innocence in return, all beneath the shelter of the American Constitution. Those who believe, believe. Those who don't, don't. The Masquerade remains shakily intact. What a fine line these self-proclaimed messiahs walk.

Some of these programs mean well. They're as legitimate and sincere as any small-town doctor. Others, however, spread a thick veneer of respectability over a rotten core. The leaders of these groups can have many reasons for forming the cult, but ultimately, they take on a commercial attitude. You'll see them hawking audio and video tapes on late-night television. They rely on their converts to spread the word about their seminars. You'll have friends recommending you come to an expensive weekend retreat, for your own good. Once they get you there, they slowly, insidiously try to take over your life. They use isolation tactics to quickly break down your ego. From there, they refill the void they made with their own platitudes about the road to health, wealth and happiness. They ingratiate themselves to you. They ingrain themselves in your self-image. They praise you. They make you believe that only through their teachings can you become the best.

Once they've got you hooked, they send you out to find more victims. They take your money, and lots of it, and they give you a whole new language around which to base your identity. Aesthetic Realism, a group formed in 1941, taught members about being "completely fair." The founder and original leader, Eli Siegel, established his own definition of this extremely ambiguous term, a definition that the members *think* they understand. Siegel also used many other cultic techniques to ensure a loyal following among members. He took his own life in 1978 because the world "resented his greatness." Others stepped in to take his place at the head of the organization. Siegel was martyred.

You have to admire those shadowy figures who took what Siegel built and turned it into something useful to themselves. They carefully chose the next figurehead, a woman, to cry for Siegel and appeal to the sensibilities of the members. Tonight, the organization has almost a hundred followers, all based in the New York area. They wear badges that state "Victim of the Press" in honor of Siegel's belief in a conspiracy among the press to keep his philosophy of Aesthetic Realism from spreading.

The puppet masters of this organization have distilled Aesthetic Realism down into something that the general public can swallow. As a result, they've attracted members from all walks of life. In particular, they appeal to the movers and shakers on Broadway, the actors, directors and producers with influence. They have also drawn an up-and-coming politician into the mix. Of course, the majority of its members work as secretaries in offices, on Wall Street, and around the city. Never underestimate the importance of these cogs, however. The secretary knows as much, if not more, about what's happening in her offices than her own boss does. Power isn't always so blatant and showy.

Sexual. The Sexual Revolution did great things for cults. Free love, swinging, orgies æ it all became accepted and even common. Tonight, they call free love polyamorism, a term that I find reminds me ironically of the phrase Pollyanna. Polyamorous people have open relationships. They may share other lovers or go freely into other beds on the side. Everyone likes a good fuck (well, everyone who's still alive…). Cults that not only offered therapy for overcoming sexual hang-ups but also provided a venue for "practicing" have become extremely popular. As time passed, these cults evolved parallel to society's growing tolerance of all things sexual. The boundaries they pushed in the early nights, charging boldly into homosexuality, swinging and bondage, no longer hold the same appeal. The frontier of society's comfort zone has shifted. Because they have stayed on the cutting edge — pardon the pun — cultic sex groups have stretched the limits of accepted behavior.

Sex plays such an integral role in everyone's life that it should surprise no one that most cults have a sexual aspect to them of some sort. Either all the *chicas* in the group take turns with the male leader, or the cult dictates who can do whom, how, when and where. Many people join cults merely because they get the feeling they're loved. Touchy-feely groups attract the lonely, the rejected, the depressed, the lost and the horny. Certain cults free you from the inhibitions and guilt imposed upon you by the rest of society. They not only give you permission to fuck, they provide you with partners who also have permission to fuck. Everyone is ready, willing and able. Kick ass! Where do I sign up?

The problem comes when peer pressure begins to insidiously turn consent into guilt, and guilt into coercion. Groups cross the line when they tell you there's something wrong with you if you don't want to participate, try to make you think you're closed-minded or judgmental, and accuse you of being frigid and unenlightened if you resist. You're not into sharing? You must be a right-wing, fascist stooge who can't have an orgasm. If you want to grow and learn, and become enlightened, you must spread your wings and fly. Trust me.

Right.

Political. As an example, the feminist movement has fostered a number of radical groups that prey upon their members. These organizations use cultic methods to isolate the women within them, impose belief structures, break down the ego, discourage contrary thinking and talk, and even violently impose loyalty. The term feminazi insults many women, with good reason. These groups do exist, but they're not healthy. Many have an embittered, rage-filled leader with enough charisma to spread her hatred among her followers. These organizations hide behind a mask of human rights issues, and all the while, they're discouraging free thought and individuality among their own members. Members are either 100% with or 100% ostracized from the organization.

Other radical organizations have the same history. Ecoterrorist groups often use extreme methods to indoctrinate and maintain their membership. Whether they're on the extreme right or left doesn't matter — both use cultic tactics. Whether they support racism, isolationism, territorialism or environmentalism, they're still cults. The methods they use tell the real story.

Some of these organizations have a Kindred at their core or at least among them. One Nazi Ventrue or territorial Gangrel who has seen far too many nights and is too out of touch decides that he can fix all the world's problems. He decides to take his antiquated visions, form a strike team and apply some pressure to the politicos. Nice. Unfortunately for maniacs like this, you can't just kill people in tonight's society, not like you could hundreds of years ago. However, you can bribe, blackmail and lobby. The larger your organization and the more money you have, the more clout you carry. Welcome to world politics.

Commercial. Although organizations like Amway vehemently deny cult status, many academics and anti-cult activists believe that multilevel marketing companies actually practice cultic methods toward their members. Once the government outlawed pyramid schemes, multilevel marketing rushed in to replace it. In pyramid schemes, you make more money the higher you are on the pyramid. Theoretically, the money flows upward and the person at the pinnacle gets a piece of everyone's pie. Those on the very bottom layer get screwed. With multilevel marketing, the schemers have managed to exploit a loophole that makes their structures legal. Strangely, the outcome remains the same. The person at the top makes a shitload of money. Those at the bottom stuff envelopes, hoping to trick someone else into occupying a new niche below them.

These organizations push recruiting because they know that the more people below you on the totem pole, the more money you'll make. They guilt you into feeling like a failure if you don't produce, don't sell and don't recruit. Whether you're selling vitamins, household products, make-up or magazines, you must use your own products because no one trusts a salesperson who doesn't use their own products in their home, and the more you spend on your own merchandise, the more money goes up the chain. It's quite efficient, really, and there's a sucker born every minute.

Multilevel marketing organizations appeal to the Kindred because once they put the structure in place, the system itself requires little maintenance. A public appearance, twice a year or so, satisfies the masses. These events happen at night, because most MLM salespeople have day jobs as well. Each level of the hierarchy has its own perpetual motion because the people at each level want to make more money. If individual salespeople work hard and increase their income, the income of those above them automatically increases as well. Thus, the entire structure is self-supporting. If one arm falls off, another grows to replace it. The Kindred must periodically check the books, do a bit of discipline or toss out morsels of wisdom to the masses. Otherwise, the founder can relax and count his money.

Aliens. I saved the most odd for last. Would you believe it if I told you that some Kindred actually believe they came from outer space? You've heard all the theories. Many different cultic groups believe in extraterrestrials who visited Earth millennia ago and who will return one night to retrieve the brethren they left behind.

The Aetherius Society, for example, believes in the Great White Brotherhood, or the Brother/Sisterhood of Light, a "multi-dimensional, interplanetary, intergalactic organization of beings who choose to serve the divine cosmic plan in this universe" (Spiritweb, www.spiritweb.org). The organization believes in Ascended Masters, historical figures who had connections to the Aetherius Society, including Jesus, St. Germain, El Morya and Lord Buddha. They also believe that, in 1954, a man named George King received a message during a meditative yoga state. The Cosmic Master Aetherius spoke to him and told him that he was appointed the Voice of the Interplanetary Parliament, headquartered on Saturn, for Earth.

Described as a mystagogue, George King performs miracles. He has "mastered" the "sciences" of Raja, Gnani and Kundalini Yoga, which allow him to consciously attain the state of Samadhi. It is this power that allows King to communicate with beings from other spiritual energy spheres. George King took the name of Primary Terrestrial Mental Channel for the Cosmic Masters, while his followers bestowed him with the full title of Sir George King, OSP, PhD, ThD, DD, Metropolitan Archbishop of the Aetherius Churches, Prince Grand Master of the Mystical Order of St. Peter, HRH Prince De George King De Santori, and Founder President of the Aetherius Society.

The Aetherius Society originated in Great Britain where, in 1959, the BBC broadcast King while in a Samadhic trance, channeling wisdom from the Great Cosmic Masters. In 1960, King established a center in the United States. Can you guess where? Hollywood. Of course. The Society has since also opened a center in Detroit and on every other continent in the world.

King died in 1997. During his lifetime, he received over 600 transmissions from the Cosmic Masters, including an expansion on the Sermon on the Mount from Master Jesus, now residing on Venus. Oddly, his last transmission took place approximately 35 years before he died, in 1961. It came from the Lord of Karma on Mars Sector Six and explained the steps one must take in the journey toward Cosmic Consciousness.

Another, similar organization, known as the Karmic Wheel, believes that a more advanced, extraterrestrial civilization uses Earth as its prison. It sends criminals to Earth for retraining. Once a person has evolved properly, she may return to the Hub, a centralized community located millions of light years away. Until then, she works through lifetime after lifetime of lessons. Beings from other planets return from time to time and sift through the souls incarcerated on Earth. Those who have proven themselves worthy may rise up to the Hub. Members of the Karmic Wheel equate this entire process with the Christian concept of Judgment Day. They believe Earth to be Purgatory.

I've spoken with the true leader of this organization. He, a Toreador, maintains a low profile and works primarily through his partners, but he does take a somewhat active role in the cult's direction. He prefers his Hub name, which he claims is Santauri X, and he believes that Cainites come from a distant planet. He believes they committed horrible crimes in order to earn their punishment in Purgatory. Furthermore, he told me that he believes that every person on Earth has Kindred blood, that the Embrace merely awakens the vitae within a person, that Kindred reincarnate just as mortals do, and that they can learn to awaken their own supernatural powers without the aid of the Embrace. While I visited, he offered me a demonstration of this. A handful of his followers gladly volunteered for the experiment. They meditated and fasted for two days in preparation. When the time came, they each drank a mixture of their own blood and poison. They died believing that, through the strength of their willpower, they could become one of the walking undead. They just died. Santauri X, saddened, assured me that they would figure out the puzzle one night soon.

Cults We've Known and Loved

Wake up. Here comes the fun part. The following list of cults gives you an overview of the ones that failed. Some of these had Kindred influence either governing them, using them as a front or shutting them down. I say they failed, and yet some of them remain intact. Despite the atrocious endings to their stories, a few have managed to negotiate a sequel. Watch for them as they begin to rebuild their influence and membership. Perhaps they learned from their mistakes. Perhaps they didn't. What victims have they targeted for next time?

The People's Temple

Jim Jones believed in an impending nuclear holocaust that would destroy the entire world, except for the towns of Ukiah, California, and Belo Horizonte, Brazil. He believed that he was the reincarnation of Jesus and Lenin, reborn to a Klansman in order to lead his people to salvation. He led them to Ukiah to wait for Armageddon and called them the People's Temple.

Eventually, he grew bored in Ukiah and gave up on the end of the world. He moved his group to San Francisco. There, he made a name for himself, receiving many humanitarian awards and becoming the chairman of the city's Housing Authority. On his days off, he and his temple practiced a ritual he called White Nights, in which they prepared themselves to protest racism and fascism by committing mass suicide.

Jim's weirdness escalated. In 1977, he moved his followers to Guyana, South America. Isolated in the jungle there, he lost all touch with reality. He built his perfect community, called Jonestown, and gradually descended further and further into insanity.

Reports of human rights violations in Jonestown reached the US Congress. They sent Congressman Leo Ryan from San Francisco on a fact-finding mission to the jungle compound. During Ryan's short visit, one of Jones' followers stabbed the congressman. Although the injury was superficial, Ryan decided the time had come to leave. He took his team, and 18 temple members who also wanted to return to the United States, and drove to the airstrip. Other members of the cult followed. At the airstrip, they opened fire on the departing congressman. They killed Ryan, three journalists and one of the leaving temple members. They injured 11 others.

Jim knew the time had come for drastic action. He ordered his followers to make a giant vat of grape-flavored Fla-Vor-Aid laced with potassium cyanide and tranquilizers. That done, he ordered them to drink from it. All of them did. More than 900 people died as a result. The children croaked first — all 276 of them. Babies had the poisonous mixture squirted into their mouths with syringes. The adults went next. While the grand majority drank willingly, some were forced to do so. Security guards shot those who attempted to flee or who refused the drink. The Reverend Jim Jones himself had a bullet through his head, though no one knows for sure whether he put it there himself or whether someone else did us the favor.

Over the next few months, other members and ex-members of the People's Temple, located outside Jonestown, also committed suicide and murder. One mother slit the throats of her three children. A year later, People's Temple critics, three ex-members (Jeanne and Al Mills and their daughter Linda), who were giving speeches about their experiences in the People's Temple, were shot to death in their home.

The People's Temple stands as a testimony to the power of cultic methodology. Some even believe that an agency of the American government set up Jonestown as an experiment in mind control. Now that's an interesting theory, isn't it? Or maybe it was some other organization performing the experiment. Think about it.

Anyway, now's the part where you expect me to implicate some frantic Malkavian. Sorry to disappoint you, but this was purely a mortal thing. I included it as an object lesson. Wanna start a cult? Find the people who are willing to drink poisoned Kool-Aid at your command. Feed them your blood instead. There are people out there who are bugfuck enough to do it.

The Branch Davidian Seventh-Day Adventists

The story of David Koresh and the Branch Davidians actually begins much earlier, in the mid-1800s, when a man named William Miller planted the seeds that would grow into the Seventh-Day Adventist church. This church predicted the Second Coming of Christ several times, and it was wrong each time. Its followers prepared, each time, by selling all their belongings and traveling to the prophesied site to await Christ's arrival. Each time, they were disappointed and found excuses for why it didn't happen. Finally, David Koresh decided that Christ wouldn't show up until the church had made itself pure. His interpretation of pure provided some interesting times for the members of the Branch Davidian group.

Political and legal intrigue surrounded the Waco faction of the Seventh-Day Adventists. A handful of prophets came and went. David Koresh (born Vernon Howell) was the Seventh Angel, or prophet. He espoused the belief that church members must purify themselves in order to prepare the way for the Second Coming. He imposed a special diet upon his followers that included fasting while he himself ate whatever he pleased because he was the Seventh Angel and had knowledge they didn't. Koresh also had a penchant for other men's wives and for young girls. He had several "wives" himself. Among them were 13-year-old Karen Doyle, Michelle Jones (aged 12), Robyn Bunds (17), and up to 11 other underage women. Koresh reportedly described his "marriage" to Michelle Jones in this way, "So I go to Michelle, right, and I climb into bed with her. She thinks I'm trying to get warm. I reached for her underwear to take 'em off. She didn't know what I was doing so she struggled. She didn't know what I was trying to do with her. But I was too strong and I was doing this for God. I told her about the prophecies. That's how she became my wife."

The entire scene ended badly when the Bureau of Alcohol, Tobacco and Firearms (BATF) began to investigate Koresh. Tensions built until the BATF raided the Waco complex on February 28, 1993. Four law enforcement agents lost their lives that day. A stand-off ensued between the FBI/BATF and over 100 Branch Davidian Seventh-Day Adventist men, women and children. The siege lasted 51 days. It ended on April 19, 1993, with the deaths of approximately 86 people in a fire that swept the compound.

Not many people realize how long the Seventh-Day Adventists have existed, nor do they notice that the cult has continued even without their Seventh Angel, David Koresh. They have found a new prophet to lead them. The Eight Angel has promised to lead them to the true Second Coming. This prophet remains in the background for now, protected among the members of the Seventh-Day Adventist church, but the day will come when the Eighth Angel will lead the chosen once again to Mt. Carmel to await "The Second Great Awakening."

Sure he will.

Falun Gong

In 1999, China banned the Falun Gong cult and systematically arrested its members. The cult, accused of killing more than 1,400 people, practices a combination of traditional slow-motion exercises and meditation. It incorporates aspects of Buddhism and Taoism. Since its founding in 1992, the group has acquired more than a hundred million followers worldwide. The majority of them reside in China. Contrarily, the government officially estimates that Falun Gong has only about two million members in China.

The size of the organization alone poses a threat to the Chinese government. In an environment of persecution, where the government forbids groups to gather without pre-approval, the cult has staged several protests. Furthermore, the cult has appealed to international governments for help in establishing their human rights. Both these acts have put the cult in disfavor with the Chinese government.

The Order of the Solar Temple

The long and sordid history of this European cult hit the news in 1994 when 53 people simultaneously committed murder and/or suicide in several locations in Switzerland and Canada. The order's dual leaders were listed among the dead. Luc Jouret and Joseph di Mambro both died in Switzerland. Jouret had called for the suicide when his popularity began to dwindle. He felt his power slipping, and felt the members beginning to drift away. Obviously, he also lost his mind. In one last, dramatic move, he led the mass suicide.

The cult, which still exists, believes that these fiery murder-suicides transport the members to a new home on the star Sirius. To ensure the trip, the victims, including some children, are shot in the head, suffocated with plastic bags over their heads or poisoned. At the time of their suicides, Luc Jouret and Joseph di Mambro wrote a letter that stated that they were "leaving this earth to find a new dimension of truth and absolution, far from the hypocrisies of this world."

The Order has its origins in the Knights Templar of medieval fame. Over the centuries, the Knights Templar organization fractured, split and evolved in many different directions. One such splinter group eventually became the Order of the Solar Temple.

Shortly before Christmas, in 1995, a second mass suicide ritual took place on a plateau in the French Alps. The police found 16 charred bodies arranged in a star formation, each with its feet pointing to the ashes of a fire. Each of the victims died by stabbing, asphyxiation, shooting and/or poisoning. Many of these victims left behind suicide notes. One of these said, "Death does not exist. It is pure illusion. May we, in our inner life, find each other forever." Isn't that romantic? Though, you have to feel for the French ski champion, Jean Vuarnet, whose wife and son were among the deaths that day.

Even more bodies turned up in 1997 in a burned house in St. Casimir, Quebec. Four people died in that incident, their bodies arranged in the shape of a cross. The members of this group, however, chose to spare their children. According to their reports, the teenage children discovered that their parents and cultist friend had placed propane tanks and electric hot plates on the main floor of the two-story house. They were trying to burn the place down. The teens complained and begged to be spared. The parents agreed, but insisted that the children, Fanie (aged 14), Tom (13) and Julien (16), take sleeping pills and sleep in a workshop near the house. One would presume they made the children do this so they couldn't call for help and stop the suicides. The three teens went to sleep, and when they awoke, their parents were dead.

Any organization that descends from the Knights Templar, unless in an utterly superficial claim, has deep roots in history, mysticism and secrecy. From the outside, the Order of the Solar Temple seems like little more than the narcissistic masturbation of its leaders. This, however, is only what those in power want you to believe. Look deeper, and you'll probably find ancient beings behind both the cult itself and the murders of its members.

The Jombola Cult

The Jombola Cult appeared in Sierra Leone several months after the signing of a peace accord between the federal government and the Revolutionary United Front in 1996. The cult has reportedly killed more than 30 people in order to advance their own political agenda in the southern districts of Bo, Pujehun and Bonthe.

Pa Santigie Murray Kawa, a resident of the Lugbu chiefdom in Bo, stated, "We are not exactly sure how many people have been killed by cult members who clearly have supernatural powers." The Jombola possess the ability to transform into certain types of animals, such as bats, dogs and felines. Many residents have also claimed that the sight of these transformed Jombola mesmerizes their victims.

The authorities managed to arrest one member of the Jombola Cult. That young man said, "Our objective is to overthrow the government and the local hunters' militia æ Kamajors æ and we are doing this not only by force of arms, but through the power of the dark." Apparently, the Jombola also use traditional feminine wiles to overcome their victims. The same cultist admitted that, "We use our womenfolk to overpower male victims, often sexually."

Aum Shinri Kyo (Aum Supreme Truth)

The leader of this Japanese cult, Shoko Asahara, demands that his followers treat him as a "living incarnation of god." Blind and extremely charismatic, the cultist has led his organization with great success, accruing a net worth estimated between $20 million and $1 billion. He makes no room for insubordination among the ranks of his organization, and he has often killed those who rebel.

Asahara preaches that killing brings good karma. Through a complex twisting of established Tibetan Buddhist philosophies, he claims that whenever a person kills someone, the murderer saves the victim from the horrors of everyday life and keeps him from accruing further negative karma. The murderer basically does the dead person a favor. How thoughtful. Because of his good deed, the killer earns some sort of spiritual redemption. The cult also believes that the world will soon end and everyone will cash in their karma pools. Asahara has some fucked-up ideas, but what's amazing is that he has managed to convince more than 50,000 followers to follow his radical philosophy.

In 1995, Asahara's followers set off bombs of Sarin gas in a handful of Tokyo subway stations. The gas killed 12 people and injured more than 5,500 others. The Japanese police suspect them of initiating a similar attack in Matsumoto, north of Tokyo. The harmful gases released that time killed seven and wounded 144. In addition, they're suspected of killing anti-cult activists who spoke out against them and of plotting to overthrow the Japanese government.

The Aum Supreme Truth cult resembles an army. They have an enormous cache of weapons and the means to mass-produce deadly nerve gas originally invented by the Nazis. At one point, they hired a Russian physicist to help them develop a nuclear bomb. Their success remains undetermined. It hinges on whether they actually managed to procure the weapons-grade uranium required for the bomb's production.

Asahara established himself as the indisputable leader of the cult. He sells his bath water for his followers' drinking pleasure. He claims the water has healing and strengthening properties. Though the price isn't cheap, the consumers line up to consume. He has sold other byproducts as well, including strands of hair and vials of his own blood (for approximately $8,000 each). His followers pay exorbitant fees for the privilege of communion during the initiation rituals when they drink some of Asahara's blood.

Asahara finally landed in jail after the gas attack on the Tokyo subway. He disappeared from his cell after only three nights of incarceration. The manhunt continued for weeks, but they never found the mysterious and enigmatic visionary.

Conclusion

Have you wondered why I took the time to show you some of the cults of the past century? It's important for your understanding of the whole picture. The world never could be as simple as the Camarilla and the Sabbat would like to have you think. Each of those cults I described, as well as those formed by Adolfo de Jesús Constanzo, Ervil LeBaron, Charles Manson, Yahweh Ben Yahweh, Woo Jong-min, and Jeffrey Lundgren (to name a very few), is a microcosm of Kindred society. Even though these cults were not publicly led by one of our kind, even if they didn't even have a Kindred lurking off-scene, they had a valuable lesson that the wise Kindred could take to heart. The society of the Damned is a cult of our own making. Whether we choose to be a part of it or not, the choice itself is an acknowledgment that such a thing exists.

If you examine the diversity of the different cults, their methods, their achievements and their goals, you find that not all cults manage to make a huge impact on the world. Don't let appearance fool you, however. Asahara, for example, built a vast network of followers that stretched from Japan to Russia and included pockets in various other strategic countries. What seems, at first glance, like nothing more than a group of wackos with lots of money and lots of guns begins to make a little sense when you ask yourself what they accomplished. Think about it. The cult had millions, if not billions, of dollars. It had access to an impressive arsenal. It had a nuclear physicist willing to make an atomic bomb for it. And what did they do with all that clout and firepower? They gas the subways and kill less than 200 people? Does that make sense to you? Or do you suppose you're seeing a diversion, a ploy or some other clever distraction from the true horror and danger — and utility — inherent in the cult? Who do you suppose covered up their real activities? Asahara has lived for several centuries or so the story goes. His blood held power that his followers never could have suspected. When Asahara disappeared from jail, he returned to his previous godlike rule over his cult and now he works from behind the scenes. Because they have failed so completely to find him, the Japanese police believe him dead. What do you think?

This is the lesson I want to share. You can never trust the media's interpretation of events. If you find a cult, you can rest assured that you don't have all the information about that cult's activities. Insanity happens, but not nearly as often as the media and the judicial system would like us to believe. The more organized and the more powerful a group becomes, the less likely it is that the leaders have lost their minds. Look closely. Look again at the cults I've described. Let go of your preconceptions and think of their leaders as sane and extremely clever liars who present one image to the world while they heft their real clout to enforce their will. Seek out the conspiracy. It exists.

The Birth of a God

There's something particularly sexy about how people sell themselves — mind, body and soul — to a single leader. The dedication required by cultists overshadows that demanded by wedding vows. You can divorce your spouse, and many people do. A cult, however, becomes so deeply engrained in your psyche, ego and life that you must tear out a part of yourself in order to escape it. Even then, you can never know for sure that your fellow cultists won't come after you and demand that you pay for your betrayal with your life.

From the shadows of night, where vampires lurk and scheme and plot and plan, the view of cults has a seductive appeal. In order to truly excel in the world, you need mortal resources. You need the worker bees to keep things running smoothly while the queen grows fat on royal jelly. Realistically, no Kindred can support that many ghouls. Fortunately, she doesn't have to rely on ghouls at all. She can select a few of the most important ones to receive her vitae. She then uses other methods to ensure the loyalty of the rest.

Genesis

Some cults arise spontaneously. An idea whose time has come attracts supporters. People recognize truth and wisdom appropriate to their experience. Sometimes, a philosopher or religious leader presents a concept that rings true to a whole generation. Sometimes, it touches only a small number of people hungry for meaning in their lives. Groups form. People talk and share. They network. Word spreads. A leader emerges and rises to the top. A cult is born.

By far, however, the grand majority of cults result from the careful plans of a clever leader. The leader begins with a goal. With that goal in mind, he forms the pathways along which his followers will travel. These pathways lead the cultists to support the leader's goal. The leader directs the cult's growth, from germination through blossom, from its first meetings in an abandoned train car to a sweeping convocation at a convention center. This requires a cunning and manipulative mind, a political mind, in order to transform a population of individuals into a tight-knit group of like-minded cogs in the cultic machine. Propaganda rearranges the members' beliefs, perceptions, desires and aspirations until they align with those of the leader.

Look around in these modern nights — wouldn't you agree that people are inherently lonely and unfulfilled? If that weren't the case, cults would never develop. Every member of every cult wants something. The cult offers that something to the member, whether it's a sense of belonging, a promise of salvation, secret information, financial opportunity, ego stroking, hot sex or any number of other perks. Hell, some freaks even seek out the Kindred because they just want to be fed upon. Once all parties agree on the product and the fee to acquire it, the cult becomes a living entity, self-propagating and regenerating. It can justify its actions with the greatest of ease. In many cases, it can rationalize even heinous acts of aberration, from statutory rape to adultery, from theft to contraband, from emotional abuse to coerced suicide, and from murder to mass homicide. The Camarilla stands as a perfect example of one such self-renewing cult that has perfected the ability to justify its every step and misstep via particular application of its laws.

Oh. Oh, there I go, speaking aloud what few dare to voice. Shame on me.

Your Very Own Cult

By now, you've undoubtedly come to understand that I use the term "cult" in its broadest sense. Not every cult has a Cainite puppeteer pulling its strings. Numerically speaking, few do, in fact. The possibilities, however, are endless. Have you ever thought about what you could do if you directed your talents toward something more productive? Have you ever considered becoming the architect of your own greatness? Many have. Many will. Do you prefer to follow, or will you lead?

I've given you the background on cults. You know what makes them cults. You know what cults have existed and failed. In other avenues of your unlife, you'll probably discover cults and secret societies that continue to prosper. If you're part of a sect, you're already in one. What more do you need? Well, if you want to truly delve into the darkest parts of the mind, you have to consider the possibility that you could join them in their deviance. Have you ever considered what end it might serve to start a cult? To relieve the weight of centuries or to build a private cabal? Doesn't the thought of coercing masses of mortals into worshipping at your feet, or doing your bidding as one amoebic entity, without questioning, titillate your mind and thrill you? It does mine, I admit. That, more than anything, makes me aware of the danger. Such power addicts. Would it be worth it?

In this section, I'll talk about cult leaders and give you some ideas on how to start your own organization. What kind of person can create a cult of personality? What resources does it require? What planning must you do before undertaking the development of a cult?

What? Do you think all this talk of the inner workings of cult development sucks the romance right out of it? Don't fool yourself. Very few of these organizations have a spontaneous origin borne from the zealous and inspired mind of a messiah. If that were going to happen, you wouldn't be reading this. You'd be out there selling your philosophy, following it and becoming slowly insane within its confines. I presume that, since you're here, you want to know how to make it happen from a cerebral standpoint. I can tell you how to do it.

The other half, of course, is that since I've come this far, it's not like I'm going to make it out of this unscathed. Fuck it. If they find me, they'll at least have something to kill me for.

Pick a Goal

Before you do anything else, you have to know why you want a cult. What purpose do you want it to serve? You have to understand that you make a commitment to the organization, just as your followers will be making a commitment to you. Unless you choose to remain completely anonymous, the great and powerful Oz hiding behind the screen, then you risk your followers turning on you if you falter and appear to betray them. Don't try this lightly, kids. It could just as easily blow up in your face as make your ass comfortable. Anonymity doesn't always protect you either. If you remain anonymous, you give up a good portion of direct influence over the organization. As Kindred, of course, you have ways of making them behave — and isn't it the ultimate rush? But, beware. You will make enemies, and those enemies may have supernatural advantages, too.

So find your cause. Do you want your cult to do nothing more than adore you, give you blood and kiss your ass? Do you want it to spite your enemies? Smite your enemies? Do you want it to make you boatloads of money? Do you want it to create great works of art for your pleasure, like the slaves who built the pyramids? Do you want to create something lasting yourself, a work of art made from the supple bodies of your followers? When you think about it, forming a cult really does resemble molding clay or applying layers of thick oil paint. You create your masterpiece with the lives and wills and souls of your followers. Delicious!

Every artist, however, starts with a vision. You can't set out with a blank canvas, apply paint randomly and expect to step back and discover that you've *accidentally* created the Masons. You have to have an idea of what you're trying to portray. That's not to say that the piece won't evolve over time and potentially become something completely different from your original intention. It very well may. However, you need to have a solid starting position from which to ground your cult.

Choose a Leader

You may decide to step into the pulpit yourself and lead your cult. Many have. You'd be surprised, perhaps, at how many of the thousands and thousands of cults in the world have Kindred at the head of their tables. You don't really believe that all of the Damned belong to either the Camarilla or the Sabbat, do you? Many go rogue. How bold of them, hm? Solo flyers who prefer to mingle among the mortals they've known and loved, and continue to know and love, and eat. Why become just another small fish in a big pond among other vampires when you can be Neptune among weak humans? Good question.

Mortals. Many Kindred choose a mortal leader to represent them in the cult. This person takes the bullet. She can go out during the day, and she diverts the speculation of nosy bastards who would seek out cultists (or Kindred…) and muck in their business. She must have the personal magnetism to pull it off. She must be charming, eloquent and authoritarian, and she must give you her complete loyalty. That's easy to manage, of course. When the time comes, if it's what you desire, she can drink the cyanide-laced lemonade along with the bulk of your members and become your martyr. Then you find another leader to replace her. You rebuild the cult after she's gone, and her memory strengthens the bonds with which you hold your cultists.

Childer. Does your leader have special needs? Does he have to produce miracles? You can accomplish this by Embracing your leader or placing an existing childe at the helm. In an isolated environment, away from all other Kindred, you can teach your childe any damn thing you please, and he will believe it. You can Embrace the childe and instill in him the belief that he is Jesus reincarnated. He won't know any better. You have the perfect puppet if you then subject him to the blood bond. You become the voice of God for him. How beautiful is that?

Your success then pivots upon this childe, however. You must prepare yourself to destroy him in the event that he becomes a liability. You must take great care to protect him and shield him from the influence of other Kindred. Even this, though, shouldn't be too difficult. If you play your cards right, a childe will never have any reason to know other Kindred exist, much less their sprawling society.

Allies. Would you prefer to have an undead partner in this cultic endeavor? You could. Perhaps your idea birthed one night as you and an acquaintance were mourning the scarcity of vitae in the ever-more-paranoid modern nights. You weren't serious, at first, but the idea began to grow on you. "What if…?" you mused.

Herds, Coteries and Cults

Are you wondering what the difference is between a coterie and a cult? Do you see your cult as nothing more than a glorified herd? If that's all you see, you're in the wrong business. A coterie brings together like-minded and sometimes not-so-like-minded Kindred for the purpose of meeting a particular end. The coterie may stay together for safety, because everyone knows there's safety in numbers. It may work as a team to oppose a threat. Its members may just like each other. A cult, on the other hand, rarely has more than one Cainite, or maybe two, involved. The bulk of the membership usually has no idea that Kindred exist and would never consider calling their leader a vampire. They might use words like "mystic" or "psychic" or "miracle-worker" or even "messiah," but never would it even occur to them to call their patron a blood-sucking freak of the night.

By the same token, a cult can become a herd, and a herd can become a cult. However, if you want nothing more than blood from your cult, then you're underestimating its value and cheating yourself of a broad opportunity. The pretty young things in your herd bend their necks to you and sigh as you sink your fangs into their succulent flesh. The pretty young things in your cult may do that as well, but they will also do whatever else you've asked them to do for you, so long as you've done your job as a cult leader. They will kill for you. They will rob banks for you, if only you give them a good reason to do so. It takes a touch of good looks to form and keep a herd. It takes savvy to run a cult.

Your counterpart loved the idea. To your surprise, the discussions continued over the next few weeks, months or even years, until one night, you finally decided to take that first step. The time had come to decide on a leader. Your fellow wanted to take the more public role. He has the smile and the twinkle in the eyes required to draw followers. You prefer to work out of sight. You discuss the idea that you'll both be leaders, equals. But, what do you do if, one night, you disagree?

In any cultic organization, room exists for only one big dog. Alpha male or female, one person has to have the final say. Otherwise, petty disagreements will splinter the group. Establish your pecking order up front. If you have to, eliminate the other half the minute problems raise their ugly heads. Dispatch all competition. It doesn't matter whether you're behind the scenes and he's center stage. You make the decisions. He's dispensable. Don't ever forget that, or your masterpiece will crumble around your ears. If he was smart, he would have rid himself of you by now, too.

Establish Your Dogma

You have to build the architecture of your particular philosophy. This key element will draw new members to you and keep them at your side long after they've come to disdain you or your chosen leader. You may choose to present your dogma as a religious doctrine, as bylaws, as a corporate mission statement, as therapeutic psychology, as political philosophy, as occult knowledge or as any other such set of rules that dictates what your followers believe and what they do. Keep in mind that your dogma, your rules, your religion, your philosophy, whatever, must establish the boundaries within which your followers may act. Also, keep in mind that your public dogma may differ greatly from your secret agenda. As a matter of fact, you'll have so much more fun with your cult if that's the case.

Belief. What do you want your cultists to believe? Do you want them to believe in the divinity of their leader? Do you want them to believe in the inevitable end of the world and all life? Gehenna cometh; take what you can while you can? Or, do you want them to maintain hope that a silvery spaceship will swoop down and save them from their fates? Do you want them to continue to strive for a way to stop the apocalypse against whatever horrible odds they face? Do you want them to believe that no one in the entire world could ever understand and accept their differences? Do you want them to believe they're ignorant, powerless and unworthy compared to you, so they never rise up and oppose you? You have so many choices.

The beliefs that you instill in your followers serve the purpose of keeping them subordinate, keeping them forever hopeful that the organization can save them from the worst of life's unhappiness, and keeping them loyal. You can wrap them around your little finger without much effort if you put true genius in the fundamental principals upon which you build your organization. If you set it all up right, you won't have to work too hard to maintain things either. The more structurally sound your "religion," the more likely the organization will become self-sustaining. Theoretically, it could continue on even after your own Final Death, ad infinitum. God forbid, of course.

Trouble in Paradise

"But," you ask, "what about the Masquerade?" What about it? Whose dogma is that anyway? Whose rule, philosophy, corporate mission statement or whatever is that? Don't panic. Put away your Pavlovian responses. I understand the reasoning behind the Masquerade, though it takes on an edge of paranoia when you begin looking around at all the Kindred out there who walk the line without causing so much as an eye-blink from these supposedly dangerous mortals. Once you begin educating yourself on the world outside the Camarilla, you begin to realize just how puckered that Camarilla ass really is. Then, you begin to wonder why it's like that. You don't really believe they're trying to avoid a second Inquisition, do you? You think they're protecting you? Or does it make more sense that everything they do has a self-serving motive behind it? I wonder what that motive could be? Do you do their bidding? Do you adore your leaders? Do you play their games? I thought so.

In all the time that I've studied cult phenomenon, I have never found an instance in which a Cainite broke the Masquerade in such a way as to endanger all other Kindred. I've seen newspaper articles that spoke of mind control, ESP, feats of strength, disappearing tricks and even references to lycanthropy. I've read about blood cults and human sacrifice. None of this makes the mortal world blink anymore. They've all become so numb to it that they either brush it off in disbelief or they accept it as fact and look the other way. The Camarilla can't find and cover all these leaky bits. They have help. Mortals themselves have put up a shield of disbelief or ambivalence against the weirdness that is the Curse of Caine. In these modern nights, this shield gives us much more leeway to play.

The Media

On March 26, 1997, 39 members of the Heaven's Gate web design cult decided to commit mass suicide. This event, so bizarre, attracted the immediate attention of the media. Camera crews swarmed onto the lawn of the house in San Diego County, California. They hit the Web to find the cult's site and shared the link with the public. They ate up the video suicide notes and had a field day with images of the bodies being removed from the ranch house.

The Heaven's Gate mass suicide changed how the media approached cults. During the coverage of that event, they found "experts" on the subject of cults and interviewed them. Each new expert had a more sensationalist story to tell, frightening viewers with talk of brainwashing and abuse. The darker the information the expert shared, the better the station's ratings. Oddly, experts had to manifest suddenly. They didn't exist prior to 1997.

Since Heaven's Gate, the media has kept a sharp eye out for cultic activities. It swarmed the area surrounding the Branch Davidian complex, hoping for any chance to capture the action on camera. Television news shows have investigated various organizations, made them out to seem like cults and completely exaggerated the seriousness of a group's activities. They delve into occult groups, into covens of Satan-worshippers and compare them with the team-building activities of vitamin salespeople. The public laps this stuff up like it's melting ice cream. They love it, and each new story, each new sensationalized account, each new stretched truth brings them one step closer to numbness or disbelief.

Room for One More

Afraid you'll end up alone and lonely? Afraid no one will buy into your scheme? Afraid you'll have no followers? Don't be. It doesn't matter who you are or what you're preaching, you'll find someone willing to jump on your bandwagon. People are stupid. They want to belong. They want someone else to think for them. You send out the message that the grass is really red, but that pollution has turned it green, and it's a sign of the end of the world æ you'll find someone to shout, "Amen! Down with green grass!" You give people permission to be naughty, to fuck at will, to fight, to kill, to eat flesh… and they'll love you for it. Try it.

Three little boys die brutally in the woods, tied up and slashed to death. A jury hears the evidence and convicts three men of the terrible murders. Despite this, and despite the police's belief that the men committed the crime, one such TV show did a slanted exposé on the crime and managed to convince many intelligent people that the jury had convicted three innocent men. Whom do you believe? Even the Waco situation has its apologists. How can you pardon a man who fucked

children because he thought God told him to do it? Oh, don't think me hypocritical — you *want* people this stupid, this desperate to believe. They're the key to your cult's success. You think *smart* people are going to believe you when you tell them you're the reincarnation of a Mesoamerican blood priest?

Anti- and Counter-cult Movements

Certain organizations have taken it upon themselves, in a very cult-like manner, to oppose cults in general and in specific. They feel deeply bound to warn everyone. They work primarily through volunteers who have subscribed to their philosophies and who see the value in the organizations' goals and principals. They work diligently and with devotion to the cause.

These organizations dedicate themselves to educating others on the practices of the cult or cults. Some spend enormous sums of donated money printing flyers that debunk a cult's teachings. They publish journals and magazines. They conduct interventions. They create in-depth websites whose functions involve building themselves up while tearing down the credibility of the cult(s). The members of these organizations, and any others who have at least a passing morbid curiosity, gather at conferences to discuss the current state and future ramifications of cultism. They pontificate and share their clinical findings. They tell inspirational stories of how a certain group "saved" them from their cults.

These groups come in two basic formulas. Anti-cult organizations make no attempt to replace the lost cultic beliefs with their own, once they've wrenched you from the jaws of certain death or eternal gardening. They just want to get you out from under the cult's influence. Counter-cult organizations, on the other hand, have a lovely feast of dogma laid out for you. They force-feed you their own philosophy to refill the belly they pumped free of whatever ideological food had been sustaining you in your cult. It's all for your own good, of course, rather like the law that requires you wear your seatbelt. Needless to say, you must choose your remedy more carefully than you chose your poison.

The Final Word

You're beginning to understand, aren't you? Yes. You see the foolishness of pride. Join me in my crusade.

The "Old" Cult Awareness Network

One particular counter-cult organization once took strong action against cults. They worked hard to educate the public on cults. Unfortunately, they also seemed to use terrorist methods to "rescue" people. A young man, Jason Scott, sued the organization. He claimed that Rick Ross kidnapped him from his home and held him captive for five days for deprogramming. They tried to get him to renounce his church's beliefs. Jason's mother had paid Rick Ross, a professional deprogrammer referred to her by the network, to do this to all three of her sons. Jason sued. He settled with Ross for a reported $5,000. Eventually, the old Cult Awareness Network was ordered by the courts to pay Jason $875,000 in actual damages and $1 million in punitive damages.

The Church of Scientology continued to pursue Ross and the old Cult Awareness Network. The network filed for bankruptcy in 1996. The CAN assets went on sale to the highest bidder, in order to pay off their debts. Ironically, a member of the Church of Scientology purchased the Cult Awareness Network name, logo, PO box, hotline telephone number and other assets. The money to purchase these assets came from private donations, not from the church itself. The owner set up a new corporation in 1997 called the Foundation for Religious Freedom and changed the message delivered by the old organization.

Now, before it's too late. Although your heart may no longer beat, it can feel. You are special. Only those among us who can see the Destroyer for what it is can keep it at bay. We must stop those who would drag us down with them into Gehenna. We can reverse the putrefaction of our society. We can cut off the diseased and gangrenous limbs. We can return the balance. I will lead you, all of you, through the end of the world to a new night. You have come to me because you see what others cannot. Join me. Follow me to peace.

Chapter Four: Sins of Power

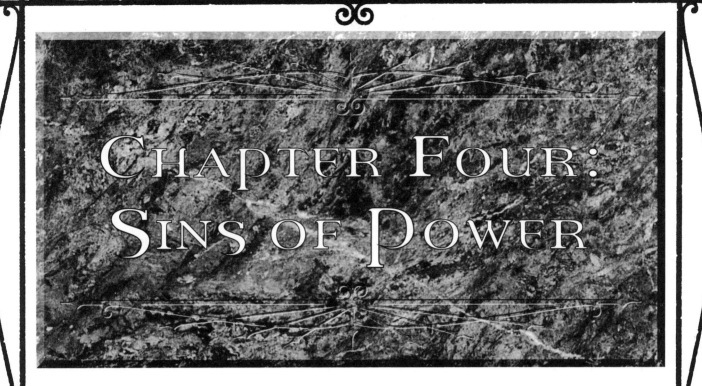

It is a man's own mind, not his enemy or foe, that lures him to evil ways.
—Buddha

What price, power? The ability to do what one wants has always been a hallmark of the Jyhad, with Cainites cutting deals, forging alliances, breaking alliances, stabbing each other in the back, committing diablerie… the list goes on an on. It might be said that personal power is the goal of the Jyhad. Insofar as we know the Antediluvians, their plots seem to pit them and the Kindred who work for them (wittingly or otherwise) against each other in a bid for ultimate success when Gehenna comes.

The only problem for many Kindred with regard to acquiring power is the time and effort it takes to cultivate it. It's easy to *decide* to learn an impressive array of Disciplines, but it's another altogether to find a willing teach and master the applications of the powers themselves. It can take what feels like forever to reap the benefits of influence, as well, requiring contact with those who provide the influence and perhaps favors to convince them to let one use that power.

It is no wonder, then, that some Kindred take the quick-and-dirty route to gathering power. It is to them that we devote this chapter.

As always, though, we'll deliver the standard words of warning concerning infernalism: Use it sparingly. Characters in league with the Devil lack any moral gray area — they've aligned themselves with evil. Such characters sometimes make for interesting Faustian dilemmas, but more often, they're better suited to be antagonists. Storytellers need not let players' characters have access to these powers.

New Dark Thaumaturgy Paths

As with other Thaumaturgy paths, when the character wishes to invoke a power, the thaumaturge's player must roll Willpower with a difficulty equal to the power's level +3 and spend a blood point. If the roll succeeds, the power takes effect according to its description. Failing the Willpower roll indicates that the power has no effect. A botch costs the thaumaturge a permanent Willpower point.

More information on Dark Thaumaturgy (as well as lengthy warnings against its misuse) may be found in the **Guide to the Sabbat**.

Storyteller's Options: The Devil's Price

These Dark Thaumaturgy paths present a unique option that Storytellers may choose to use should such demonic "miracles" make their way into his game. Each of these paths includes a price, exacted by the demon who teaches the thaumaturge this forbidden knowledge. Instead of leaving it open to interpretation of the Storyteller, we've chosen to make the demon's payment forthright, as it relates specifically to the path. Storytellers, feel free to adapt prices for other paths or to excise them altogether. As always, you have the final word, particularly with setting elements that should scare the characters *and* the players.

The Path of Pain

Physical discomfort fuels this path: In the right hands, the Path of Pain can flay flesh from the body, shatter bones and rupture internal organs with a single look or word. Infernalists who practice this path derive as much pleasure from inflicting pain as their victims suffer. However, pain is also an opiate — an addiction that requires the thaumaturge to subject himself to intense torture and agony. Only by reaching the depths and depredations of sadomasochism can a thaumaturge unlock the true potential of this wicked art. Ritual scarring and maiming is common among practitioners of the Path of Pain, who often walk a fine line between self-mutilation and self-destruction.

Price: Addicted to Pain

Upon learning the third level in this path, the infernalist is addicted to pain, needing it almost as much as vitae. Whenever the thaumaturge takes a single health level of damage, he will do nothing to stop the source of the injury unless the player spends a Willpower point. However, if the character suffers a single health level from a weapon, attack or effect that causes a variable amount of damage, she will not necessarily have to withstand it again. Note that this effect applies only to a single health level. A character will not stand idly by while being mauled by a Gangrel whose player just happened to roll poorly, for example, nor will she perforce tempt a gunman to shoot her again in hopes of suffering only one health level of damage.

The pain addiction is insidious, however. It applies to Path of Pain powers that require the thaumaturge to inflict health levels of damage on himself, but only when the player fails his initial Willpower roll. If such is the case, the thaumaturge will continue inflicting the same number of health levels he sacrificed every turn until the player spends a Willpower point.

The character will indulge his addiction a maximum of three times consecutively in each situation. Note that a character will not do so if it would render him Incapacitated.

Example: Vaughan tries to evoke Shattering. Before his player rolls Willpower and spends a blood point, Vaughan breaks a finger (one health level of damage) to initiate the casting. When it comes time to roll, however, the player fails the Willpower roll. Every turn afterward, Vaughan, lost in the throes of pain, will continue to inflict a health level of damage to himself unless his player spends a Willpower point. He keeps it up until he does it thrice more or would risk becoming Incapacitated.

• The Numbing

Broken bones, torture and ritualistic scarring are all a source of delight for many on the Path of Pain. Thaumaturges studying this path must first learn how to control and resist their instincts to avoid pain. Once mastered, the Numbing allows the infernalist to explore the limits of pain without becoming weakened or incapacitated by it. However, overriding the Beast's instincts to avoid pain has caused many dark thaumaturges to destroy themselves — literally reducing their bodies to ashes.

System: For each success scored on the Willpower roll, the thaumaturge can ignore the dice pool and movement penalty for one health level of damage. This effect lasts for a scene. The Numbing does not work with wound penalties incurred from aggravated damage.

•• Anguish

A thaumaturge on the Path of Pain can flood his target with sensations of pain without having to actually wound her. Although the injuries are not real, the pain is. With a simple touch, the thaumaturge can send his victim reeling in agony to the point of rendering her unconscious or even comatose due to shock.

Sins of the Blood

System: The practitioner needs to touch his target in order to use this power (possibly requiring a Brawl roll, at the Storyteller's discretion). If the character does so, the player can roll Willpower and spend a blood point as normal. For every success, the target suffers the dice pool penalty associated with losing the equivalent number of health levels (starting with Hurt, not Bruised), but he doesn't suffer actual damage. When used against mortals, nothing can be done to stop the pain. If the target reaches Incapacitated, she falls unconscious. Vampires and supernatural creatures can try to resist by rolling Willpower. Each success on this roll cancels one of the thaumaturge's successes. A vampire may be Incapacitated by this pain, but it will not force him into torpor. Furthermore, a point of blood heals one level of Anguish "damage." The effects of Anguish last for a scene otherwise.

••• Shattering

At this level, the thaumaturge can break bones and rupture organs, crippling his victim. The resulting cacophony of compound fractures and bursting organs are, more often than not, the last sounds the victim ever hears.

System: The thaumaturge can use this power on any one target within eyesight. To invoke Shattering, he must sacrifice a health level in order to channel the pain to the target. Once he does so, a point of blood and a successful Willpower roll complete the process. For each success, the thaumaturge inflicts a health level of lethal damage that cannot be soaked. Vampires can roll Willpower to resist the effects of the Shattering; each success on the victim's Willpower roll negates one success of the thaumaturge. Additionally, creatures with the ability to do so (Kindred, ghouls, etc.) may spend blood points to heal the damage as normal.

•••• Agony Within

This terrifying power allows the thaumaturge to create hooked tendrils out of his target's own blood that course through his veins and rip him to shreds. In some extreme cases of this power's use, the blood-barbs actually burst the victim's flesh, ending his life in a gory display.

System: In addition to the blood point expenditure and Willpower roll, this power may require the thaumaturge to wound himself to create the blood chains. For each health level of bashing damage that the thaumaturge inflicts on himself (minimum one), the player can add one to the total number of successes from the Willpower roll. This total is then applied as lethal damage to the victim, as the blood tendrils bite into and rend the hapless victim asunder from within. Mortals cannot soak Agony Within damage, and vampires may use only Fortitude. However, the target is allowed a Willpower roll with a difficulty equal to (6 + the number of health levels that the thaumaturge inflicted upon himself [maximum 10]). For every two successes on the Willpower roll (round down), reduce the damage of Agony Within by one.

••••• Hundred Deaths

The ultimate expression of pain known to practitioners of the Path of Pain, Hundred Deaths lacerates the victim with countless deep cuts that constantly heal and reopen. The pain drives the victim insane before killing him outright.

System: Hundred Deaths requires the thaumaturge to inflict upon himself a single aggravated wound, achieved by the player succeeding a Willpower roll (difficulty 6) first. If successful, the player can then roll Willpower and spend a blood point to evoke Hundred Deaths. Each success inflicts one health level of aggravated damage on the target, which can be soaked only with Fortitude. The pain debilitates the target completely, rendering her shocked by pain and unable to do anything, including heal herself, without the expenditure of a Willpower point. If the victim does not receive medical attention or some form of supernatural healing, she will suffer an additional health level of lethal damage every night for each unhealed level of aggravated damage that remains.

The Path of Pleasure

Perversion comes easily to vampires, being creatures of strong emotional echoes and stronger desires, but practitioners of the Path of Pleasure take decadence to unnatural depths. They are masters at infecting others with their own indulgence and manipulating their desires, fanning them into self-destructive infernos of depravity.

Forbidden pleasure, often fueled by obsession, guilt and self-loathing, is a gateway to corruption, a downward spiral that damns those who walk it. Making matters worse is the fact that everyone, from Setite temptresses to the local preacher, keeps forbidden desires hidden and locked deep within themselves. To the thaumaturge, these desires become a tool with which to bend the will of others to their own needs — whether for the sake of pleasure, power or something less definable.

It is whispered that Toreador and Malkavian infernalists crafted the Path of Pain during the orgies of Rome, and that to this date, they gather in secret locations to indulge their wanton desires.

Price: Desires Sated

Infernalist practitioners of the Path of Pleasure sacrifice more than their souls to learn this path. They open themselves to the basest desires of their Beasts, crafting their power from its unnatural hunger. To represent this effect, all frenzy rolls suffer a +1 difficulty modifier once the thaumaturge attains the third level in the path. This penalty is cumulative with other frenzy penalties. Brujah beware.

> **Side Effects**
>
> The Path of Pleasure has a drug-like effect on its victims. They may become addicted to its effects and seek out any opportunity to indulge in it again. Each time a thaumaturge invokes any Path of Pleasure power successfully, the target's player must roll Self-Control (difficulty 6) after the effects of the power have passed. If the player fails the roll, the character develops the Obsessive/Compulsive derangement (see **Vampire: The Masquerade** p. 222) for a number of weeks equal to the level rating of the power used. During this time, the victim will do nearly anything to experience the sensation again — which might not necessarily involve the use of the Discipline.

• Ecstasy

The thaumaturge can make the target feel intense pleasure, tailoring the sensation from general sexual arousal to mimicking the euphoria of the strongest drug around. This power works regardless of the subject's tastes, simulating any kink or fetish, or stimulating simpler, less complicated pleasures — whether the victim consents or not.

System: Ecstasy requires the Willpower roll only if the thaumaturge uses this power on an unwilling target. Otherwise, physical contact and a blood point are all that are needed. Once she is under the effects of Ecstasy, the victim is flooded with physical sensations so intense that she must score more success on a Wits + Self-Control roll (difficulty 7) than the thaumaturge's player's Willpower roll to do anything *except* enjoy herself. This power lasts as long as the thaumaturge continues to touch the target. Once physical contact stops, the effect wears down over the course of a number of turns equal to (10 – the subject's Willpower). During this time, the victim exists in a mollified, sluggish state and suffers a +1 difficulty to all actions.

Whatever sensation the thaumaturge used becomes the focus of the Obsessive/Compulsive derangement if the victim's player fails her Self-Control roll.

•• Intrusion

Intrusion functions much like Ecstasy, however, the thaumaturge doesn't need to touch the target. He can communicate the pleasure through telepathic means.

System: Intrusion can be used on any individual within eyesight of the thaumaturge. If successful, the infernalist overwhelms the individual with a pleasurable physical sensation of his (the infernalist's) choice. Because of the unexpected nature of the pleasure, the victim suffers one bashing health level of damage for each success scored on the Willpower roll. Note that this bashing damage isn't "painful" as such. It reflects the subject being immediately overwhelmed by pleasure. Mortals cannot soak this damage, but vampires can resist with a Willpower roll (difficulty 7) of their own. Each success negates one level of the bashing damage.

In all other respects, this power works like Ecstasy, including Willpower and blood costs, as well as requiring a Wits + Self-Control roll (difficulty 7) to ignore the pleasure long enough to take an action.

••• Daisy Chain

This orgasmic power allows the thaumaturge to spread pleasure to other people in a chain. Each person that the infernalist touches becomes a vector for the chosen pleasure, "infecting" anyone with whom he comes in contact.

System: The Daisy Chain works exactly like Ecstasy, however a Willpower roll is needed even if the target consents to its use. For each success, the thaumaturge can spread the sensation to another target (at the rate of one per turn), who then experiences the same sensation. Furthermore, each target can affect another individual through touch (the new victim is allowed a Self-Control roll to resist). Daisy Chain functions only if the thaumaturge remains within eyesight of the victims, or until a subject resists successfully, which also ends that particular vector's "contagion."

•••• Deadening

This insidious power allows the thaumaturge to make an individual numb to physical sensations and even most emotions. While under the effect of Deadening, the victim can feel nothing including pain or pleasure. For all intents and purposes, he is dead to any and all sensations. He exists as if in a daze, aware of being unable to feel anything and incapable of doing anything about it.

System: This power requires the standard blood point and Willpower roll. The target is allowed to resist by rolling Willpower (difficulty equal to the thaumaturge's Manipulation + Empathy). If the thaumaturge scores more successes, Deadening is successful. While he is in this emotionally torpid state, the victim cannot spend Willpower points, and any Virtue roll is at a +2 difficulty. The number of successes scored determines the duration of Deadening.

1 success	One turn
2 successes	One hour
3 successes	One day
4 successes	One week
5 successes	One month

This power is exempt from the price: desires sated

••••• The Garden of Earthly Delights

With this power, the thaumaturge can totally overwhelm a victim with pleasure until it renders her catatonic, existing only in her mind and unaware of her immediate surroundings or even her physical body.

System: To use this power, the victim must already be under the effects of Ecstasy. Once this criteria is met, the player makes another Willpower roll and spends an additional blood point. If this second roll is successful, the infernalist can flood the victim with pleasure until she becomes comatose, her mind entering a dream-like state where all she experiences are visions and sensations of pleasure. To resist this power, the victim needs to score more successes on a Willpower roll (difficulty 8) than the thaumaturge scored upon invocation. Remember, though, that the target first makes a Self-Control roll as per the Ecstasy rules before this power even becomes a possibility.

For each night a victim is under the effect of this power, her body takes a level of bashing damage unless the victim is being treated at a hospital. Vampires can resist this damage with Stamina (and Fortitude). Successes determine the duration of this power.

1 success	One night
2 successes	Three nights
3 successes	One week
4 successes	One month
5 successes	One year

Path of the Defiler

Few Dark Thaumaturgy paths, except perhaps the Path of the Unspoken, are so reviled as the Path of the Defiler. Under the auspice of this path, a thaumaturge can warp and taint others as easily as a gardener can make plants blossom or wither—even other infernalists loathe the corrupting influence of the defilers. The thaumaturge's hatred and jealousy of the normalcy of others fuels this insidious and perverse school of Thaumaturgy. Many infernalists come across the path through a desire to see people debase themselves—not by perverting them through pleasure or suffering — but by tainting their own perceptions of themselves and all that they hold dear.

Many Inquisitors consider this path to be a variation of the more traditional Path of Corruption, and they charge the now defunct Tremere *antitribu* with its creation. The fact that it continues to exist, and attract new practitioners even after the disappearance of the Sabbat Warlocks, suggests that more malignant forces are at work.

Price: Jealousy

Defilers are extremely territorial, especially when it comes to their victims. Once the thaumaturge uses Path of the Defiler on an individual, he becomes possessive, even protective of his victims. Like an overprotective parent or lover, the infernalist guards his victim jealously. If another vampire, or even mortal attempts to harm, seduce, use any Discipline or even help the victim while in the presence of the thaumaturge, she must succeed on a Self-Control roll (difficulty 7) to prevent herself from flying into a possessive frenzy. This territoriality lasts for as long as the victim is under the effect of a power from the path or the thaumaturge uses the Path of the Defiler on another target. A Willpower point can be spent to override the urge for a scene.

• Call the Weakness

Defilers are adept social predators, able to surmise an individual's passions and weakness by engaging in idle conversation. From a simple answer or a casual gesture, the defiler can piece together a complete mental picture of the individual. The thaumaturge can use this information to bring the victim under her sway.

System: Aside from the blood point and Willpower roll needed to evoke Call the Weakness, the defiler must engage the victim in conversation. For each success, the thaumaturge can ask the Storyteller a single question about the target, which then must be answered truthfully. Information that can be gleaned this way includes, but is not limited to, Nature and Demeanor, Willpower ratings, derangements, blood bonds and Virtues that the character observes — in effect, any single aspect of the character's emotional or moral self.

Furthermore, each success adds one to the thaumaturge's dice pool when making any Social roll against the target. This aspect of Call the Weakness lasts for an entire scene.

•• Tainted

With this power, the defiler can plant the seed of doubt and self-loathing in an individual, slowly infecting the victim with shame and guilt. With a well-timed comment or action, the thaumaturge can break the victim's spirits, rendering him hollow and empty. An artist will be ashamed of his work, a priest's faith will falter, and a prince might lose all confidence. Once under the spell of Tainted, the victim becomes an easy tool for the defiler to bend to his own ends.

System: Tainted requires the thaumaturge to first use Call the Weakness to discern the victim's most cherished quality of herself. This can be something tangible like a prized possession, or an intangible quality, like a Trait, Ability or even a less quantifiable characteristic. The player then rolls as normal, and the target can resist with a Willpower roll (difficulty equal to the thaumaturge's Manipulation + Subterfuge). If the thaumaturge is successful, the victim must spend a point of Willpower to use or acknowledge the Trait or quality in question. For example, an artist will cease to paint, possibly pushing him into depression, unless he spends a Willpower point very time he picks up a brush. Likewise, a priest's sudden lack of faith might lead him toward sin as his moral resolve is stretched to the limit.

The duration of Tainted varies, based on the number of successes the thaumaturge scored.

1 success	One scene
2 successes	One night
3 successes	One week
4 successes	One month
5 successes	One year

••• Degradation

With this power, the defiler not only taints an individual's source of pride, but he can cause drastic personality changes as well. Once under the effect of Degradation, the victim becomes a whole new person, unrecognizable to his friends and family, and governed by strange obsessions and desires.

System: Degradation allows the defiler to change a target's Nature. Doing so has the immediate effect of altering the victim's personality and how he regains Willpower. Most infernalists choose a new Nature that is contradictory to the target's old one, forcing the target to debase himself in order to regain Willpower.

Alternatively, with Degradation, the thaumaturge can infect the victim with a derangement of the defiler's choice.

The number of success rolled determines the duration of the Degradation.

1 success	One scene
2 successes	One night
3 successes	One week
4 successes	One month
5 successes	One year

•••• Poisoned Soul

Far more potent than Degradation, Poisoned Soul removes any moral or ethical inhibitions from an individual. Without the need to conform to social mores, victims of Poisoned Soul succumb to their most base and perverse desires, indulging in rape, murder, torture and other heinous crimes to provoke any emotional response at all from herself, much as a Kindred with low Humanity does. Poisoned Soul, like other Path of the Defiler powers, is subtle and insidious, even though the results seldom are.

System: The player spends a blood point and rolls Willpower as normal. The victim may resist with a Conscience roll (difficulty equal to the thaumaturge's Manipulation + Empathy). If successful, the victim resists. If the victim fails, every success that the infernalist scored reduces the victim's Humanity rating by one. The effect occurs at the rate of one Humanity point lost per night.

Furthermore, each night that the victim's Humanity rating is affected, he is compelled to perform one sin according to his new Humanity rating unless he spends a Willpower point. In addition, the target incurs any penalties associated with his new, lower, Humanity score. If reduced to zero, the victim becomes a mindless beast for as long as Poisoned Soul remains in effect.

Downward Spiral's duration is based on the number of successes scored on the thaumaturge's Willpower roll.

Successes	Duration
1 success	One night
2 successes	Three nights
3 successes	One week
4 successes	One month
5 successes	One year

This power also affects Kindred who follow Paths of Enlightenment.

••••• Chancrous Blossom

The thaumaturge can transform the target's perversion, self-loathing and guilt into a physical cancer that either turns her into a hideous mass of boils and sores or kills her outright. The effect is disturbing to witness as the victim's skin literally erupts with lacerations and ulcers that ooze a black, malignant ichor.

System: The thaumaturge must catch the target engaging in some depraved act (as determined by his Humanity/Path score). The player then spends a blood point and rolls Willpower as normal. For each success, the victim suffers a health level of aggravated damage. Additionally, the victim cannot heal these wounds for a number of nights equal to the thaumaturge's successes.

Path of the Unspoken

Many thaumaturges believe that the Path of the Unspoken is a legend, superstitious babble spawned from the absinthe-addled dreams of florid mortal poets. Even the Tremere denounce it, having found no substantial proof of its existence — at least, so the Warlocks claim. Mere mention of this path often causes knowledgeable sorcerers to prick up their ears in many domains. Those who know the truth, however, know that the Path of the Unspoken is no legend.

With the vanishing of the Tremere *antitribu*, many considered the path a dying one, practiced by only a few thaumaturges deranged enough to walk down the road of heresy. However, a disturbing number of rumors involving the path have surfaced in the last few years. Luckily (or unluckily), many of these infernalists have since been destroyed, not by fellow vampires, but by mortal witch-hunters.

Price: Memory Lapse

Infernalists drawn to the Path of the Unspoken hunger for knowledge — even to the point of sacrificing their own mental integrity. The path has such a pervasive and insidious influence over the infernalist that it begins to affect his psyche, clouding memories and slowly making the thaumaturge forget what he already knows in his desperate rush to learn more.

For every level of mastery in the Path of the Unspoken, the infernalist loses more of his memories. Eventually, he forgets even who he was originally. This memory loss is so total that even written accounts of the thaumaturge, such as diaries and journals, fail to trigger any recollections.

To reflect this effect, any time the character needs to use a Knowledge, his difficulty increases by one for every level of the Path of the Unspoken he possesses, to a maximum of 10. He simply can't remember the finer points of his vast memory. If the character's Path of the Unspoken score ever exceeds his Willpower, he has difficulty remembering even things about himself, such as his clan, the location of his haven or even his name.

• Whispers of the Unborn

The infernalist opens himself to the raw power of entropy, and for a few seconds, he can hear what can only be described as the voices of the unborn. Immediately, a chorus of childlike voices and screams flood the thaumaturge, who can then discern warnings or glean information from the resulting cacophony.

System: The player rolls Willpower and spends a blood point. For each success, the player can decide to gain an answer to a single question, or receive a premonition of danger, or a combination of the two.

If used to gain information, the "voices" can articulate only rough answers of no more than three to five words (Storytellers are encouraged to be as vague as they wish), yet they do seem to be omniscient. Storytellers should also be cryptic, as the unborn have no real reason to care about the outcome of the living world's problems.

If used for premonitions, Whispers of the Unborn lasts for a scene. During this time, the player can subtract one from the difficulty of one roll for each success achieved.

•• Scribing the Unknown

Entering a trance-like state, the thaumaturge can subconsciously scribe the contents of a written document — regardless of the language and without needing to see the original. As long as something is written down, whether on vellum or as magnetic data on a hard drive, there is no way of keeping it a secret from the infernalist.

System: For the thaumaturge to enter the trance, he first needs to know the source of the information he wants to transcribe (the name of the book, author of a letter or file name is often enough) and the player must spend the blood point and roll Willpower. The copy is rarely exact, and unless the infernalist has some skill in forgery, the transcribed material will look nothing like the original. Even that isn't enough in some cases, such as a handwritten version of a computer document.

The number of success determines the accuracy of the transcript.

1 success	Largely incomplete. Many sentences are missing, and some words are replaced with others of different meaning; 20 percent accurate to the original document.
2 successes	Vaguely complete; 40 percent accurate.
3 successes	Partially complete; 60 percent accurate.
4 successes	Mostly complete; 80 percent accurate.
5 successes	Functional; 95 percent complete.

••• Shadow Thoughts

This mysterious power allows the thaumaturge to peer into anyone's shadow and glean information about him. As the saying goes, nobody knows one better than her own shadow.

System: Evoking this power requires the usual blood point and Willpower roll. In addition, the thaumaturge needs to be standing in the shadow of his intended victim. Any successes achieved on the Willpower roll allow the thaumaturge to look into the target's past, enabling him to witness any actions or thoughts as if the infernalist was present. She will be unable to affect the outcome of the events, though.

The number of success determines how far back in time the thaumaturge can gaze.

1 success	One night
2 successes	Three nights
3 successes	One week
4 successes	One month
5 successes	One year

•••• Fragments of the Forgotten

With Fragments of the Forgotten, the infernalist can transcribe information even if the source no longer exists, or was never written down. Entering a similar state to Scribing the Unknown, the infernalist can write fragments of the original *Book of Nod*, paint DaVinci's lost masterpieces or pen Shakespeare's original copies of his plays.

Because these tattered memories are invariably incomplete, however, Hell has been known to "fill in the blanks" when it sees fit. As a result, no information this power generates should ever be completely trusted. Then again, if the person the infernalist reveals it to doesn't know the source….

System: Fragments of the Forgotten works the same as Scribing the Unknown, except that the thaumaturge can now transcribe to paper any written document even if it no longer exists. However, this power is nowhere near as precise as Scribing the Unknown. Although Fragments of the Forgotten allows the thaumaturge to transcribe lost or destroyed documents, the hellish minions who provide the information ultimately taint the process. The final document, though close to the original, is also extremely subjective and not entirely accurate.

The number of successes on the roll determines how accurate the document is. The Storyteller should conduct this roll in secret — as the information no longer exists, even the thaumaturge should have no idea what parts of it she can trust and what she can't. Demons misdirect, occlude and outright lie about such things, even to infernalists. Also, Storytellers will obviously have to make some parts of this information up for themselves.

1 success	Occasionally sensible garble; five percent accurate to original document.
2 successes	Partially intelligible; 10 percent accurate.

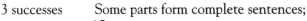

3 successes	Some parts form complete sentences; 15 percent accurate.
4 successes	Rambling, but largely cogent; 25 percent accurate.
5 successes	A clever reader can spot the lies by context; 50 percent accurate.

Alternatively, the thaumaturge can use Fragments of the Forgotten to write down prophecies or premonitions about the future. If used in this manner, the prophecy gives the infernalist a vague impression of what *might* happen. The number of successes dictates how clear the prophecy is. The nature of the premonition is again left to the Storyteller's discretion.

••••• Forsaken

The few infernalists who have attainted this level have the power to literally make people and things vanish from the collective subconscious. Although the thaumaturge cannot destroy the target physically, he can cause it to disappear from the mind's eye. With Forsaken, the thaumaturge alters people's perceptions and memories about someone or something to the point that they seem to cease to exist without actually doing so.

System: Forsaken makes it nearly impossible to find, remember or even see the person or object in question. In addition to the normal mechanics for casting, the thaumaturge's player must spend permanent Willpower point and suffer a permanent loss of a health level, subsuming the person's legacy into a suppurating wound. Once this power has been invoked, anyone wishing to interact with the target of Forsaken must first make a Perception + Occult (difficulty [5 + 1 for each success the thaumaturge scored]) to do so. If he succeeds at this roll, he can interact with the target of Forsaken as normal (such as have conversations, remember the subject's location, etc.) for as many nights as he scored success on the Perception + Occult roll. Once this time expires, the fugue of Forsaken returns.

If the thaumaturge uses this power against inanimate objects such as paintings or sculptures, the objects become virtually impossible to find, even in plain sight. Books collect dust on library shelves, overlooked by everyone, including their owners, or they sit in huge warehouses never to be read again — or even unwittingly destroyed as needless junk.

If used against a person, Forsaken blurs people's memories and perceptions so that all forget every meeting with the victim. The victim still exists, and he can act as normal, but once out of sight, he is forgotten. Even if the victim manages to remain in sight, he is often overlooked and ignored. This effect might have obvious advantages, but they are outweighed by the drawbacks. While the prince's ghoul might overlook the target, so may the bus driver.

Forsaken remains in effect until the thaumaturge is destroyed, chooses to end the effect or evokes this power on another target. If the thaumaturge ends the effect, he rises the next night with his original complement of health levels. The thaumaturge can evoke Forsaken on only one target at given time.

Path of Pestilence

While hate may bring a thaumaturge to the Path of Pain and pride to the Path of the Unspoken, nihilism brings the desperate and forsaken to the Path of Pestilence. A subconscious desire to destroy everything, even themselves, drives the practitioners of this art to revere all that is vile and corrupt. Beneath the filth and decay, the practitioners of the Path of Pestilence long for the final kiss of death, but they are often too craven to end their own existences. Instead, they satisfy their urge by inflicting pain and suffering on others — killing them through wasting diseases, plagues and cancers born from the thaumaturge's own self-loathing and misery.

Once learned, the Path of Pestilence warps the minds and bodies of its practitioners. They become infatuated with decay and drawn to torment. Like carrion, they flock to places where despair reigns supreme, all too pleased to indulge in its agony. They forget everything that once brought them joy, able only to focus on their wasting desires. Their bodies, too, become hosts for different viruses and plagues. This telltale sign, known as the Rot, is near impossible to hide or disguise — further pushing the thaumaturge underground.

Price: The Rot

Upon attaining the first level in this path, the thaumaturge develops the Infectious Bite Flaw (see **Vampire: The Masquerade** p. 297) but earns no additional points for it. Once the thaumaturge progresses to level three and beyond, his body becomes riddled with diseases and viruses — acquiring the Disease Carrier Flaw (see **Vampire: The Masquerade** p. 298) for no points as well. At undefined intervals, a new sickness manifests (both the illness and the frequency are up to the Storyteller), which is impossible to conceal unless the thaumaturge spends a point of blood every night to "heal" the symptoms temporarily.

• Illness

Although he is still only a student in the Path of Pestilence, the thaumaturge with this power can make his victim succumb to symptoms that are common among many illnesses. With a simple touch, the victim can suddenly develop a fever, chills, internal bleeding,

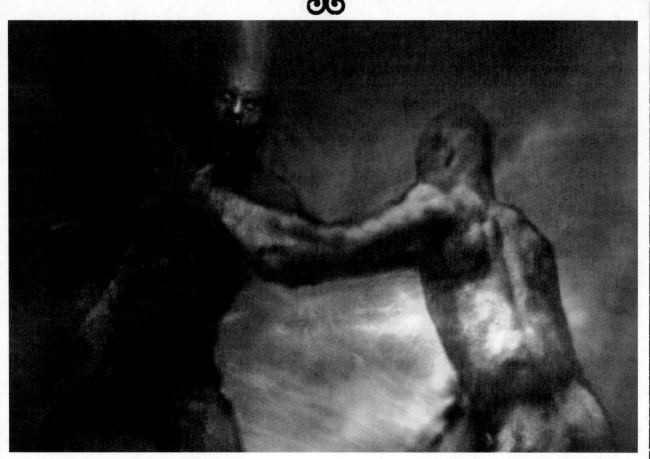

stomach cramps, vomiting, nausea and even open sores. The effects are never long lasting, but they are nonetheless debilitating and unpleasant to experience.

System: Illness requires the thaumaturge to touch his victim. The player may then roll as normal, while the victim rolls Stamina + Survival against a target number equal to the thaumaturge's Path of Pestilence rating + 3. If the victim scores more success, Illness fails to take effect. However, if the thaumaturge acquires more successes, each success subtracts one from one of the victim's Physical Attributes or Appearance, at the thaumaturge's choice. If any Physical Attribute drops to below zero, the victim falls unconscious and remains bedridden. This power can affect vampires, but they can spend a blood point to nullify the effect of Illness. Each point of blood used reduces the Attribute penalty by one.

Illness cannot be healed normally, but the victim recovers a point in each Attribute every four hours.

•• Infection

At this stage of understanding, the thaumaturge can infect a victim's wounds causing further injury and even death. With the right incantation, maggots will burrow deep into flesh, gangrene will set in and other complications arise from even the most incidental of cuts. Among mortals, Infection usually spells a death sentence — even with modern medical attention.

System: Evoking the right incantation (and succeeding at the appropriate Willpower roll as well as spending blood) allows the thaumaturge to infect a normal wound. As long as the victim has suffered a wound recently (whether bashing, lethal or aggravated), the thaumaturge can use Infection to cause an additional level of aggravated damage per individual wound. Mortals cannot soak this damage, and only vampires with Fortitude can try to resist.

••• Miasma

A thaumaturge this far advanced in the Path of Pestilence is usually riddled with countless diseases and sores allowing him to exhale a noxious gas from his mouth and pores. The resulting miasma affects all creatures that breathe, while vampires are blinded by it.

System: If the player spends the blood point and succeeds at his Willpower roll, the thaumaturge exhales a cloud of diseased breath around himself. The cloud lasts for a number of turns equal to the thaumaturge's Stamina rating and expands at a rate of five feet per turn. Players of characters caught in the miasma must roll Stamina (difficulty 6). Those who succeed can do little except move out of the miasma cloud. If they fail, all difficulty ratings increase by one for each success scored on the casting Willpower roll for the duration of the turn. Furthermore, for every two successes the thaumaturge rolled, those affected by Miasma suffer one health level of bashing damage (round down). This damage can be soaked with Stamina. Vampires take no damage. Instead, they suffer the difficulty penalty if they failed their Stamina roll.

•••• Parasitic Possession

This strange and unnerving power allows the thaumaturge to take control of an organism riddled with disease. As long as the target is currently suffering from a viral or other infection — even something as innocuous as a common cold — the infernalist can command the host's body as if it were her own. The thaumaturge can use Parasitic Possession on any visible organism (anything from insects to large mammals), but is not restricted to living beings. With this power, the infernalist can literally raise the dead, animating the parasites inhabiting the carcasses.

System: Parasitic Possession has a number of distinct applications, however, all require the standard blood point and Willpower roll. Commonly, this power allows the thaumaturge to take control of a victim's body to perform an action of his choice. If used in this manner, each success translates into a single physical action that the victim must perform. The target can resist by spending a Willpower point to nullify one forced action. Dead "hosts" may not spend Willpower to resist, but Kindred may.

Alternatively, infernalists can use this power to summon and command pestilential insects and small vermin. Each success determines the size of the swarm called. However, the thaumaturge can issue only simple commands such as attack, eat all food or bite.

1 success	One tiny animal (a rat), a few insects
2 successes	One small animal (a raccoon), a small swarm (a one-foot cube)
3 successes	One medium-sized animal (a dog or wolf), a medium swarm (a three-foot cube)
4 successes	One large animal (a horse), a large swarm (a five-foot cube)
5 successes	One massive animal (a bear), a veritable plague of insects.

For more information on swarms, see pages 304-305 of **Vampire: The Masquerade**.

Finally, the thaumaturge can animate a single dead organism, as long as it is a host to insects or other parasites. Once animated, the thaumaturge can issue a single, simple command, which the carcass follows until Parasitic Possession wears off. Successes determine how long the body remains animated:

1 success	One turn
2 successes	Five minutes
3 successes	One hour
4 successes	Three hours
5 successes	Until sunrise

••••• Vector

Mastery of the Path of Pestilence grants the thaumaturge the ability to infect a target with any virulent disease. Once infected, the victim succumbs to the virus almost instantaneously, exhibiting all the symptoms and accompanying agony in a matter of minutes.

System: Vector is a devastating power. If successful, the thaumaturge infects his target with a disease of his choice, which then plagues the victim for a duration dictated by the infernalist's Willpower successes. Victims are allowed a Stamina roll (difficulty 8) upon contracting the disease. Should they fail, they succumb to the accelerated effects of the disease, suffering a number of health levels of bashing damage equal to the thaumaturge's total successes, plus whatever the disease itself imposes upon the sufferer. For mortals, death is almost guaranteed with Vector.

The disease imparted by Vector has a supernatural duration, so it is unaffected by medicine or hospitalization, but medical science may allow characters to heal the damage they suffer from it. Healing Disciplines will abate health levels of damage, but not the disease itself unless the user of the healing effect knows that Discipline at a higher level than the thaumaturge imparting the Vector.

1 success	One night
2 successes	One month
3 successes	One year
4 successes	Seven years
5 successes	Permanent

Players of Cainites may add Fortitude to their Stamina roll. Should their characters fail, they contract the symptoms of the disease for the duration of Vector, but instead of losing health levels, they lose blood points.

Finally, there is a chance than witnesses and those who come in contact with the victim may contract the disease in question and become carriers. Any living being within a 10-foot radius must roll Stamina (difficulty 6) or contract the disease normally. Such "secondhand" infections are normal, and they may be healed and treated as such.

No Rest for the Wicked

For those Storytellers employing the optional price rules for Dark Thaumaturgy, we suggest the following prices for the paths from the **Guide to the Sabbat**. Those who think that these prices are too lenient are encouraged to make them as fierce as they wish. After all, the Devil doesn't make a bargain that doesn't favor him in the end.

Fires of the Inferno Price: Hell's Aura

Upon attaining level two of this path, the character suffers a change in her aura. Immediately visible to those using Aura Perception on her is a baleful green flame. This aura is visible to *anyone* using that power on her successfully, and it does not count toward the normal amount of information the character receives from such uses.

Path of Phobos Price: Nightmares

The very dream-forces that the character uses upon others ravage their way through his own mind while he sleeps. Any character who learns this path at any level acquires the Nightmares Flaw (see p. 299 of **Vampire: The Masquerade**), but receives no additional points for it.

Taking of the Spirit Price: Arrogance

All too accustomed to watching the will of others erode before her own, those who practice this path suffer the effects of the Megalomania derangement (see **Vampire: The Masquerade**, p. 223) for the duration of any scene in which this path's powers are invoked.

Other Forbidden Ways

Not all "heretical" powers wielded by the Kindred are infernal in nature. Some of these forbidden gifts are blacklisted because of reasons presented elsewhere in this book. Some have grave social repercussions, some rely upon restricted acts and others are simply so alien that they unsettle the Kindred observing them.

Remember, though, that heresy survives underground. While a few worldly Kindred may have witnessed these powers or heard of them, the very fact that they have been widely restricted means that few have had much real contact with them. When a Kindred whispers that the Ritual of the Bitter Rose has earned all Tremere the prince's distrust, he's saying such more out of rumor than personal experience. Even so, he's probably saying it to Kindred who have never even heard of it before.

Thaumaturgical Rituals

For those who are unable to distinguish between Dark Thaumaturgy and the non-infernal, "normal" Thaumaturgy of the Tremere, the difference is probably moot. Witchcraft is witchcraft, regardless of its origin, and the effects of these rituals are every bit as unpleasant as the paths of infernal sorcery.

Thaumaturgical rituals require an Intelligence + Occult roll to invoke, with the difficulty equal to the level of the ritual + 3 (maximum 9). Only one success is required, and a botch signifies a catastrophic failure, as always. Unless specified otherwise, thaumaturgical rituals take five minutes per level to perform.

Spite of the Harridan (Level Two Ritual)

Wives' tales of less enlightened times spoke of the ability of witchcraft to strike them barren, to steal children's breath and to leave them without issue. This ritual may be the origin of some of those stories. Invoking this power allows the thaumaturge to terminate any pregnancy, regardless of its stage, so long as the child is not yet being born. The caster must crush a snake's egg in her hand for this ritual to take effect.

System: This ritual must be performed in the presence of the subject, though she need not know that the thaumaturge is there. The pregnancy's termination is messy, obvious and often painful to the erstwhile mother.

Ritual of the Bitter Rose (Level Three Ritual)

Although this ritual has almost passed wholly from the face of the world, its reputation makes it one of the most fearsome weapons in the arsenal of the Tremere. The Ritual of the Bitter Rose allows multiple Kindred to gain the benefit of diablerizing a single vampire. Many elders rightly fear this ritual; nothing encourages a bloodthirsty coterie more than a chance to bring themselves closer to Caine and the opportunity for all of them to do it at once…. Needless to say, it is almost unthinkable that someone would teach a childe or protégé this ritual, as the potential for having it turn around and harm her is too great. Scholarly Tremere suspect that perhaps a half-dozen or so transcriptions of this ritual exist outside the one copy carefully locked away at the Vienna chantry.

System: The diablerie victim must be drained of all but a single blood point. This in itself may prove difficult, and those players of vampires drinking this blood from the Kindred may have to make a Self-

Control roll (difficulty 7) to halt their characters at the proper time. Thereafter, the victim's heart must be cut out and ground into paste with a marble mortar and pestle and mixed with a small amount of red wine. The thaumaturge adds to this mix a bit of ash from a burned alder stake and a pint of pure water. In old accounts of this ritual, the "pure water" comes from a mountain stream, but the few accounts of this ritual being used in the modern nights indicate that even purified tap water or store-bought distilled water works as well.

Each character wishing to take part in the communal diablerie must imbibe the concoction. The player of the character performing the ritual then makes the necessary roll. If the roll is successful, the ritual works correctly, and a number of characters may lower their generation. If the ritual fails, the concoction is sterile and no one gains any benefits (or suffers any detriments) of the diablerie. If the roll botches, the mixture becomes poisonous, inflicting three unsoakable aggravated wounds on each Kindred who partook of it.

The number of Kindred who can benefit from this ritual is equal to the number of generation steps between the diablerized vampire and the vampire of the lowest generation participating in the ritual, even if he's not the one performing the ritual. That is, if an eighth-generation vampire, a 10th-generation vampire and an 11th-generation vampire use this ritual upon a fifth-generation vampire, all three can benefit from the ritual (as the difference between generations eight and five is three). If the number of steps yielded by the difference is less than the number of vampires participating in the ritual, the Storyteller should lower the generations of those Kindred with the highest generations first until all of the steps have been accounted for. For example, if four vampires participate in the ritual and the lowest-generation diablerist is only two steps removed from the victim, only the two Kindred of the highest generation would gain any benefit from the ritual. No Kindred may gain more than one generation step through use of this ritual at any one time.

Anyone who participates in the ritual suffers the drawbacks of diablerie — loss of Humanity, veins in the aura, etc. — even if they did not gain a benefit from it.

A lesser known aspect of this ritual is that it requires exceptionally potent blood for it to take effect. It would seem that only Methuselahs (and, presumably, the Antediluvians themselves) have rich enough vitae for the ritual to take effect. A few reports have surfaced stating that the blood of vampires of the Sixth Generation work, but all of these Kindred were of advanced age, if not generation.

Rumors, of course, abound regarding this Discipline, from the paranoid to the credible. A few sources say that particularly robust vitae might lower a diablerist's generation by more than one step. Others suggest that one variation of the ritual always yields a poisonous ichor. Yet another claim suggests a rite that allows the would-be diablerists to be "taken over" by the elder upon whom they have foolishly chosen to slake their thirsts. None of these rumors have been substantiated, but the possible repercussions have helped to keep this ritual suppressed — the risk, as far as most Kindred are concerned, far outweighs the benefit. Still, more than one Kindred has been willing to got to any length to strengthen his bond to the mythical First Vampire.

Quenching the Lambent Flame (Level Six Ritual)

The origins of this ritual are surrounded in mystery. Some claim that it was developed as a way to censure unwholesomely ambitious Tremere while others suggest that it's not Hermetic in origin at all, but rather a survival device for Kindred in underpopulated areas, such as the Mayan territories where it was first discovered. Still others suggest that it is the penultimate punishment for diablerie, more effective than Final Death because it leaves the subject with the knowledge of the power he once had and the pale echo with which he is left after this ritual affects him. The ritual increases the generation of a Kindred to 13, regardless of his original distance from Caine.

System: This ritual takes one hour to perform. The thaumaturge must draw a circle with a mixture of his own blood and that of the subject. The subject must then lie motionless in the center of the circle for a full hour for the ritual to take effect, which requires that the subject be staked in the case of unwilling Kindred. If the subject is willing, the difficulty for the roll is 7, otherwise it is the normal 9 (ritual level + 3).

Koldunic Sorcery Rituals

The witchy magics of the Tzimisce are practically heresies in and of themselves. By calling upon the spirits of their homeland — which some call demons — the Fiends who are skilled enough to be called *koldun* work their will upon the night.

The rituals of Koldunic Sorcery require a successful Intelligence + Koldunism roll (difficulty of 4 + the level of the ritual). Additionally, unless specified otherwise, a sorcerer using these rituals must spill one point of blood when calling upon the spirits, though it needs not be her own.

Enlightenment (Level One Ritual)

All things in nature contain a spirit of some type, which are referred to as *lèleks* (pronounced LAH-lek; Hungarian for "spirit"). Koldunic Sorcerers must first be able to recognize a nature spirit before they can manipulate them into servitude properly. This ritual is requisitely cast often, thereby reinforcing the *koldun*'s attunement to the land and nature. Many of the old *koldun* did not simply trust that their attunement to the land would remain intact. Rather, they dedicated one night out of the week to completely reconnect with the spirits of their land. These *lèleks* are more recognizably "felt" rather than visually perceived. A *lèlek* traveling on a breeze close to the *koldun* might instill a static sensation in the back of the sorcerer's neck. Healthy trees might seem to have a faint verdant glow about their trunks. Whichever way he believes to perceive these spirits, the *koldun* awakens to a new sense after casting this ritual.

System: The *koldun*'s player spends one point of blood and makes the roll. Each success he accumulates increases the duration of his attunement to the nature spirits of the four natural elements.

1 success	One hour
2 successes	One night
3 successes	One week
4 successes	One month
5 successes	One year

Mephistophelean Minx (Level One Ritual)

Old wives tales tell of the inherent perils of allowing a cat near sleeping children for fear that it will suck out the child's soul. The *koldun* casting this ritual substantiates these tales by enlisting any small feline into his service, as the cat will search out any sleeping individual it finds and mystically draw out some of his soul.

System: The player makes a normal activation roll. By feeding a cat one point of his blood, the *koldun* brings the feline into temporary servitude. Once the blood is fed to the cat and the ritual is cast, the cat will immediately seek out any child in the area who is asleep. The cat will then crawl up to the victim's face and mystically draw out some of his spiritual "essence." This essence will funnel through the cat, acting as a conduit to the *koldun*, who will then temporarily gain a point of Willpower that may be spent at any time during the night. This Willpower point must, however, be spent in the same night it was stolen, otherwise the "essence" will mystically dissipate and return to its rightful owner. Every point of blood spent in feeding the cat spurs it to visit another victim, resulting in another point of temporary Willpower. Willpower gathered in this way may not exceed the *koldun*'s permanent Willpower Trait.

Alternatively, the koldun may feed one point of blood to multiple cats, thereby reducing the amount of time he must wait for one cat to complete multiple tasks.

Storytellers may decide how much time it takes for the feline to hunt down a suitable slumbering victim. A child who has had her essence stolen for three nights in a row dies before waking the next day.

Service for Souls (Level Two Ritual)

In casting this ritual, a *koldun* summons the attention of nature spirits to his person, enticing them by offering a part of his own essence to them. These spirits are vital in their own right, and they have mystical powers that aren't easily defined; they are free to act as they will. If they do accept the *koldun*'s essence, they are bound to perform the duties as part of a Koldunic Sorcery ritual would require. Otherwise, they may roam free to live their lives.

System: The *koldun*'s player spends a blood point and makes his roll in order to awaken the spirits from their natural settings and attract their attention. Then the caster enacts this ritual, spending at least one more blood point. For every blood point he spends, he may bind one nature spirit of the land into servitude. Although they do occupy space in his body (and thus count toward maximum blood pool), these blood points remain "inert" within the *koldun*'s body and unavailable to him. He cannot use them to fuel Disciplines, heal wounds et cetera for as long as he intends to keep the nature spirits bound to him.

The lèleks summoned by the sorcerer may take any number of actions, but they may not typically affect physical objects other than those they inhabit. Even these are singular. The spirit of a tree may affect only that one tree, as opposed to all trees. Most often, these spirits are used as spies, emissaries or witnesses to some pact between the *koldun* and a greater spirit. They remain bound to the *koldun* for as long as their original agreement or until the Fiend chooses to relieve the lèleks of duty, whichever comes first. At such a time, a lèlek will disperse into the night air, absolving the *koldun* of the promised vitae.

Withering Agony (Level Two Ritual)

By pulling the spirit from a sick tree and coaxing it into the body of a mortal or Kindred, the *koldun* infects his victim with a physically debilitating malady. When infected, the victim will decrease in weight, caused by the exfoliation of a thick sap-like substance from his pores. Hair will fall out, and skin will degenerate to an ash gray. Bones are more brittle, and breath comes in laborious gasps.

System: The *koldun*'s player spends a point of blood and makes the appropriate roll while the character marks his victim with a bloody glyph. A spirit inhabiting a sick tree is then enticed to flee the dying wood and make its new home inside the marked victim. Over the course of a night, the adverse effects of this ailment will take effect, causing the victim to suffer a –2 to all Physical and Social dice pools. The afflicted also suffers one health level of unsoakable bashing damage due to the atrophy the body endures. This damage may be offset through rest or blood expenditure normally thereafter.

Kindred are similarly affected, suffering both the penalties to their Physical and Social dice pools and the associated damage. They also lose one additional blood point on top of the normal one point spent at the beginning of their night.

Withering Agony lasts for one week.

Note: Although mortals and Kindred aren't normally affected by nature spirits, the lèlek infecting victims are dying spirits and do not "join" with a host so much as they "invade" their health, similar to a virus.

Raze the Lélek (Level Three Ritual)

A *koldun* casting this ritual may destroy inanimate objects by severing their spirits from their material shells. By severing an object's spirit, objects like stone pillars turn to chalk and dust, cell phones malfunction and break into a small pile of wire and plastic, and clothing frays to become tatters of cotton and leather.

System: By expending the appropriate number of blood points, a *koldun* may rend a spirit from its inanimate housing, permanently. He may do so to any object within his line of sight.

The number of successes the player achieves determines the degree of the *koldun*'s success and the size of the object he may destroy.

Successes	Object
1 success	A fountain pen
2 successes	A cell phone
3 successes	A television
4 successes	A sofa
5 successes	A small car

Rumors of elder *koldun* using this power to great effect persist, especially among young Tzimisce, practically becoming legends in the telling. One such legend involves a Fiend reducing a rival's very haven to brittle shale, while another suggests that a jealous Tzimisce transformed a scorned lover into a pillar of salt before she could turn against him. None of these tales have been substantiated, however.

Beyond the Wall of Death (Level Four Ritual)

This ritual was created by a *koldun* toward the end of the medieval struggle against the Warlocks, in an attempt to preserve the knowledge possessed by fallen sorcerers. After this ritual is cast over the dead body of a newly slain *koldun*, its spirit will appear to the caster. As long as the *koldun* is aware of the specific sorceries that were possessed by the recently deceased, he can entice it to mentor him in these Ways.

System: The player spends a blood point and makes the necessary roll. While standing over the body of a recently deceased *koldun* and chanting his name, the caster summons the spirit into his presence. The *koldun* must have prior knowledge as to what powers the spirit possessed when it was itself a *koldun* before he asks to be mentored in the Ways. On a successful roll, the spirit will grudgingly abide to mentoring the *koldun*, as long as the character is explicit in his question and the player has the experience enough to buy the specific power. The spirit will mentor the caster in only one level of a Way, but, before moving on to its final rest, it will grant enough knowledge of the Way so that the *koldun* no longer requires a mentor to continue his progression. Once the spirit has completed its task, it will be banished from existence, and it will not be accessible again.

A spirit will be compelled to instruct the *koldun* only in other powers of Koldunic Sorcery and its rituals, not other Disciplines. Neither will it reveal other knowledge.

This power does not work on a subject who has been diablerized.

Incubus Visage (Level Four Ritual)

During less progressive times, people born with defects or abnormalities were thought to be touched by demons and devils while in the womb, so they were treated as outcasts. Similarly, Tzimisce *koldun* would cast this ritual as punishment for sexual or theft crimes committed by their *boyars*. The *koldun* seduces one of his bound nature spirits to warp the physical features of a mortal or Kindred, distorting facial features by elongating the nose, bulging the eyes, extending the teeth and chin. Mucus runs freely from the nose, saliva drools out of the mouth, boils and pock marks break out over the entire body, open sores drip a yellowish ooze and a hump swells between shoulders. Very soon, the victim resembles the most hideous of mortal beings and is reviled by society.

System: The ritual must be cast on the night of a half-moon, and the *koldun* must ingest and spend one blood point from a boar, along with a piece of the victim's skin. For every success scored, a victim will suffer the adverse effects of Incubus Visage for one phase of the moon, for a maximum of another half-moon phase. The victim's Social Attributes drop to zero, and he gains the Flaw: Eerie Presence (see **Vampire: The Masquerade**, p. 302).

Merging of the Souls (Level Four Ritual)

Before they had revenants at their disposal, Tzimisce *koldun* learned to amalgamate the ghouls and *lèleks* in their sway, thereby enhancing the ghoul's physical prowess. Many of these ghoul hosts end up either with multiple personalities, abnormal physical features or are altogether destroyed by the dangerous rigors of merging with a nature spirit. Still, they make efficient brutes, useful for keeping unquiet peasants in line and even finding use in the modern nights.

System: The player makes her roll and spends a blood point, the blood from which is used to mark the ghoul. By marking one of her ghouls with this extra point of vampiric vitae, a *koldun* entices a nature spirit to "join" with the ghoul. One of the ghoul's Strength, Dexterity or Stamina may be increased for every nature spirit that merges with him, for a maximum of three spirits and three points. Enticing more than one spirit into a ghoul requires marking him with more than one point of vampiric vitae. Any more than three nature spirits attempting to "join" with a ghoul will cause his consciousness to be shoved out from his control, and his body will warp and rip into a creature resembling something with no place in nature. For each *lèlek* beyond the third used to augment the ghoul's body, the ghoul gains a derangement of the Storyteller's choice or loses one point of Appearance, which lasts as long as the augmentation itself.

A ghoul's Traits may be increased above and beyond their normal maximum of 5 with this ritual to 6 for as long as this ritual lasts.

This ritual lasts for one night per success that the *koldun*'s player scores on his activation roll.

Normal mortals are unable to withstand this sort of transformation process. Not only is their blood too weak to sustain the amalgamated spirit, the *lèlek* would immediately warp the victim's physique, causing it to change into an inanimate object in nature. Kindred are too far outside the realms of nature to properly benefit from the merging of *lèlek*, so this ritual does not affect them.

Elemental Savior (Level Five Ritual)

During the centuries-old conflict with the Warlocks, some Tzimisce *koldun* desperately needed their *lèleks* to effectively aid in the fight, and they eventually created this ritual to make that possible. Once this ritual is cast, a nature spirit will become physical, in the form of an animated element in nature. The most common form that these spirits took was that of man-sized mud golems. When in this form, the *lèlek* can obey only basic, one-sentence commands. It was not long after the *koldun* created this ritual that the Warlocks came up with their own form of elemental manipulation, which more than evened the odds in this blood feud.

Years later, in the modern nights, when this ritual was rediscovered and cast, the *lèlek* was surrounded by artificial, man-made creations and took the form of a large concrete golem, made up of concrete, asphalt and rebar.

System: A spirit already in the employ of the *koldun* (through some other ritual) will readily take to an elemental form after the caster bleeds four points of vitae onto the object he desires to have animated and the player makes a successful roll. Once the spirit animates an element, it will respond only to simple, one-sentence instructions from the *koldun*.

A *lèlek* can remain physical for a single night before it is forced out of its elemental state and return to the spirit world.

Embracing the Demon (Level Six Ritual)

Many centuries ago, a renowned brood of *koldun* was known to barter directly with powerful evil spirits, and it eventually wound up being destroyed by these untrustworthy creatures. Although it may seem senseless to risk life and limb to enlist a "true" demon into one's employ, the benefits reaped by the *koldun* who were not torn apart almost totally eclipses this peril. Following this mode of thought, *koldun* of the modern nights have re-adapted this ritual of demon-conjuring by requiring the body of a newly dead neonate, one that was blood bound to the caster. When summoned, the demon inhabits the dead body, thereby removing it from its natural element and reducing its overall power. Doing so ensures that the demon will not have enough

---

Koldunic Elemental Traits

No matter what elemental form a nature spirit takes, from a large oak tree to age-old stone, to roiling river water, its potential always remains the same.

Strength 4, Dexterity 3, Stamina 5

Willpower: 2, Health Levels: OK, OK, OK, -1, -1, -3, -3, -5, Banished

Attacks: Melee strike for 4 (does not account for Potence)

Disciplines: Fortitude 2, Potence 2

Abilities: Brawl 2

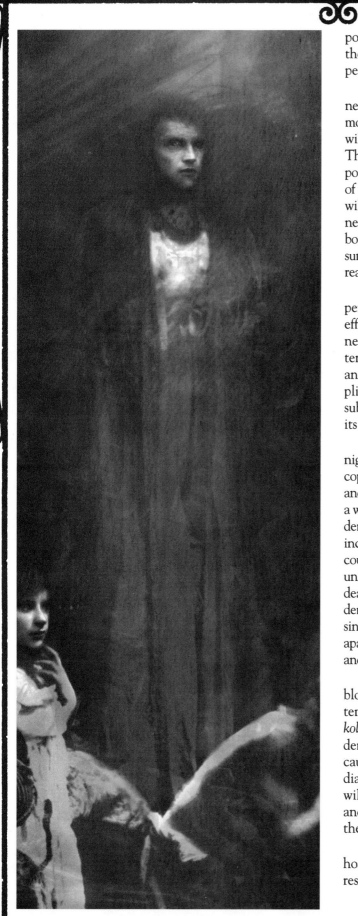

power to simply destroy the caster on a whim. However, the host body grants it enough of its mystical energies to perform most of its "required" tasks.

System: The caster must first sacrifice a blood bound neonate. The fledgling vampire cannot have spent any more than 20 years as Kindred (otherwise the dead body will decay too rapidly for it to host a demon properly). Then the *koldun*'s player makes his roll, spends a blood point and casts this ritual, all the while chanting the name of the demon he wishes to summon. The demon, in turn, will be drawn from its infernal realm and forced into the newly dead vessel body. As long as the vampire was blood bound to the *koldun* before she was destroyed, the demon summoned into her body will not have the capacity to readily defy its master.

Once it is within the vessel body, the demon may perform any of a number of tasks, from performing as an efficient bodyguard to serving as a mentor for teaching new Disciplines. It possesses all of the physical characteristics (Attributes, Talents, etc.) of the host vampire and all of the supernatural and mental capacities (Disciplines, Attributes, etc.) of the demon. It is considered subject to the blood bond, and it cannot actively harm its master, even though it almost certainly resents him.

The demon will be physically weak for the first few nights after the summoning, as it grows accustomed to coping without the full range of its tremendous powers, and it will be restricted to the limits of the body. Within a week, it will "grow" into the body, causing it to take on demonic features. Its Attributes and powers may also increase with time (at Storyteller discretion). Over the course of a month, the body will degenerate into an unsuitable vessel for the demon, caused in part by both the dead body's decay and its inability to accommodate the demon's increasing powers. After a month has passed since the demon's summoning, the vessel body will fall apart, and the creature will be released from its servitude and immediately sent back to where it originated.

A demon summoned into a vessel body that was not blood bound before it was killed may consistently attempt to break free from its term of servitude. The *koldun* must make a Willpower roll every night that the demon remains in the vessel body. While a failed roll causes the *koldun*'s sway over the demon to slip, immediately releasing it from its mortal chains, a botched roll will ultimately end in a bloody conflict between demon and caster, of which the outcome is almost assuredly in the demon's favor.

Mortal vessels are wholly unsuitable to properly host a demon for any length of time, and any test of this restriction will always result in the body melting into puddles of flesh and viscera almost immediately after this ritual is cast.

Assamite Sorcery

The very concept of Assamite Sorcery is itself heresy in some circles. Still, some practices among the Children of Haqim see more use than others, largely because those others have fallen out of favor and are practiced only in hidden cabals and cells in forgotten corners of the world.

The system by which the rituals of Assamite Sorcery are performed is similar to Thaumaturgy. The player rolls Intelligence + Occult at a difficulty of the ritual's level + 3 (to a maximum of 9). Success brings about the desired result. Failure indicates that nothing happens. Prior to using the ritual, the sorcerer must partake of *kalif* in one form or another (see **Blood Magic: Secrets of Thaumaturgy**).

Kafir's Bane (Level Three Ritual)

Although their potential is more in line with judgment and stealth, some Assamites are willing to go to any length to fulfill their purposes. Those Assamites of the warrior or assassin caste have been known to use this ritual to steel themselves before any situation in which they might find themselves exposed to overt combat. Through this rite, the Assamite harnesses his Beast and turns it upon his doomed foe.

Among conservative Assamites, this ritual is scorned because it allows the Kindred to grow too close to his Beast.

System: The player makes the roll to activate this ritual and the character partakes of *kalif* smoke or blood. If the Assamite enters frenzy as a result of combat, he does not need to roll to see if he can keep it in check; this ritual allows him to "ride the wave" of the frenzy automatically, as described under the Instinct Virtue on p. 287 of **Vampire: The Masquerade**. Such is the case even if the Assamite does not have the Instinct Virtue. This works for only the first combat that incites frenzy after the Assamite performs the ritual. If the Assamite fails to enter a combat frenzy before the end of the night, the ritual expires with the sunrise.

The Sire Impotent (Level Four Ritual)

It is unknown whether this ritual was developed as a punishment or as a warning to neonate Assamites. Regardless of its origin, this ritual renders a given Kindred's vitae inert for the purposes of siring new vampires. Using this ritual requires the caster to partake of the *kalif* blood, not merely inhale the smoke.

System: The player makes his roll, and the character ingests the blood of a vessel under the influence of *kalif*. The subject must either be a descendant of the sorcerer, or the sorcerer must have the fang or tongue of the subject. If the roll is successful, the subject is unable to sire childer for a year and a night, or until the Final Death of the sorcerer, whichever comes first. Potential childer drained of blood will simply die if the Kindred attempts to Embrace them.

Using this ritual destroys the fang or tongue once the ritual is complete. If the ritual fails, the fang or tongue is destroyed anyway.

From Marduk's Throat (Level Six Ritual)

This ritual, the hallowed means by which the Assamites lowered their generation while under the influence of the Tremere curse, has largely fallen into disuse. A few cults of the clan still observe it out of humility or habit, and these Kindred are among the schismatics and ur-Shulgi loyalists, respectively.

Full details for the ritual may be found on p. 126 of **Blood Magic: Secrets of Thaumaturgy**.

Merits and Flaws

Blessed (7-pt. Supernatural Merit)

You are favored by some higher power to the extent that the corrosive touch of Hell does not harm you. You are unaffected by the paths and rituals of Dark Thaumaturgy. Characters with this Merit may never learn Dark Thaumaturgy themselves, and they are affected by "normal" Thaumaturgy as any other character is. Storytellers, if a player wants to take this Merit without it fitting the character concept or having any rational reason, kick the stinking gumby out of your game.

Indomitable Soul (7-pt. Supernatural Merit)

In the horrific event of your diablerie, the Kindred who commits the act gains none of the benefits of diablerie (generation, Disciplines, etc.), but he does suffer the drawbacks (aura veins, loss of Humanity, etc.). Obviously, this won't do you much good, but it is an excellent way to give one final "Screw you!" to your murderer. And the members of your former coterie can always avenge you.... A vampire with this Merit will never become a wraith. Instead, she goes into the unknowable beyond upon her diablerie.

Devil's Mark (1- or 7-pt. Physical Flaw)

Somewhere on your body, you have a mark of the Devil upon you. For one point, it appears as a patch of scaly skin, a "witch's claw," a mark resembling the Number of the Beast or something similar. For seven points, you have been obviously disfigured in a diabolical-looking way — vestigial wings, backward-bending knees, cloven hooves — that reduces your Appearance by one and no doubt raises all manner of questions. As if this weren't bad enough already, you're going to attract a lot of attention that may threaten the Masquerade. You may take this Flaw at either point value only if you have not made any pact with the infernal. If you *have* dealt with demons, you're going to earn these all by yourself. If you take this Flaw and later earn another disfigurement through truck with demons, you must pay off the point value with experience points as soon as possible.

Spoiled Beast (3-pt. Mental Flaw)

What the Beast has had before, it wants again, and it wants it now. Any time the player must make a Willpower roll in order for her character to resist a desire, she does so with only as many dice as she has in her Willpower pool, as opposed to her rating. That is, she rolls her current Willpower as opposed to her permanent Willpower. This Flaw can be particularly debilitating when it comes to staving off hunger, for example.

Unrepentant Beast (4-pt. Mental Flaw)

The Beast leaves its mark on you long after it has run its course and had its way with you. If you ever botch a Self-Control (or Instinct) roll to resist (or ride the wave of) frenzy, you immediately acquire a compulsion derangement (see **Vampire: The Masquerade**, p. 222, listed under Obsessive/ Compulsive). The Storyteller should determine the nature of the particular compulsion, and you may indeed gain a wide and varied spectrum of compulsions.

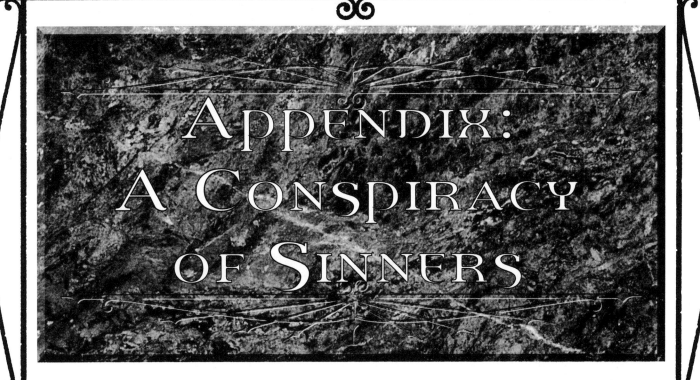

Appendix: A Conspiracy of Sinners

Sin bravely...We will never have all the facts to make a perfect judgement, but with the aid of basic experience we must leap bravely into the future.
—Russell R. McIntyre

Sin cannot exist without sinners, and each group herein has stepped outside vampiric "society" to pursue an endless parade of vices, goals, and political agendas that have been shunned by Sabbat and Camarilla alike. Some are civil dissidents uninterested in the often black-or-white mentality of either sect, while others truck with baleful entities best left to whatever hell humanity forgot.

The following is a sampling of groups that have flourished in the Final Nights. They are not indicative of any new power players ready to contest the Sabbat or Camarilla's rule, but given the chance, justicars, paladins, archons, Judge Inquisitors, alastors and even scourges would willingly end such heresies. Some cults represent an ideological threat, some a political obstacle and some... they're just different enough to frighten the status quo. Yet, they are not simply disposable antagonists for characters who are spoiling to fight; they are not slavering beasts looking to re-enact the Rape of Nanking. These groups are intelligent and articulate organizations with private and dedicated agendas. Most will not threaten characters who discover their existence (at least initially). Instead, they seek understanding, allies and even converts. They are the Storyteller's tools for confronting characters with moral dilemmas and alternative solutions, a means of forcing them to face and question their existence regardless of the result.

The Associates

Members of the Red Rose Sabbat pack thought that they were being funny when they grabbed Arnold Fleschner, Embraced him and locked him in a freezer truck with a dozen other "recruits" during a mass Embrace. They never expected him to survive. Arnold was a clean-cut, high-priced lawyer during the early '70s, who defended the rich and infamous in Detroit's halls of justice. This mousy defender was a tiger in the courtroom, who methodically ripped apart cases in which his clients were accused of assault, larceny, rape and even murder. Prosecutors called it "guilty until the check clears" style justice. Arnold was perfect fodder for the Sword of Caine.

Needless to say, the Red Roses were slack-jawed when Arnold emerged from the truck first, dusted off his mangled suit indignantly, and demanded to know what was going on while closing the door on a woman's head, pushing her back inside. Since that time, the Lasombra Arnold has been a member of the Sabbat, although he sometimes questioned why. The sect's blind faith and religious fervor seemed alien to him, and although he participated in the Vaulderie and various *ritae*, he never felt connected to the Sabbat. The Red Roses, in turn, could not turn him into any more of a monster because he was already detached, abrupt and "a cold fish" by their description. He killed and tortured with distracted interest, and he rarely exhibited any emotional commitment one way or the other outside of feeding. For him existence seemed hollow.

That all changed when the Red Roses adopted Marylenna, a Tremere *antitribu*, following the destruction of her pack. Nobody realized that Marylenna was an infernalist who had sacrificed her packmates to her demonic master. She could not afford to kill more Cainites without arousing suspicion, but she did manage to bring the Red Roses under her satanic sway, member by member, before she finally came to the mousy lawyer. Arnold was not stupid, however, and he recognized the slow change that was overtaking his allies. In his trademark deadpan fashion, he confronted Marylenna, not to condemn or expose her corruption, but to understand her infernal activities. Delighted to find a willing audience (and ready to destroy him the minute he betrayed her), Marylenna explained her concourse with demons and the pacts in which she engaged in exchange for power. Arnold immediately realized that the demons were handing Marylenna the short end of the infernal stick, and he advised her on how to handle subsequent negotiations. In exchange for Arnold's help and expertise on contractual bargaining, Marylenna taught him Dark Thaumaturgy.

Arnold discovered that while infernalism lacked any real allure for him, the prospect of haggling and negotiating with the ultimate lawyers, demons, was just as thrilling as working for a law firm again. Arnold realized that he missed the intellectual challenge of facing opponents of like or even greater skill, and set about learning all the nuances of Dark Thaumaturgy to best represent the Red Roses during negotiations. Because Arnold was always bargaining on behalf of someone else, however, he discovered methods to offset his own contact with the unholy host. In fact, even to this date, he justifies his services to clients as altruistic and necessary. "After all," he claims, "if someone is willing to damn their souls to serve demons, then I might as well help them make the best deal possible." Few realized that Arnold was negotiating deals behind their backs....

Marylenna taught Dark Thaumaturgy to willing acolytes while Arnold negotiated on their behalf, turning the Red Roses into an infernal enterprise. Over the next decade, Arnold gathered or Embraced other lawyers, forming an underground pack of advisors who were skilled in matters of Hell. Privately calling themselves the Associates, they acted as roving advocates on behalf of Cainite clients who did not possess the skill to bargain with demons. The business was going well for the while, but matters really picked up after Marylenna and all Tremere *antitribu* vanished. What most considered a tragedy, the Associates saw as an opportunity. Without the Tremere *antitribu*, many would-be infernalists lacked the skill to learn new Dark Thaumaturgical paths or avoid the pitfalls that demons used against amateurs. The Associates realized that they could tap the vacuum left in the wake of the disappearance of the Tremere *antitribu*. Their clientele would include not only infernalists, but those Cainites who did not want the brimstone stench of demonic concourse on them. The Associates would act as advisors, intermediaries and negotiators. For a higher fee, they would even bargain on behalf of clients (Cainite and kine alike) who did not want any direct connections with Dark Thaumaturgy.

In the short time since Marylenna vanished, senior partner Arnold and the Associates have established several dummy businesses using under-the-table financing from some of their oldest clients. The Red Rose pack still exists and serves as a front for Arnold's cohorts and their legitimate dealings with the Sabbat. The Associates, however, now maintain "offices" in New York, Detroit, Las Vegas, Miami, Washington and Atlantic City under various names including Prescott & Childers Legal Services, Habbib & Habbib Financial Advisors, Atlantic Union & Partners and Madam Moon's Tarot Readings. These businesses are dummy corporations and shell companies, however, with fake addresses, but real phone lines connected to answering machines for anyone calling them. The Associates access their messages through multiple terminal points, and only answer those prefaced by "[such and such] referred me to you." Even payments and financing of these companies is handled automatically through Swiss Home Banks, with anonymous depositing and a paper trail of fake names. It has proven invaluable against the Inquisition, which knows a little about the Associates but has been unable to track them down.

Meanwhile, the Associates only handle their oldest, most trusted and richest clients directly. All others discover their services through the underground rumor mill, and even then, they are lucky if they have a phone number. While the Associates are very careful to avoid the Inquisition, the secrecy also comes from infernalists who keep their contacts carefully guarded.

Unbeknownst to many except for Arnold and his principal partners, they succeed for one reason alone… the demons want them to appear successful. A Cainite's soul is already damned, but the chance of redemption, however frail, always exists. Infernalists sacrifice that hope in pursuit of their powers, believing that the trade is equitable. The truth is far from equitable, but most Cainites are at least possessed of enough of a self-preservation instinct that the mere hint of damnation frightens them into playing it safe. The Associates, however, offer a supposedly safe avenue for dealing with demons, promising to absorb the risks and danger of infernal stains on behalf of their clients, in exchange for a substantial fee. This offer draws more Cainites out from the woodwork — certainly more than would practice infernalism normally — most of whom think that the peril of bartering with demons is thus diminished. This development pleases Hell's hierarchy because the truth is, any deals with the devil, be they direct or by proxy, still result in damnation. It's called intent, and Hell's built on it. The difference is that those who deal with demons themselves know that they have signed away their existence. The others never realize it until it's too late.

The Associates know this truth because Arnold realized it while first learning Dark Thaumaturgy. The only way to placate demons, save one's skin and still earn more power is to set someone else up as a dupe, a patsy. Arnold keeps his infernal corruption to a minimum because he uses a sacrificial lamb in his stead. By negotiating as a client's proxy (call it power of attorney), he establishes any contract he wishes with demons in exchange for offering the clients power, sparing his existence and advancing his skill in Dark Thaumaturgy. The contract also remains valid because it was never the demons that broke or lied about their contractual obligations with the client. The Associates did, however.

Currently, the Associates number just under a dozen agents, including Arnold, who claim havens across North America; only they handle negotiations and infernal dealings directly. Their center of operation is Detroit, home to the Red Rose pack, but they do not limit their activities to Sabbat cities alone. While they deal with Camarilla enclaves as well, their limited connections with the sect hamper their current efforts. They are looking for sympathetic, gullible or mercenary Kindred to serve as further inroads into the sect. Given the Camarilla's limited experience with infernalists, the Associates are considering dealing exclusively with Kindred, but Arnold and several others still consider themselves "loyal" to the Sword of Caine due to both the Vaulderie and the Sabbat's effective propaganda efforts. Still, the Associates cannot deny the lure of a sect that lacks an internal force like the Inquisition to hamper its activities.

Serving each lawyer are three to four Sabbat enforcers who bear the taint of Hell to varying degrees. These right-hand-men all owe the Associates a major boon for helping them negotiate tough deals or saving them from committing terrible mistakes. The enforcers conduct thorough background checks on potential clients, act as the lawyers' intermediaries for the first few meetings and pursue errant payments. Additionally, the enforcers also eliminate clients who exhibit devilish marks and infernal deformities, since such direct evidence of infernal taint would not reflect well on the Associates who are supposedly negotiating good deals on behalf of third parties. Destroying such obvious taints also robs the Inquisition of potential witnesses.

Below the enforcers are peripheral scouts — unwitting ghouls and mortals. Before New York's fall, the Associates had received payment from the city's bishop in the form of eight Zantosa revenants. These ghouls had fled the New York estate massacre that claimed over two dozen of their family, and they now serve the bishop secretly in return for refuge. Already degenerate, they made easy targets for further corruption at the hands of their patron, and they now serve the Associates in the same capacity. The revenants act as scouts in Washington by exploring its seedy underbelly, and by helping the Associates determine which politicians are ripe for the plucking. Unlike the enforcers, these ghouls know nothing of the Associates themselves, and instead work through a handler. The Zantosas bear minor infernal staining, but given the Sabbat's existing disdain for them, the sect might easily dismiss their peculiarities as their typical inbreeding.

While the Associates have been very careful to avoid attention, the Inquisition knows of them at least by name. At first, the investigating Judge Inquisitors believed that the infernal society resided solely in Detroit, but their most recent information indicates that the Associates dwell within several Sabbat enclaves within North America. This information worries the Inquisitors, who believe that they may have an epidemic on their hands. Of course, the Inquisition must conduct its investigation under utmost secrecy. If Sabbat fledglings discovered that the Associates offered deals with the infernal "without direct risk," Cainites might flock to Hell's advocates and risk personal damnation.

Serapis Ex Machina

The arrival of the Christian calendar's first century was supposedly significant because it marked the birth of Jesus Christ, and the formation of a novel religion based on compassion, faith and salvation. The truth, however, is that Christianity was far from the first or last religion to espouse these ethics under the guise of monotheism. The worship of the singular, supreme deity existed with the veneration of Mithras (who found acolytes across the Middle East and Europe among the Hindus, Romans, Zarathustrians and Manicheans) and the Yoruba who venerated the supreme Oludumare in Africa. Both religions followed a system of strong moralities and righteous behavior. Nor was Christ the only messiah of the region aside from Moses, Zarathustra and the later-born Muhammad. The first Christian century also saw the miracles of Apollonius of Tyana.

Apollonius of Tyana was born in Turkey at the time of Jesus, and he died at a far more venerable age between AD 96 to AD 98. Like Jesus, Apollonius healed the sick and raised the dead. He wore his hair long and traveled as far west as Italy, and as far east as India. Where he journeyed, he studied the local wisdom and culture. He took up Pythagorean thought while exploring Greece, and he studied Buddhism in India. Apollonius observed a strict vegetarian regimen to the point that he refused to wear furs, leather or any garment of animal origin, and he avoided Palestine because the Judaic Temples spilt sacrificial blood in honor of God. Even in death, Apollonius ascended into heaven, much like the Christian messiah. Unlike Christ, however, Apollonius

mysteriously fell into virtual anonymity, nearly forgotten by history had it not been for the writer Philostratus who compiled an account of his life over a century later....

The organization named *Serapis Ex Machina* began with a group of autarkis who simply gathered for mutual protection in the mid-70s. Tired of fleeing near-destruction at the hands of Lupines and overeager sectarian vampires, a handful of autarkis converged around Cyrus Benjamin, a Ventrue outcast with a haven in Hull, just outside the Camarilla stronghold of Ottawa. Cyrus enjoyed the protection of Ottawa's prince for private reasons, so he was able to exist with little interference from local Kindred (with occasional exception). The growing autarkis coterie enjoyed the same considerations as long as they remained hidden, which they did in the interest of self-preservation. Cyrus suspected that the prince tolerated this arrangement because Hull provided Ottawa with a kind of buffer against Sabbat excursions from Montreal and Toronto. Any attempts to infest Ottawa would use Hull as a beachhead to "enlist" Sabbat recruits and provide a steady blood supply. Cyrus and his lot were fodder to delay the Sabbat should the local Kindred need to retreat to Ottawa or organize a counter-strike.

While Hull suffered the occasional raid, Ottawa was not truly besieged like New York. Cyrus and his autarkis allies, however, chaffed under inactivity and grew bored from simply existing. More so, they knew they would deplete their considerable pooled resources eventually. Slowly, the group extended its influence over Hull. Their activities proved to be exercises in subtlety to see how much wealth or power they could accrue through patience and diligence. The first simple experiments included bribing Hull's politicians to vote a certain way on local by-laws or siphoning funds from community programs into their accounts. Soon, the group established minor money-laundering networks and swindled cash through real estate schemes. Each venture increased the scope of the next and brought more autarkis into contact with Cyrus' cell.

Cyrus eventually realized that Hull could no longer support the group and that if the Camarilla learned of his schemes and growing flock, it would cast a leery eye toward them. The group needed to "buy" freedom and find a place where neither sect would bother or plague it. After considerable brainstorming, the coterie eventually hit upon a dying town, one whose central employer had left, and revitalizing its commerce. With the North American Free Trade Agreement, doing so was an easy chore. Several automobile manufacturers were closing their small-town operations in favor of opening cheaper plants in Mexico. Carroll, Iowa was one such "statistic." The local plant and town's principle employer had recently closed, signaling a mass exodus of locals to neighboring cities and states. Cyrus and his entourage escaped Hull quietly, nearly bankrupting the city by embezzling money from the government's coffers.

By the time the autarkis arrived in Iowa, Carroll was practically deserted. The core members settled in, but the remainder waited in neighboring cities and towns because the local herd could never sustain them. Then, Cyrus and his scattered cohorts began their new and highly ambitious project... *Serapis Ex Machina*.

Forget the cults dedicated to the self-castrating priests of Cybele or the mysteries of Isis. *Serapis Ex Machina* is mother to a brand-new and fabricated religion. Cyrus chose the name from the Greek-Egyptian god Serapis, an entity manufactured by the Greek rulers of Egypt, the Ptolemys, who built a common deity that would unite the Egyptians and Greeks, and maintain civic order. Philosophers and poets created Serapis by studying and then borrowing from a wide field of values and outlooks to create a unifying theme between the two peoples. Serapis was the Frankenstein's monster of gods. Building from this lesson, *Serapis Ex Machina* decided that the ultimate corporation was organized religion. Cyrus surrounded himself with the brightest autarkis he could find, combining his business savvy with Toreador aesthetics, Lasombra organizational tact, Malkavian inspiration and Nosferatu faith and scholarly acumen. They studied and debated the strengths and weaknesses of the different religions, hoping to learn from their mistakes.

Tonight's faiths, they determined, labored under a history of atrocities, hatreds and twisted interpretations. To establish a wide-base appeal, however, *Serapis Ex Machina* still required "God" so as not to alienate potential adherents. What they needed was a different messiah, one who already existed and died, one few could question directly. They decided that Apollonius of Tyana was perfect messianic figurehead, since few existing records could dispute his actions (unlike Mithras) and because he remained untouched by the established influence of the monolithic institutions of Christianity, Judaism or Islam. Apollonius was also reputedly born on December 24th, meaning that adherents could still celebrate Christmas and remain a part of Christian practices. Additionally, Apollonius' embrace of Buddhist philosophy, vegetarianism and yoga (according to the cult) would easily attract those interested in New Age and Far East philosophies. Through Philostratus' texts, Cyrus and his brood then created the Apollonius Bible, complete with numerous contradictions and obscure phrasing for the purposes of debate.

Serapis Ex Machina has used its ill-gotten gains to fund the formation of several temples and monasteries to Apollonius' way of life through dummy corporations a mile deep. The group even influenced the priest of Carroll's beleaguered church to follow Apollonius (through visions and "suggestions") dragging the congregation of destitute townsfolk along as well. These new adherents are now employees and ministers-in-training of the Apolloniun faith, and they will eventually head the monasteries and temples being built elsewhere. Some are even New York- and LA-bound where they plan to open teen shelters to siphon lost souls to the principle temple in Carroll, Iowa.

Outwardly, the Apolloniun Church espouses the principle tenets of Christianity. It even welcomes Jesus as brother and one in a long line of messiahs, but it says that Apollonius continued where Christ had left off. In fact, the newly ordained ministers of this faith even believe that Apollonius may have been Christ returned after the Resurrection. Currently, though, the religion is still "under construction" and months away from becoming public. Nobody knows yet that it exists. *Serapis Ex Machina*'s business plan is to turn Apollonius' teachings into a new brand of belief savvy to the needs of the modern word, with 1-976-hotline confessionals, Internet mass offered via webcams, PDF Bibles, CDs of Apollonius Temple Maidens chanting, videocassettes for Apollonius Yoga-Prayer Techniques and vegan cookbooks. Cyrus' coterie has already copyrighted Apollonius-specific terms, and it plans to launch the religion through late-night television advertising and infomercial blitzes. By then, the new temples will be open, the Internet sites will be on line, and Carroll will be ready to receive the influx of lost souls journeying to the mouth of wisdom. Instead of trying to "manipulate" millions or create blood-cults, *Serapis Ex Machina* is in it for the money and independence. This is a business like any other, and the score of Kindred involved with the project nationwide have no wish to become gods or prophets.

Tonight, the atmosphere of Carroll, Iowa is as unsettling as the ominous serenity before a storm. A bevy of construction sites dot the townscape, and those citizens who have not converted keep their mouths shut. Many townsfolk have fallen for the new religion partly out of desperation, partly because of the promise of employment and partly through Cainite-style influence. Community leaders including the temple ministers undergo a blood bond, if only to help keep the locals in line through their devotion. The worshippers of Apollonius are not violent, but nobody wants to spook the new "investors" who are promising to employ folks regardless of their religious affiliations. Some locals find the sudden birth of this cult scary, but they stay quiet for the sake of feeding their families. Cyrus does not even lift a finger to silence any dissidents. The townsfolk do it for him through social pressures. The Apollonius Temple is still being built, but mass takes place in the converted church. Two warehouses in the old automotive plant also contain thousands of boxes with Apollonius-related products, from books to videocassettes and CDs, all ready to be shipped out a week before the launch.

Currently, *Serapis Ex Machina* claims the abandoned automotive plant as its haven, and the members have set booby traps for any intruders. Due to a population count of just over 10,000 people, Cyrus requires the other four Cainites with him to slake their thirst with animal blood lest they tax the herd too heavily before it can support them. Cyrus hopes that once the religion launches, enough people will flock to Carroll to support the autarkis there.

Serapis Ex Machina already possesses its share of enemies. Cyrus' theft of Hull's budget did not escape the attention of Ottawa's Nosferatu prince. Unfortunately, that prince allowed the autarkis Cyrus and his cohorts unsupervised movement in Hull, which means that the theft reflects badly on him. Rather than report the incident to the Inner Circle, the prince is privately funding volunteers to investigate the matter quietly and to find Cyrus wherever he is hiding. Additionally, a member of the Society of Leopold recently heard about the suspicious behavior of Carroll's priest and its entire congregation. Given the recent explosion of blood cults and heresies, the Society is investigating the matter. Whether the group merely discovers the presence of Cyrus and other autarkis is debatable since the Cainites are not assuming positions of spiritual power or importance. They are in it for the business, not the adoration, which could throw the mortal Inquisition off.

Because Carroll is not entirely isolated from the world, some townsfolk are trying to convert relatives and friends elsewhere despite the main temple's requests for secrecy at this time. Mortal watchdog groups concerned with cult activities are hearing rumors about this cult-like behavior, but these organizations already have their hands full with similar reports from around North America. The Camarilla, however, also watches the watchdogs in case they encounter breaches of the Masquerade. While Carroll, Iowa does not warrant the full investigative brunt of justicars and archons, the Camarilla is considering sending in a small, scouting coterie to determine any potential vampiric involvement. What they do not realize, however, is that Carroll itself barely supports five Kindred, meaning one to three autarkis from *Serapis Ex Machina* are scattered throughout all neighboring cities and towns, acting as early-warning sentries. Any Kindred or Cainites fishing for information on Carroll in an adjacent district will probably attract the attention of at least one sentry, allowing Cyrus and the others to hide.

Despite all this attention, *Serapis Ex Machina*'s greatest enemy is its own ambition. All this preparation has emptied the group's coffers, nearly bankrupting the religion months before its launch. Cyrus and his cohorts are planning several smaller scams to keep *Serapis Ex Machina* operating for a few months, but they lack the time to pursue these ventures subtly and diligently. Kindred in nearby cities may notice an unknown Kindred skulking about, and local populations are small enough that *any* new Kindred is likely unknown. Even Kindred in cities far from Carroll but renowned for their finance may notice their own influences and resources challenged, funneled back to… well, eventually Carroll. In some instances, it even appears as though someone sloppily used Dominate to simply order people to give them donations for some organization or another — again, all headed back to Carroll.

The Tapestry

Some secrets are a terrible burden that only a chosen few can carry. What happens, however, when even the secret's bearers are ignorant of the truth that they possess? Synonymous with ancient Alexandria was the Great Library, the largest repository of written words in the ancient world, as well as a center of learning. Founded between 300 to 290 BC, the Great Library's charter allowed it to search all ships berthed at the port and uncover and copy any original texts. It then returned these copies to the owners while storing the originals at the Mouseion, or main library.

After Julius Caesar laid siege to Alexandria and nearly destroyed 70,000 scrolls in a blaze, a group of Cainites decided to take additional measures to protect the more valuable arcane texts. After months of debating, the Alexandrine Cainites finally arrived at a set of books that they deemed important to mortals and Cainites alike. These works spoke of eldritch divinities and a coming darkness. They spoke of the world's true face and chthonian entities that swam below the seas of consciousness. For their own reasons, the Cainites chose works that they believed were grave truths and necessary for future survival. So, with the help of Tzimisce *koldun* from the distant Carpathians, they developed a ritual to protect these scrolls by linking them to Cainite *saiti*, divine custodians. The rituals ensured that should certain key texts in the Mouseion fall to destruction, then the contents of that particular scroll would manifest in a *saiti* for safekeeping until such a time when she could transcribe them elsewhere. Unfortunately, while the texts remained safe from harm for a time, each disaster that claimed the city, whether by invaders or local riots, also killed off the rare *saiti*. Even worse, when the Great Library suffered its final indignity in AD 624 at the hands of Muslims and fell to the flames, the destroyed texts did not manifest on those *saiti* who survived Alexandria's fall. The entire process appeared to be a failure, and the attempt eventually fell from the memories of most Cainites.

Matters changed in 1978, when the FBI first used an argon laser beam for fine fingerprint analysis, which would help in identification of old fingerprint residues. A few Kindred, however, worried that this technique would finally uncover a vampire's prints. Previously, Cainites rarely left complete prints behind since they do not secrete oily residues normal in mortals. The argon laser, however, picked up any faint trace normally invisible to standard operating procedure of the time. Unfortunately, these worried Kindred could not act until the late '80s, when computer technology facilitated the notion of remote crimes. The Inner Circle used its best hackers (and even Embraced a couple for the job) to infiltrate the FBI's Identification Division, search through any files potentially relating to Masquerade breaches and eliminate the evidence. It proved a failure since the FBI kept copies of stored data, but the hackers did discover a series of separate Federal investigations dealing with "script-prints" that they had recently uncovered. The argon laser proved sensitive enough to detect vampiric fingerprints, but it also registered several cases where the print ridges appeared to be compacted script. The resolution was not high enough to determine the actual text, but the Kindred moles surmised that the discovery bore some great significance. The hackers copied the information weeks before the NSA stepped in and claimed jurisdiction under the blanket aegis, "It's a matter of national security."

The matter made it to the attention of the Inner Circle, which tasked the Tremere with investigating the unusual prints given that clan's facility with the arcane. The Warlocks, in turn, spent years tracking down any relevant information they could find, calling in boons and even secretly approaching sympathetic factions among Noddist Sabbat. After considerable investigative work, the Tremere finally found an Alexandrine Setite named Hussan who knew portions of the story through the tales of his sire and grandsire. Afterward, the Tremere surmised that the ritual to protect the scrolls worked, but in a manner undetectable to the vampires of that time. The script not only manifested in their fingerprints, but when a *saiti* sired a childe, their progeny also became *saiti* as well, carrying on the responsibility unknowingly. This feature, it seems, came about thanks to the Tzimisce *koldun*, who were assumed to have used some fleshcrafting component in creating the ritual. This transfer of obligation proved worse in Sabbat cities where the descendent of a *saiti* would dispatch the script into a multitude of progeny. In fact, thanks to the Sabbat, some scrolls actually survived into the modern nights even though dozens probably died along with the last Cainite of certain *saiti* lineages. Through their investigations, the Tremere determined that these "carriers" possessed long-lost information, and they were in the process of compiling an index of Alexandrine descendants in the Camarilla when someone stole their master list. They never determined who did it.

Elsewhere in 1996, Beirut's Kindred were recovering from a rocky three decades of war. Among the hardened survivors was Sedirah Milhim, a harpy of the local Kindred, and preeminent among the city's Mushakis (Brujah). Surprisingly, despite the religious strife that marked the conflict, Beirut's Kindred were a tightly knit faction. The mortal conflict had degenerated into a maelstrom of violence, and soon, nobody knew who they were fighting anymore. Indiscriminate sniper and mortar attacks wreaked havoc with everyone's lives and unlives, and when the Israelis stepped into the mess, all hell broke loose. If the Kindred took sides initially, they abandoned that strategy in favor of survival and non-aggression pacts with other vampires. Following the war, many of Beirut's Kindred knew and bore a wary respect for one another, so when several strange vampires appeared in the city and reported directly to the region's prince, everyone knew about it within an hour. When Sedirah received a strange phone call from the prince's aide-de-camp telling her to go underground now and hide, she did so without question.

Sedirah's existence turned instantly turbulent, which was no mean feat for someone of her experiences. The prince issued a blood hunt for her, grudgingly and without reason, and he told the local Kindred to cooperate with the gloved and mysterious visitors. Sedirah managed to hide in secure havens that she used throughout the war, and with the help of allies who "overlooked" her potential hiding spots, eluded the visitors who eventually left. The blood hunt continued with some local and many visiting Kindred (who were eager to commit the Amaranth) on her trail. Sedirah, however, possessed enough allies to survive the following months. Eventually, a visiting Nosferatu found her, but not with the intention of committing diablerie. The Sewer Rat, named Ethan Fouri, told Sedirah about the strange script she bore in her fingerprints, and how he shared them as well. The Tremere, while missing the master register of Kindred targets, still possessed enough information to hunt key individuals whom they knew were *saiti*. With blessing from the Inner Council (which apparently believed that the *saiti* carried dangerous information), the Tremere approached target cities and placed confirmed "carriers" (as they called them) under a blood hunt through the prince.

The *saiti*, however, were not alone. The "someone" who stole the master register did so after realizing that he bore the script-print as well. While the Tremere knew nothing of him, this secret patron warned as many *saiti* as possible to vanish underground. The Tremere, however, were still beating him to some targets, as in Sedirah's case. Fortunately, the Tremere have been trying to keep matters low-key by approaching each prince privately. Were various cities to suddenly discover the flurry of multiple blood hunts, many might question the reasons. Therefore, targets of this directed Lextalionis rarely appear on records outside the city, so carriers can escape the hunt by leaving their domains and traveling far away.

With little choice in their fate, Sedirah and Ethan have traveled the world for the last few years, guided by their mysterious patron's missives, seeking others like themselves for mutual protection, trying to salvage this ancient knowledge that has supposedly condemned them. They are not the only *saiti* coterie out there, but Sedirah and Ethan are making the most concerted efforts of creating a network of alliances with other cells and uncovering the truth. Sadly, they do not possess the technical acumen to access equipment sensitive enough to read or record the delicate script (like electron microscopes and laser scanners), unless they break into a major research facility or protected law-enforcement bureau and force someone to help them. Doing so, however, would undoubtedly earn them the attention of their Tremere hounds.

Currently, the coteries and individual *saiti* are gathering in Britain, Germany, France and North America where they have the best chance of finding the necessary equipment to transcribe their entire print scripts and translate it from whatever ancient tongue marked the original scrolls. Sedirah's and Ethan's main challenge, aside from being virtual autarkis, is that despite their efforts to unite and pool the *saiti*'s resources, many refuse to cooperate or even meet with others of their kind. A foolish few met Final Death or other, less final but no more pleasant, fates when they turned themselves over to the local prince in exchange for leniency. Others believe that they can survive on their own rather than joining a coterie and presenting the Tremere with an easy target. Several are just too paranoid to trust anyone anymore, and most of these examples belong to the Camarilla. Sedirah and Ethan are loath to consider the number of Sabbat *saiti* they will never reach. None of them want the Sabbat to find out about the script for fear that the sect will uncover the *saiti*'s secrets and use it in the war against the Camarilla.

Unlike most cults, groups and organizations, the *saiti* are isolated and barely able to survive. The *saiti* have no center of operation, and the two strongest leaders, Sedirah and Ethan, are currently traveling across the United States wholly incognito. The patron remains a mystery, but he does maintain a private digital archive protected by a surprisingly complex firewall (password: *saiti bennu*, which is the phonetic transliteration of the hieroglyph for Divine Custodian of the Phoenix). The archive is little more than an update on where the Tremere hunters are concentrating their efforts, any potential leads into the meaning of scriptridge passages, and information on any *saiti* currently alone who needs help fast. (Whether someone chooses to help is another matter.) The patron offers access to this site only once a *saiti* goes underground. How he stays ahead of the Tremere, knows which *saiti* is a traitor or not (which has happened), or knows about their activities remains unknown, but the fact that he can make these distinctions does signify that he is at least an elder, if not older.

Unbeknownst to Sedirah or the other *saiti*, the mysterious hunters who ordered the initial blood hunt

by sanction of the Inner Council and harangued the carriers across the Middle East, North America and Europe are not actually Tremere. They are six alastors assigned to this case directly, and while they might not conduct the hunt themselves, they oversee the chase with the help of local chantries. Most Tremere, including the order of Pontifices, however, know nothing of the script itself. The alastors carry the seal of the Inner Council and the Tremere Council of Seven, meaning that they have carte blanche when requesting assistance from the clan of Warlocks. Few can challenge or question their authority save another justicar or archon. These alastors are exceptionally potent in political power and authority, and the *saiti* patron is one of them. His own proficiency with Thaumaturgy hides his ridges and his position keeps the other *saiti* safe… for now.

The Cold Man's Children

This innocuous name hides a particularly dangerous little group. During the '60s, a Cainite named William Loddard stalked the members of a small new-age commune. Loddard had been a member of the Sabbat, until the rest of his pack died. Rumors among the Sabbat claim that Loddard had been appointed lookout and had failed to warn the others of approaching danger. Since that time, Loddard went autarkis and preyed only on groups. He would select a likely group, usually small and isolated, and then observe them for months, eavesdropping on their meetings, spying on their nightly activities and learning all of their habits and routines and secrets. In his own mind, Loddard symbolically become a member of the group, filling the void left by the death of his pack. Then, when Loddard felt comfortable as an unseen member of the unit, he would burst into their midst and kill them all, completing the cycle. But this time, a strange thing happened to him. While listening to his herd of vessels-to-be talk about religion, Loddard found himself pitying them. The group consisted of atheists and agnostics, all searching for a higher purpose and a sign of the divine, and they were all becoming disillusioned since nothing miraculous had ever occurred to them. He discovered a sympathy for their plight, similar to his own musings over the ultimate meaning of existence, and their growing doubt matched his own despair at the repeated loss of his small family, as if each time he were begging for an intervention that never came. One night, Loddard listened in on a commune gathering, held in its meeting hall. He watched as the commune's leaders turned to each religious symbol in turn — they had large versions of several major symbols on the wall, in the hopes that these would focus their efforts and perhaps attract attention from the deities in question — and prayed for a sign. Something snapped in Loddard, and he leapt from his hiding place, burst into the room, ripped the man-sized crucifix from the wall, tore it to bits and threw it aside. Then he drew himself up to his full height, awing the commune, and announced, "You prayed for the divine, and I have answered." Half of the commune fainted. Several tried to run. But the remainder fell to their knees and thanked him for finally appearing before them.

Naturally things did not stay this simple. After waking up, many of the commune members refused to believe Loddard's claim of divinity. Many accused him of being a charlatan, while others claimed that he must be some sort of monster, preying upon their weakness in order to gain power over them. Loddard killed the first one of these unbelievers by snapping his neck and tossing him through a window, but he realized that such violence would not strengthen his case. Instead, he instructed the commune members to observe him closely. One of them had been a medical student, and the young man quickly realized that Loddard did not have a pulse, or a heartbeat. This realization stunned the commune members. Several still insisted that he was a monster, but the cries of charlatanism disappeared. Loddard acknowledged their concerns and vowed that he would not hurt any of them. Those who wished to leave were free to do so, but those who wished to stay were welcome, and he swore to watch over them as a loving father would his own children. He did not tell them of his vampiric nature, of course. Instead he called himself the Cold Man and claimed to be a creature of nature, the darker side of the cycle, which included death and decay and led to rebirth. Loddard insisted that he only wanted to protect the commune, and he announced that he would demand nothing in return but love, obedience and an occasional offering of blood to warm his cold body. But in return, he would grant them his divine blood and his favor, and he would guide them to redemption. Weeks passed before the commune leaders reached a decision. Several members departed, and Loddard allowed them to leave. With each departure, though, the faith of the remainder grew stronger, for their avatar had demonstrated his mercy and his honor. At last, the leaders agreed that the Cold Man was clearly divine, and clearly beneficent. Those remaining members who doubted were asked to leave. Fifteen stayed behind, and thus the Cold Man's Children were born.

The group has now grown to outlandish size with 82 members, all ghouls to Loddard. They believe fervently in the Cold Man's divinity, and they will defend their leader against any who belittle him or question his existence. Loddard has instructed them to bring other believers to him, that he may extract their offering and share with them his divine strength. Over the decades, he has come to believe his own hype, and he now genuinely thinks of himself as the Cold Man, god and deliverer.

The Cold Man's purpose is simple — to save his "children" and guide them to eternal life. Unfortunately, eternal life is not the province of the Cold Man. His realm is the night, and his strength is a gift from Mother Earth and Father Death. Therefore, his Children are instructed to search for the answer themselves, by scouring the mortal coil for every trace of the divine and the miraculous. Children of the Cold Man are distinguished by their nocturnal schedules, their unusual strength and their lack of proselytism. They do offer pamphlets in various stores (particularly new-age stores and nightclubs), but they do not preach, they do not go door-to-door, and they will not beg someone to come to their commune. Only true Children are welcome in the commune, and those will choose to enter without being forced to it. This tactic apparently works, for the Children's numbers are slowly growing, and many of the anarchs in Northern California area know of them. The Cold Man's Children all wear his sigil — a small marble replica of his face, complete with ruby eyes — but otherwise, they wear any type of clothing they like.

The Cold Man's Children still inhabit the same commune they did in the '60s, located near San Jose. The compound has expanded to fit their increased numbers, and it is now largely self-sufficient. Members do travel to San Jose on a regular basis. Some have night jobs, others sell fruits and vegetables and crafts from roadside trucks, and the remainder travel the highways in search of fellow Children and in search of miracles. They are insatiably curious about other religions, about faith healers, about amazing new cures or about anything else that carries a hint of the unexplained. The Cold Man himself stays in his haven at the compound, in which the Children have constructed a windowless room at the back of the meeting hall to serve as his chamber. During the day, he rests and "communes with nature," restoring his strength and considering the best path for his children. At night the Cold Man rises, bestows a blessing on his flock, then grants audience to any Children who wish to speak with him. (Once a month, this blessing involves taking blood from each of the Children in turn and replacing it with some of his own, thus renewing their cyclical bond.) He listens to the Children's problems, offers direction and imparts his strength to bring them closer to the divine. He also listens to the information that they have gathered the previous night, and he advises which stories should be pursued and which are merely urban legends or outright fabrications.

The Cold Man's Children are not normally dangerous. However, if they are threatened, they have been granted permission to defend themselves with deadly force. They may also attack anyone who is destroying a potentially "miraculous" event (for example, someone assaulting a "faith healer," or polluting a "fountain of youth"). Some of the Children are provoked to violence by insults to the Cold Man, but such is the case only in extreme situations, as the Children have been taught to view other opinions with tolerance.

The Cold Man's Children are well known to other religious groups in the area. Children routinely attend various services, in the hopes of finding clues of eternal life. They tend to be quiet, respectful and very attentive during services and sermons. The Cold Man's Children also seek out proselytizers and listen patiently to every argument that would-be converters put forth, even suffering long-winded diatribes and accepting every stray scrap of literature. Yet, their tolerance and attentiveness extends only so far. Despite their almost universal acceptance of other religions, the Children consider the Jehovah's Witnesses to be merely brainwashers who are interested not in religious truth but in mundane control and temporal power. The Witnesses, for their part, view the Children as arrogant, condescending cultists, who ignore the truth in order to stay wrapped in their delusion. The two groups regard one another with antipathy, and some Witnesses carry pepper spray to use against any particularly fervent Children they might encounter.

Of course, the Children have their share of enemies among the Damned. Local Sabbat are amused by Loddard's conceit, and they applaud his scheme to create a protective herd of followers. Most Camarilla members do not know of the Cold Man and his Children (and of those who do, few realize that the Cold Man is a Cainite), but the handful who know consider this a gross violation of the Masquerade. The prince of San Francisco (the nearest actual princedom) has his hands full fighting Cathayans, and he has ignored all reports about the Cold Man, assuming that the cult is harmless and most likely devoted to some graven image. Other vampires in the area are more concerned, but few are so foolish as to attack such a large group of ghouls without major support. The Cold Man has also warned his Children about the undead, calling them renegade children of Father Death, his bastard half-siblings, and stating that they are jealous of his power and divine authority. Most of the Children have never encountered another vampire, but those who have back away quickly, either to inform the Cold Man or to return with a larger group.

Of late, the Children have become more active in their search, expanding the area they explore and investigating even the wildest and thinnest of rumors. They are also more insistent with people. They take even the slightest interest as wholehearted agreement, and they assume that a polite listen is indicative of a person's complete support of their goals and methods. Whether the Cold Man has stepped up the pressure to find his other Children and attain eternal life, or the Children themselves simply see the need to increase their numbers and speed up the process, no one is certain. But more and more mortals are being enticed into the commune, and they are stepping back out as full Children, bound to the Cold Man by ties of blood.

The Questing Beast

Myths exist among even such occult creatures as the Kindred, and one of the most long-standing subjects is Golconda, a state of mystical transcendence for vampires. The legends claim that Kindred who have attained Golconda are no longer subservient to the Beast but instead control it and find balance with their undead existence. Few have achieved such equanimity, and fewer still will talk about it. Golconda is an attainable goal for some and a fairy tale for most.

For the Questing Beast, however, it is an endless pursuit and a reason for existence.

This group came to be when a Kindred named Jenna Benjamin began a quest for Golconda, in the 17th century. Jenna had been a member of the Camarilla, an esteemed member of the Ventrue and a true plotter, willing to sacrifice anyone and everyone for the sake of her own ambitions. None of that changed, but Jenna began to find the Camarilla small and insular, with Kindred always fighting against their appetites and battling down their rage and fear. Jenna wished to move beyond that, to become one with her appetites, one with her anger and her fear, in order to be stronger than those around her. Jenna had never wanted a princedom — too many mundane responsibilities — and she still did not, but at the same time, she could no longer stomach subservience to arbitrarily named princes or even justicars. So she left the Camarilla and struck out on her own, searching for the path to true contentment.

Two decades later, Jenna encountered a Ravnos named Miguel. Miguel had walked away from Kindred society, and begun to wander in search of something he could not name but which Jenna recognized as Golconda as she saw it. Upon meeting, the two of them felt their kinship, and they resolved to travel together for a time. As they traveled, Jenna and Miguel discovered something that would inhibit their ability to attain their vaunted goal — they hated one another. Every attitude, every belief, every method proved different, almost exactly so. Despite their common goal, the two could not stand being together, so they parted, promising to keep in touch.

Over the years that followed, Jenna and Miguel cooperated on only one thing — to find Golconda. They pursued rumors and chased down legends, sharing their information and their thoughts on the next step, and while many leads became dead ends, others led in new and unexpected directions. From time to time, they encountered others with the same goal, and each one was welcomed to share information as well. Some refused, but others accepted, and the distances between them gradually shrank. Members worked together more closely in order to act on new information more easily, until finally all the seekers were traveling together. And the Questing Beast took form.

The Questing Beast currently has a half-dozen members, and a few others keep in contact with it. It travels as a group, moving from place to place, investigating Golconda, seeking out those Cainites who are rumored to have attained it, hunting up ancient texts claimed to describe it and locating places and artifacts said to embody it.

Upon joining the Questing Beast, most of its Kindred set aside their old prejudices. Golconda is more important than petty concerns of clan or sect. A Lasombra works alongside a Ventrue without qualm, and an Assamite teams with a Tremere if it will help reveal important information. Golconda, after all, is not a medal or a plaque. It can be shared by all present, and if one member of the Questing Beast reaches Golconda, hopefully he can help guide the others there. This is not to say that enmities do not exist, but they are personal rather than cultural. Jenna and Miguel continue to dislike each other, but it is because they disagree on everything, not because one was a Camarilla Ventrue and the other an independent Ravnos. Old party lines no longer matter — they have been outgrown. Jyhad is no longer a concern, as the Questing Beast hopes to acquire contentment for its existence. If they can do so, they can accept their end with equanimity whenever it occurs. Many of them also feel that the Antediluvians will no longer pose a threat to them, and thus Gehenna is also beneath them.

Most vampires, of course, know nothing of the Questing Beast. Rumors do exist, and a handful of elders joke at their expense, but to others, the Questing Beast is a mere folk tale, or perhaps a symbol of vampiric folly and obsession. Those who do know the stories to be true often agree. After all, Golconda is a very personal achievement, something based upon an individual's own attitude and enlightenment. How could a group possibly achieve that? The very notion of a group striving together for personal revelation is laughable, and some old allies of Questing Beast members have tried to explain this to their misguided peers, stating that a group effort may be counterproductive for such an endeavor. Unfortunately, the Questing Beast considers itself above the advice of others (unless they have already achieved Golconda), and it believes that the group effort increases each group member's chances. The group also does not bother to announce itself, feeling that those who wish to know them will already have heard of them, which contributes to the lack of attention.

One exception to this wave of ignorance is a pair of Methuselahs that the cult approached almost a century ago. These Methuselahs are well aware of the Questing Beast, and they despise it utterly, for two reasons. First, the Questing Beast strives toward Golconda, while they do not — the Methuselahs seek power over peace, dominance above contentment. Second, the Questing Beast interfered with their plans when it approached them many years ago. Millennia-old plans for fighting the Jyhad were disturbed by the small band's investigations, plots were uncovered, and pieces were shifted without warning, all in the name of the cult and at the expense of the Methuselahs. Therefore, this ancient pair opposes the Questing Beast at every turn. Sometimes they send Kindred to harry the group, but other times they take a more devious approach. They plant false clues for the Questing Beast to find — clues that lead in an endless circle so that the group can never escape, never arrive at an answer and never interfere in critical areas. Between the Methuselahs, misleading the cult has become a game unto itself, seeing who can distract the Questing Beast more and longer.

The other Kindred who know of the Questing Beast are the Inconnu. The two groups are similar in that both have stepped away from the Jyhad, both have their own interests, and both dislike outside interference. The difference is that the Inconnu generally avoid other vampires, and vampiric society, in order to handle their affairs privately. The Inconnu do not have a set goal or common interest beyond remaining free to pursue their own interests. The Questing Beast, on the other hand, has a definite common purpose — to reach Golconda. Several Inconnu are whispered to have already attained Golconda, and the Questing Beast often seeks out those vampires for information and guidance. While most of the Inconnu dislike such fanfare, a few have agreed to speak with the group. Such discussions have proven unhelpful, however. The Questing Beast has a very set idea of what Golconda is and how to achieve it, and even being told a different route by someone who has already attained the prize cannot convince its members to change their methods.

The Questing Beast is dangerous, despite its lack of interest in lesser affairs, or perhaps because of it. The group will not hesitate to destroy any nonmember in its way (including old allies and friends) should such be necessary to protect a secret or unearth one. Only the goal remains; all other ties are ultimately meaningless. Even the Masquerade could be set aside, if that becomes necessary for Golconda, and mortals are at risk just as much as Kindred.

The Darwin Society

Sometimes the most unassuming of names can conceal the most bizarre — and dangerous — of groups.

> #### Methuselahs?
> The two Kindred who specifically oppose the Questing Beast have been left unnamed deliberately, to better fit the group into a chronicle that might benefit from the addition of a meddlesome group of self-righteous Kindred. They need not even be Methuselahs — they can be any Kindred who were slighted or had their plans ruined by interference from the Questing Beast. Methuselahs are named to give the small cult a role on the Ancients' field of Jyhad, but feel free to make them the bearers of a mere vendetta should such a large scale be unnecessary.

The Darwin Society began as a mortal organization, a college club dedicated to debating social philosophy and discussing what "survival of the fittest" actually entailed. Then one night, a Malkavian Embraced one of the members, a young graduate student named Palmer Ward. The Malkavian envied Palmer's intelligence and thought that he might become a gifted protégé, once he was suitably twisted. Two weeks later, however, the Malkavian did not appear at their appointed meeting place. It would be months before Palmer discovered that his sire had perished in a fire, possibly one set by the Malkavian himself. For several weeks, Palmer survived on his own. He was smart enough to avoid killing his victims, so he could keep his existence a secret while he gained strength and debated his next course of action.

Two months after his disappearance, Palmer returned to his old friends at the Darwin Society. He ignored their questions concerning his whereabouts, stating only that he had been studying survival firsthand. As the night wore on, Palmer turned the debate to the question of limits and constraints, including morals. He posed the question, "When does one set aside morals in favor of pragmatism?" Then, while the others discussed the topic, he grabbed the nearest of his former peers and sank his fangs into her neck. As the others watched, too stunned to move, Palmer Embraced the woman. Then he turned to the next in line. By the time any of them thought to act, it was too late.

Upon awakening, the 12 fledglings were greeted by Palmer, who informed them that a true survival test had begun, only four of them would be allowed to survive the night. Mayhem ensued. When the blood settled, five were left standing, but after a quick consultation, two of them ganged up on another, and then there were four.

Palmer appreciated the outcome, and he applauded his surviving childer. He and his four remaining progeny reestablished the Darwin Society, only now with a practical side — survival for themselves. The Sabbat heard of this little bloodbath and invited the club to join them. Since strength existed in numbers, the Society agreed. All five survived the initiation, and they became Sabbat.

But after 10 years, the Society felt that something was missing. The Cainites had grown stronger, more comfortable with their new existence, and they had carved out a small niche for themselves amid the Sabbat. However, their chances for continued survival were low due to the chaotic nature of the Sabbat itself, its sudden shifts in leadership and the growing rumors of warfare between Sabbat and Camarilla that had been planned for the East Coast. To guarantee survival, an edge proved necessary. The Society debated for several months and finally arrived at a conclusion: It would be safer among the Camarilla.

Knowing that it would be impossible to conceal its defection from fellow Sabbat, the Society left town and relocated to another city in another state. It deliberately chose a non-college town to the south because college students often migrated to such places during class breaks, which allowed a perfect cover for the group's own arrival and also allowed the young-looking vampires to blend in. Their new location fell within a Camarilla domain, and the Society members presented themselves to the local prince, claiming to be fledglings. They gave false names for themselves and did not mention their society or previous location. The youthful group impressed the prince with their tight bond and apparent enthusiasm for membership, and he acknowledged them, granting permission to reside in the city. Consequently, they were now considered Camarilla. The Society members had also done their research on the prince before presenting themselves, and they had learned from other Kindred in the area that this particular prince held a relaxed attitude toward newcomers and toward movement within the area. He also did not require blood bonds of Kindred in his domain.

For 10 years, the Darwin Society continued to play the loyal, if somewhat passive, Camarilla coterie. The coterie avoided the politics, preferring to remain neutral and ignoring games of prestation as that would simply create enemies for them. But after a decade, the Darwin Society members decided that perhaps they had been incorrect, and that their odds for survival were higher with the Sabbat. Their reasoning was that, while the Camarilla had higher numbers and more structure, the Sabbat provided a more close-knit organization and more leeway in a pack's behavior. The threat of Camarilla politics was also growing. The Society members knew that they could not stay out of that arena forever, and once they were forced to enter politics, they would acquire enemies within the sect in addition to those without. Therefore, they returned to their original town and were surprised to be greeted with relief by the Sabbat there. Apparently, a large skirmish had occurred right after they had departed, and the Sabbat had assumed the Society to be among those destroyed. The Society members quickly claimed to have been wounded and been forced to spend the last 10 years hiding and recovering. Since they had left the area, no reports had surfaced of their stint in the Camarilla, and the Society found itself once again a Sabbat pack in good standing.

The Society quickly realized that it would need to make a decision, however. The Sabbat proved more fervent and more tightly knit but smaller in numbers, and while movement between locations was open, the very closeness of the packs meant that everyone knew what everyone else was doing. The Camarilla had more members and more freedom of movement within each domain, but weaker bonds and more political infighting. Both sides had strengths and weaknesses. But which offered a better chance for survival? Ultimately, the Society decided that its best option lay in choosing both sides. The Cainites mentioned a desire to wander the countryside, and several months later, when classes ended, the Society took to the road. They returned to the Camarilla city via a circuitous route, just in time for summer school. The prince asked after their absence, of course, and the Society Kindred told him the truth. They had been traveling in order to avoid becoming too rooted to one spot and thus inflexible. Fortunately for them, the Society members were skilled debaters, and they convinced their prince (who, honestly, had not been overly concerned).

Since this time, the Society has led a double unlife. Every six months, it switches locations. In one, the vampires are loyal nomadic Sabbat members who occasionally settle. In the other, they are loyal Camarillists who sometimes undertake "research trips" for their own purposes. In the Sabbat, they are known as the Darwin Society. To the Camarilla, they are merely a nameless coterie of Malkavians. The two locations are far enough apart that only one other vampire has ever been to both — and she suffered an unfortunate accident her first night in the Sabbat town, which conveniently prevented her from recognizing the Camarilla coterie she had met weeks before. The Society is playing a dangerous game. If either side discovers its dual sect membership, the Cainites will probably be branded as traitors to both sects and hunted down immediately. If both sides learn of the duplicity, the Society could be attacked from two fronts, and it will have no safe haven. For the time being, though, the deception holds.

When in Sabbat territory, the Darwin Society behaves as a proper Sabbat pack. The members gleefully prey on mortals, they light fires at rallies, and they even participate in intellectual Games of Instinct with an amicably rival pack of Tzimisce and Lasombra. They also attend pack meetings and *ritae* in the area. When it is in its Camarilla city, the Society hides its true nature, taking only enough blood from victims to survive and explain away the attack, upholding the Masquerade and participating in any actions that the prince requires (such as the occasional blood hunt). Indeed, the Society members have earned a reputation in both locations as fierce ideological defenders of their (current) sect. They argue strongly in favor of their sect's "dogma" and methodology, always leap to oppose any of the other sect who have wandered in and insist that the only good member of the (current) opposition is a truly dead one. They do so for self-preservation, of course. Supporting the sect makes it unlikely that they will be accused of defecting, and destroyed vampires cannot reveal their secret. Meanwhile, the Society is making itself an expert in both sides, learning everything it can about the two major sects. Doing so helps the members play their dual role more effectively, but it also gives them information to trade (or blackmail with) if necessary.

The Darwin Society is not interested in politics. It really does not care which side wins. Its members do believe in the existence of the Antediluvians, and they worry about those Ancients and their plans, but the Society feels that it is strengthening itself against any eventuality. If Gehenna does occur, it will choose whichever side is strongest at the time, and ultimately the members will fend for themselves within that group. The only important thing is continued survival, and in order to survive, they will do whatever is necessary. The one thing the Society will not do is blood bond to any outsiders. They are willing to observe the Vaulderie as a pack, but being forced to answer to anyone else would limit their options, and they will use every trick and tactic to avoid such a restriction.

Redline

The Camarilla is a society with rules and regulations, therefore, it also has lawbreakers and criminals. Most crimes are minor, and they are punished immediately by loss of prestige, loss of domains or hunting grounds, physical punishment, blood bonds or possibly banishment. Some crimes, however, are too severe for such relatively minor measures. In particular, violating the Masquerade, breaking two or more of the Traditions or diablerizing a fellow Kindred. These three crimes are so offensive that most princes punish those who commit them with blood hunts. A blood hunt is an immediate and full pursuit by all Camarilla Kindred in the area, hopefully (for the aggrieved party) ending in the Final Death of the targeted vampire. Sometimes, though, the target escapes. The Camarilla has an undeniable social network in which each prince shares vital information, and those lawbreakers who escape a blood hunt in one area may find themselves targeted in another, simply as a courtesy from one prince to another.

Not surprisingly, Kindred under a blood hunt are outcast, even from some Sabbat groups. The danger of full-scale Camarilla retaliation is too great to risk for a single Cainite. Many of these vampires have given themselves up, preferring a quick Final Death to decades of pursuit, but others are not that easy. They continue to run and hide, evading pursuit at every turn. In the early 20th century, one such vampire found herself in New Orleans, fleeing a Kindred-directed mob. Upon rounding a corner, however, she ran headfirst into another Kindred who was fleeing the same mob. The two cooperated in escaping the port town, and after the danger had passed, they compared notes. Much to their surprise, they discovered a common bond — both were under blood hunts. Certain possibilities immediately presented themselves.

The two Kindred stayed together, traveling the world and listening for other signs of a blood hunt. In Africa, they found a Nosferatu hiding in a swamp. In France, a rogue Tremere fled the Camarilla's wrath. In Australia, a Lasombra had almost given in to despair. Each time, the growing group invited fellow fugitives to join. The fugitives' goals proved simple — survival, independence and bitter revenge on the Camarilla where they could take it. In each case, the invitee accepted the group's offer.

The new group dubbed itself the Redline. Every member is under a blood hunt, and they all openly defy the Camarilla by maintaining their independence. The Sabbat has offered the Redline membership dozens of times, and it has been refused each invitation. The Redline is not interested in becoming Sabbat or in joining any other organization for that matter. The fugitives were all members of one sect or the other, and they enjoy the fact that their only limits are their own preferences and common sense. Many of them know secrets about the Camarilla and some of its more prestigious members, which they expose when they have the chance. Others are simply powerful Kindred who angered the wrong prince or elder, or who became too much of a risk. But as a unit, the Redline is powerful, stronger than any group it has yet encountered, and its strength lies in its freedom and sense of personal responsibility. The Redline sees itself as an expatriate community, a gathering of Cainites who choose neither the Sabbat nor the Camarilla and yet who still wish for social interaction.

The Redline has an uneasy truce with the Sabbat. Its members will not join the Sabbat, but the Sabbat respects them and has yet to force the issue. Of course, the Sabbat also takes delight in watching the Camarilla confounded, and it can honestly claim no involvement because the Redline is not a member of the Sword of Caine. The Camarilla, for its part, has tried everything it knows — blood hunts, spells, curses, alastors, even bribes. Nothing has blunted the Redline's enmity. For the Redline it is not about politics — the attacks are personal, revenge for being hunted for so long.

Redline members maintain all or most of their old ties. Personal allies, sires, childer and other contacts are all more important than ever, for they provide the Redline's vampires with valuable information and with warning of impending blood hunts and other retribution. Indeed, the Redline seeks out new contact with other Kindred, extending its network to include anyone willing to let them survive as they are. In this way, the Redline grows, because many contacts become allies, and some have even been swayed into joining the Redline themselves to escape the power plays and treacheries of their own sects. The group keeps in frequent contact with its far-flung members, often with notes handwritten on other papers and then mailed or passed to another vampire, who then adds any new information and passes them along again. Despite their informal nature, these "chain letters" are very popular, and they often provide the only source of information that members of the group can rely upon about Camarilla and Sabbat activities.

Lately, the Redline has taken to declaring its own hunts. It will enter an area, target a leading Camarilla member, and launch a vicious campaign of "justice" until that Kindred is dead. The Redline even notifies each target beforehand, sending a message saying that Kindred has been "redlined." They dare the Camarilla to stop them from killing the target in question. Thus far, the Camarilla has failed in every attempt.

The Redline does observe the Masquerade, but only for self-preservation. Mortals are too numerous and too prone to fanaticism to be provoked into hunting Kindred. The Redline ignores the other Traditions, though, seeing them as only a form of Camarilla restriction.

The Redline has no fixed location — to stay in one spot is dangerous and counterproductive. The group is always on the move. Members sometimes go to Sabbat territory to rest and to plan, since the Sabbat leaves them alone and even offers help sometimes in the form of sustenance and local information. But the Redline never stays for long, as to do so would be to suggest membership in the Sabbat, which would weaken many of their ties to sympathetic Camarilla members.

It is difficult to say how large the Redline is. It has no formal roster, and rarely a year goes by without either a new member joining, or at least one old member renouncing ties to the faction (or meeting the Final Death). Originally, the entire group would vote on each prospective new member, but as the Redline has grown and become more of a community, the barrier to entry has lowered. All that is currently required is to be Kindred and to desire an escape from the Camarilla and the Sabbat under pain of blood hunt. For some, that escape is literal, while for others, it is merely an attempt to step away from the politicking and the ideological battles. Those Kindred among the Camarilla who monitor such things believe that less than 100 Cainites claim membership in the Redline, though for some, that means only that they sympathize with the group and contribute to Redlines.

The Inconnu do not comment on the Redline, but they may see the group as a younger, more active version of their own organization. Certainly the Redline admires the Inconnu for its ability to stay above the petty disputes of the sects. They do disapprove of the Inconnu's separation from other Kindred, however. They are convinced that such solitude can only lead to further distancing and to a loss of identity and vitality.

The Thrill Kill Club

Vampires are so damn somber. They hang around nightclubs, sticking to the shadows under stairwells, sporting long, coifed manes like somebody just Embraced Fabio's hair and looking whiter than Wonder Bread... at least according to the Thrill Kill Club (TKC). "Hell," its members say, "unlife's too long to go wasting it on some decrepit Masquerade, or fighting 'for the cause.' What does deathlessness matter if a Cainite can't take a few risks, push the limits of his nature and remind himself that he's out on the edge for a reason?" What's the solution then? Buck the system, either system, and join the Thrill Kill Club. To that end, autarkis among the TKC know how to stir shit and fight the power, all with a laugh while dancing off into the Final Nights. The Camarilla considers it an anarch band or a cult of spoiled childer who are just out to wreak havoc, but the Thrill Kill Club is a gang of vampires looking for a bit of spirited competitive mayhem. What separates them from the Sabbat is that they are not interested in the cause or the sect's paramilitary organization. The TKC is more an adrenaline junkie club if vampires still pumped adrenaline.

The irreverent Thrill Kill Club is the modern incarnation of a society club predating the 20th century. Then, it was better known as a *Salles d'Escrime* or School of Fencing, which provided normal schooling in handling blades and quick lessons for the uninitiated who were off to fight their first duel. Such schools also served as loci for gentlemen's circles. Prior to the 1850s, men of honor and station across North America and Europe fought duels to settle disagreements, slights and outright insults. Back then, such challenges were the privilege of officers and noblemen, but toward the turn of the century, the practice slowly filtered into the middle classes. Engaging in this practice proved a risky venture for anyone not of the gentry or military, and some judges from society's upper echelons even imprisoned commoners who won their duels at detriment to their opponents' lives. The aristocracy followed Victorian sensibilities and decorum, settling their disputes through sword and gun duels. Naturally, when some fell to the Embrace, they carried their practices into unlife out of habit. The pomp and circumstance of dueling even swept through Kindred society of the time, and many vampires settled their arguments in such fashion. They saw frenzying as the tasteless act of barbarians.

The Camarilla informally approved of such activities among the gentry of its sect, ancillae and elders, as long as they conducted their duels with the blessings of the domain's prince. Final Death was rare, and exchanges lasted to first wound or even torpor. Conversely, many princes inflicted the harshest penalties on any neonates caught dueling, mirroring the disparity present in kine society. This "noble" accounting proved a brief whim, however, and the Camarilla banned its practice while many European nations were outlawing dueling themselves throughout the early 1900s. Unfortunately, vampires do not change easily, and some refused to abandon the practice, at least privately. The movement went underground as a sort of gentleman's fighting club, only with rapiers and pistols, and it finally allowed neonates to join when the ranks of the old guard thinned. For invited neonates, it was a great honor to join and hobnob with elders and ancillae who might otherwise ignore the young vampire under most circumstances. It was an opportunity for social climbers and the ambitious.

Over time, the inclusion of younger generations changed the nature of the underground *Salles d'Escrime*. The older members perished or lost interest, while the influx of neonates turned the dueling society into a safety valve where they could burn off their aggression from the sect's often-stifling Traditions. Following WWII, the group moved away from standard duels and pursued exciting dares and risk-taking ventures, much like the old gentlemen exploration societies of the colonial era. The group's Kindred derived sport from traveling the world and placing themselves in real danger. Dares grew into contests, and contests became races to best one another, whether it was to bring down a lion barehanded in an African night safari, collect rare insects in the deadly Amazon rainforest or steal canopic jars from an Egyptian tomb. Unfortunately for the society, some members of the gentry who left years ago finally betrayed the group's activities and secrets to the Camarilla in a bid to curry favor and increase their personal prestige in local politics. The sect's authorities descended upon its rogue neonates harshly and decisively, banishing some, blood bonding others and destroying a handful just to prove that they meant business. Until about two decades ago, it seemed that the group had died.

A few members of *Salles d'Escrime*, exiled for their endangerment of the Masquerade, survived in the Anarch Free State, in Los Angeles. By then, they had bastardized the club's original French name into Skirmish School. For a few dozen years, Kindred such as Big Daddy Lopez and Widow Annie kept the Skirmish School active through minor dares and homegrown challenges with other gangs to keep the competitive spirit vital. Then, one night in the '80s, a Sabbat pack calling itself the Mercy Killers paid the two veterans a visit under a flag of truce. The pack knew about the competitions, and it challenged Big Daddy Lopez and Widow Annie to a game of skill and high daring. The competition was to see who could make it cross-country to New Orleans first, steal Prince Marcel's crucifix earring that he customarily wore, and make it back to LA. At the time, New Orleans was undergoing political reformations, and Prince Marcel was scrambling to keep his power base intact amid changing administrations and massive government restructuring. Needless to say, he was preoccupied. The Skirmish School agreed to the contest, and both Lopez and Annie participated alongside their own gangs.

The trek across the US proved less hazardous than crossing the Lupine-infested bayous around the city.

Both sides lost members, but both made it into the poorly named Big Easy. Afterward, Prince Marcel destroyed at least one foolish member from Skirmish School who tried sneaking up on him to rip off his earring while Obfuscated. The Mercy Killers, however, proved far more cunning for a Sabbat Pack. They discovered the prince's penchant for handsome, young men, and they simply prostituted one their pretty-boy members to Marcel, who stole the prize while they fed from each other. The trip back proved equally adventurous while the Skirmish School dogged the Mercy Killers, trying to steal the prize before they hit LA. Although the Skirmish School lost the competition, it reinvigorated the club's old adventuring spirit and infused it with the Sabbat's irreverence and devil-may-care attitude. Big Daddy Lopez and Widow Annie hosted increasingly challenging, daring and deadly competitions, widening the breadth, duration and scope of their games. Some were races against time, while others were races against each other. Contests included stealing a giant cross from Grace Cathedral in San Francisco (a challenge that has remained unfulfilled), hooking up red paint to the emergency sprinkler line in Chicago's Succubus Club then triggering the fire alarms (done) and participating in a literal dead celebrity scavenger hunt (which the late Justicar Petrodon stopped).

The Skirmish School fell out of favor with many hard-line anarchs who thought that the competitions endangered unlife unnecessarily. Matters became more heated when Petrodon's archons ripped through Los Angeles trying to find the Cainites responsible for these games. It did not help that many teams left their graffiti autographs behind at the scenes of their exploits to prove their responsibility. Anarch elder MacNeil exiled Skirmish School from the Barony of Angels, while rival gangs in outlying areas threatened to destroy the club if only to stop the archon investigation. Big Daddy Lopez and Widow Annie left LA quickly, but Skirmish School was growing rapidly. Newer members were now filming their exploits and selling bootleg copies to Kindred neonates and Sabbat fledglings who thrilled vicariously through their anarch brethren and sisters. The Camarilla was furious with this breach of the Masquerade, and it threatened severe punishment for anyone caught owning these bootleg tapes and Final Death for anyone participating. With matters on home turf heating up so rapidly, Skirmish School decided to go global with its show, in places where the Masquerade mattered little and mortal authorities had greater worries on their hands (if they existed at all).

The Skirmish School became a loose society of Cainites who traveled to the world's most troubled hotspots independently, be it Lebanon in the late '80s, Bosnia in the '90s or anywhere else that government oppression or the struggle for political freedom had Amnesty International squirming. Part scavenger hunt and part Baron Munchausen Syndrome, the contests are open to any vampire regardless of his affiliation. The Cainite with the best tale or souvenir wins. Without the North American safeguards hampering their activities, however, the Skirmish School's contests turned downright deadly and dangerous. Their more infamous exploits included:

• Stealing diamonds from Angolan mines protected by the ultra-violent National Union for the Total Independence of Angola (UNITA) rebels and Cainites.

• Hunting and scalping members of Brazil's *Commando Vermelho* (Red Command) and *Carecas do Brasil* (Skinheads of Brazil), who are among the many groups responsible for the beatings and murders of Brazil's street children, Jews, blacks and gays.

• Finding Pol Pot's burnt corpse and returning with his skull (nobody has succeeded yet).

• Participating with Sierra Leone's Revolutionary United Front (RUF) guerillas in the ritualized devouring of a victim's heart or liver. (What does one expect from an army whose units are officially named Burn House Unit, Cut Hands Commando and Born Naked Squad, and whose commanders include Betty Cut Hands and Dr. Blood?)

While some challenges might seem simpler than others, part of the contest includes traveling to the country in question while avoiding its supernatural elements (most of whom are very nationalistic, or at the very least, protective of their domains). Then, after participating in the contest itself, the contestants must survive the trip back home while fighting off the other teams for the prize. Unlike the Sabbat, there is no shame in foregoing certain events or even failing to complete the game. Aside from bragging rights, the only benefit of participation is recording the event and selling it bootleg to Sabbat packs and Kindred enthusiasts for $1000 to $5000 American. Tapes of exploits including cannibalism in Sierra Leone and a werewolf pelt hunt on the Pacific (and war-torn) island of Bougainvillea fetched $10,000 in one online bidding war before eBay shut the whole thing down.

Unfortunately for the Skirmish School, the Camarilla seized a sizable cache of tapes, so it now knows the faces of many members. As a result, archons and justicars managed to destroy several participants over the past few years, including Big Daddy Lopez. Enraged over his destruction, Widow Annie changed the group's name to the Thrill Kill Club in honor of Lopez's memory, and she upped the ante. Since the Camarilla tagged many members for destruction, Widow Annie's newest challenge is to see who can piss off the Camarilla the quickest and land themselves on the Red List. A few members are wary of this venture, but the Thrill Kill Club has seen a surge in its membership for those folks with an eye on a certain brass ring: notoriety. Some fear that the Thrill Kill Club will turn into another London Hunt Club for diablerists. Widow Annie, however, wants to teach the Camarilla a lesson in the differences between enjoying one's self and being an actual menace to society.

The Thrill Kill Club is not centralized, which makes it harder to behead. Widow Annie secretly makes her haven in Barcelona, but the group numbers at least 34 regular members scattered across North and South America and Europe. The Red List gambit, however, has brought in an additional score or so of Cainites, some of whom have already started their campaigns of terror. Camarilla justicars, alastors and archons are working overtime to nip this newest competition in the bud.

Not everyone partakes of all the challenges. Each game normally sees a dozen participants at any one time, since the competitions are always open to latecomers or vampires who like to take their time. There's currently a roster of 30 "dares" that contenders can try, five of which are still running with no victors. Joining the Thrill Kill Club is difficult since members pass around information, stories, videotapes and competition invitations by hand or mouth. Only the most trusted members earn Widow Annie's generic and falsified email address, and they are usually the ones who introduce new members or tell participants about the latest games. The easiest method to enlisting with the group, however, is finding a Cainite with bootleg copies of past events and determining his contact. This is how most members joined up in the first place. Once someone competes in one game and can prove it, he's a member.

coming next...
NEW YORK BY NIGHT

Vampire
THE MASQUERADE

main books

VAMPIRE: THE MASQUERADE
WW2300
$29.95 U.S.

The core rulebook for the game of modern horror. Hardcover.

GUIDE TO THE CAMARILLA
WW2302
$25.95 U.S.

The core resource on the foremost sect of vampires. Hardcover.

GUIDE TO THE SABBAT
WW2303
$25.95 U.S.

The core resource on the Camarilla's undead rivals. Hardcover.

clanbooks

Clanbooks contain vital character information for players and Storytellers.

CLANBOOK: ASSAMITE
WW2359 $14.95 U.S.

CLANBOOK: GIOVANNI
WW2363 $14.95 U.S.

CLANBOOK: TOREADOR
WW2356 $14.95 U.S.

CLANBOOK: BRUJAH
WW2351 $14.95 U.S.

CLANBOOK: LASOMBRA
WW2362 $14.95 U.S.

CLANBOOK: TREMERE
WW2357 $14.95 U.S.

CLANBOOK: FOLLOWERS OF SET
WW2360 $14.95 U.S.

CLANBOOK: MALKAVIAN
WW2353 $14.95 U.S.

CLANBOOK: TZIMISCE
WW2361 $14.95 U.S.

CLANBOOK: GANGREL
WW2352 $14.95 U.S.

CLANBOOK: NOSFERATU
WW2354 $14.95 U.S.

CLANBOOK: VENTRUE
WW2358 $14.95 U.S.

CLANBOOK: RAVNOS
WW2364 $14.95 U.S.

other supplements

ART OF VAMPIRE: THE MASQUERADE
WW2298 $14.95 U.S.
The lavishly illustrated art book that accompanied the Vampire limited edition now available individually.

BLOOD MAGIC: SECRETS OF THAUMATURGY
WW2106 $19.95 U.S.
A long-awaited resource that contains the most jealously guarded powers of blood magicians.

BOOK OF NOD
WW2251 $10.95 U.S.
The tome of vampires' proposed origins and history. Tradeback.

CAIRO BY NIGHT
WW2410 $15.95 U.S.

chicago chronicles volume 2
WW2235 $20.00 U.S.
Combines Chicago by Night Second Edition and Under a Blood Red Moon

CHILDREN OF THE NIGHT
WW2023 $14.95 U.S.
The masters of the undead in the Final Nights.

CITIES OF DARKNESS VOLUME 3
WW2624 $16.00 U.S.
Combines Alien Hunger and Dark Colony

DIRTY SECRETS OF THE BLACK HAND
WW2006 $18.00 U.S.
Secret rules and powers for this hidden sect.

ETERNAL HEARTS
WW2400 $19.95 U.S.
A novella from Black Dog Game Factory that examines the vampire as a sexual metaphor. For adults only.

GHOULS: FATAL ADDICTION
WW2021 $15.00 U.S.
The guide to playing vampires' human pawns.

THE GILDED CAGE
WW2420 $15.95 U.S.

GIOVANNI CHRONICLES IV: NUOVA MALATTIA
WW2097 $19.95 U.S.
For adults only.

THE GIOVANNI SAGA I
WW2098 $17.95 U.S.
The epic adventure of undead betrayal and power across the ages. Contains parts I and II of the Giovanni Chronicles. For adults only.

MIDNIGHT SIEGE
WW2422 $19.95 U.S.

NEW YORK BY NIGHT
WW2411 $17.95 U.S.

NIGHTS OF PROPHECY
WW2265 $19.95 U.S.
Secrets revealed and cycles turned in the Year of Revelations.

REVELATIONS OF THE DARK MOTHER
WW2024 $10.95 U.S.
New insight into vampire origins and the undead curse itself, in the Book of Nod tradition. Tradeback.

SINS OF THE BLOOD
WW2421 $17.95 U.S.

THE TIME OF THIN BLOOD
WW2101 $15.95 U.S.
Allows you to portray the hunted childer of high-generation vampires.

VAMPIRE STORYTELLERS COMPANION
WW2301 $14.95 U.S.
The essential screen and resource book for Vampire Storytellers.

VAMPIRE STORYTELLERS HANDBOOK (REVISED EDITION)
WW2304 $25.95 U.S.
The core reference for Vampire Storytellers. Hardcover.

for more information visit us online:
www.white-wolf.com

Vampire: The Masquerade

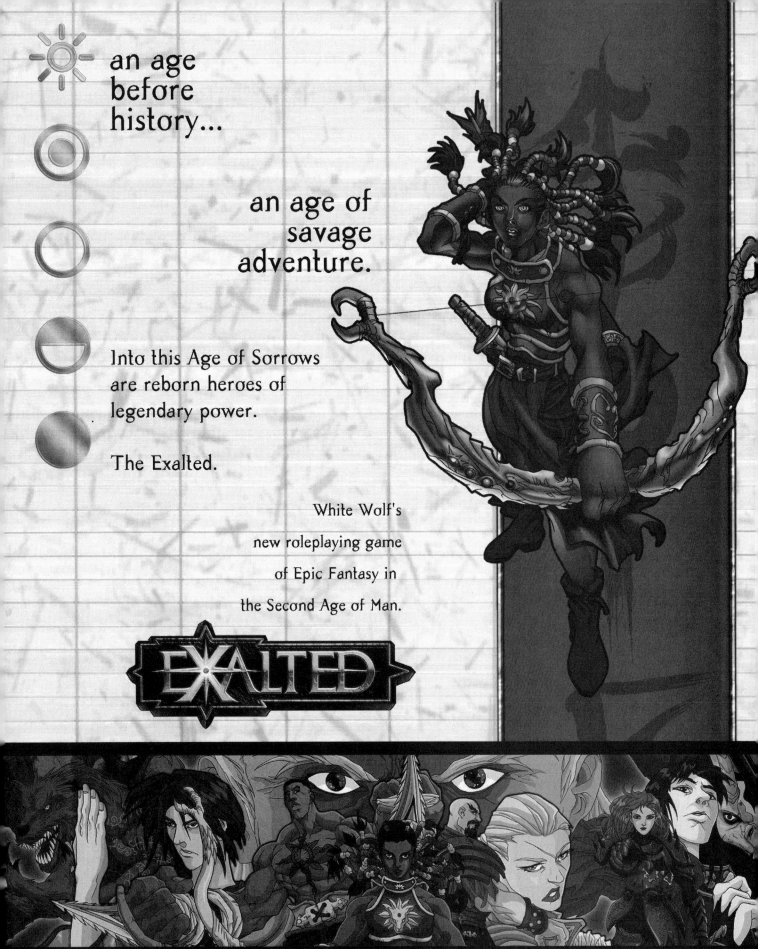